Also by Lila Riley

Best Worst
Mistake

Also by Lia Riley

Right Wrong Guy
Last First Kiss

Best Worst Mistake

A BRIGHTWATER NOVEL

LIA RILEY

AVONIMPULSE

An Imprint of HarperCollinsPublishers

Excerpt from *Right Wrong Guy* copyright © 2015 by Lia Riley.
Excerpt from *The Bride Wore Red Boots* copyright © 2015 by Lizbeth Selvig.
Excerpt from *Rescued by the Ranger* copyright © 2015 by Dixie Lee Brown.
Excerpt from *One Scandalous Kiss* copyright © 2015 by Christy Carlyle.
Excerpt from *Dirty Talk* copyright © 2015 by Megan Erickson.

EPub Edition OCTOBER 2015 ISBN: 9780062403803

Print Edition ISBN: 9780062403810

10 9 8 7 6 5 4 3 2 1

To my readers, you guys are the best

Acknowledgments

GRATITUDE, AS ALWAYS, to my brilliant editor, Amanda Bergeron, who makes everything I write way better. Special appreciation is also due to the fabulous Gabrielle Keck. To my lovely agent, Emily Sylvan Kim, you always know when to give the perfect pep talk and it's so very appreciated.

Love to my dear writing compadres: Jennifer Ryan, Jennifer Blackwood, Natalie Blitt, Jules Barnard, Megan Erickson, and A.J. Pine.

Super special thanks to my family for putting up with me. When I grunt an answer or stare off into the distance, what I'm really saying is "I love you."

To my readers, I couldn't do any of this without you. Your support means the world.

The Curious Tale of the Castle Falls Phantom

(Excerpt from *Brightwater: Small Town, Big Dreams*)

DURING THE DAWN of the twentieth century, an alleged phantom haunted Castle Falls Gulch just beyond the Brightwater city limits. Anglers and hunters alike spun fireside yarns about a so-called "watcher in the woods." A strange phenomenon was also noticed near the riverbanks above the cascades, circles of flowers, perfectly formed fairy rings.

Many townsfolk believed the area was haunted and stayed away, but a few attributed the ghostly occurrences to the Castle Falls hermit. While his existence has never been proven, sightings of a mysterious man along the riverbanks occurred on and off for nearly twenty years. Unsubstantiated rumors claimed he was everything from a ne'er-do-well hobo to a murderer on the lam to the victim of a horrendous physical malformation. As a result, Castle Falls and its surrounds were considered a place better avoided and remain unpopular to this day despite the area's abundant natural beauty.

Stories of the phantom and the enigmatic fairy circles eventually dwindled. The official cause was never determined.

Chapter One

FIFTEEN HUNDRED FEET below the plane window, smoke and flame rose from the mountainside as if a dragon prowled the forest. "McDonald! Kane!" The spotter beckoned, shouting over the Twin Otter's noisy propellers. "You're up."

Wilder Kane tightened his helmet's chinstrap and maneuvered through the aircraft's jam-packed interior, which was teeming with equipment and other smoke jumpers. The adrenaline surge added an extra beat to his heart and cleared away the mental cobwebs. After reaching the back, he jittered his boot heel against the floor while his partner, McDonald, took position in the open door.

"Got any plans for your mandatory day?" the spotter hollered, bracing a hand on the roof as they hit a pocket of clear air turbulence and dropped hard. It was a record temperature outside and Wilder's gut rolled with the plane as he breathed deep, inhaling fuel and a hint of charred wood. Friday was his day off—he had to take one every three weeks because of pain-in-the-ass regulations. He'd just as soon work through the whole damn season.

"Probably going for a ride." Free time meant thinking. Better to spend days off screaming his mountain bike down heart-pounding single track in the Rattlesnake Wilderness or Pattee Canyon.

"A couple of us are going into Missoula for the night. Come along and bikini-scope college girls down by the river."

"Nah, I'm good." Occasionally, he drove west on I-90 to the Silver Dollar or Rusty Spur and searched the roadside bars for a pretty face and weary eyes. Someone hoping to forget, if only for an hour. Someone like him. Bubbly and cheerful younger women weren't his type. He'd lost hope and innocence so long ago, it was hard to know if he ever had them at all.

"Jesus, Brick." The spotter shook his head, annoyance and amusement warring across his features. "Anyone ever try and clue you in to the fact that you're a surly S.O.B.?"

"Once or twice," Wilder replied, scrubbing the thick scruff on his jaw. "But they never made the mistake again."

The spotter's laugh boomed. "You're something else."

"Got that right." McDonald twisted around from his seated position in the door and shook his head. "Something that needs to get laid."

Wilder shrugged. He hadn't earned the nickname Brick for nothing. He caught good-natured shit from the others for the steadfast way he maintained an unflappable personal wall, a stoic face no matter the situation, but he didn't care. This job wasn't about the accolades or prestige.

He was a smoke jumper because it was the only thing he could ever be.

He knew no other way to endure himself.

For the next two minutes, he'd be a kickass parachutist, and the second he hit the ground, it was time to transform into a firefighting machine—a smoke jumper's real work. What other career required flying over desolate wilderness with a team of warriors and jumping from a small plane armed with not much more than an axe, shovel, and iron-clad balls?

Best job on earth.

The inferno devouring Lost Moose Gulch appeared to be a classic "gobbler," a wildfire hungry for destruction. Detected two days ago, following an unremarkable lightning strike in the remote wilderness, the resulting smolder took advantage of the summer's bone-dry conditions and changeable Montana weather, especially here along the Continental Divide. The calming wind left the fire vulnerable to defeat—just—providing the team could rally quick, scratch some lines to make a fire break, and hook it. If they couldn't gain the upper hand within a day or two, an extended attack crew would be sent out, the on-ground hotshots.

Wilder didn't have any intention of letting that happen. He won. That was his reputation. He threw himself against every blaze as if his very life hung in the balance, and it did, in more ways than the others ever guessed.

The spotter slapped McDonald's shoulder, and he was out the door in a blink.

"Take position," came the order.

Wilder stepped forward, licking his dry lips. His partner's parachute opened and McDonald swung around, expertly steering toward the designated jump site, a predetermined meadow.

"Get ready," called the spotter.

Wilder crouched to sitting and braced his hands on the outside of the plane, the aluminum cold against his palms. Tension hummed through his body. His muscles might as well be rendered stone. The second the spotter's hand slapped his shoulder he flung forward with every ounce of strength, giving over to the void.

He closed his eyes, in the tuck position, savoring the few seconds of free fall, the blissfully mind-numbing silence. *Goddamn.* Allowing his lips to curl into a rare smile, he exhaled a contented breath. No better place existed than this limbo between earth and sky. Once out of the plane there were no take backs, only total commitment. The buzz gave way to a moment of absolute clarity. It was about being alive, about—

A sharp jerk wrenched him back into the present, knocking his teeth together.

He twisted, glancing up. *What the shit?* His head rang as his heart rate soared. Streamer malfunction. The parachute hadn't opened right. Bad news. Really fucking bad news. He yanked the reserve but they had jumped low and at a thousand feet, there wasn't time to do much before he slammed into the earth at a hundred miles an hour.

This was going to go either of two ways: a lot of hurt or game over.

Impossible to gain orientation amid the gut-twisting free spin. Landscape flipped past in a nauseating kaleidoscope, blue sky, green forest, blue sky, green forest, a river, fuck—the river? He'd careened too far from the jump site, over the steep gulch. An inferno now separated him from McDonald. The scenic beauty of this stark, lonely landscape was a steep and jagged catch-22. Crashing into the roughest terrain east of the divide would make it damn near impossible for a quick rescue.

If there was anything left of him to save.

The tree canopy closed in. *Got to relax*. If his muscles remained rigid, the impact would destroy vital organs. Better to keep his legs moving to avoid locked limbs, cover his head with his arms, elbows forward, lacing his fingers behind his neck. Wind roared in his face. Strange how his life didn't flash before his eyes, only smoke and flame.

Figured.

A crash, a snap of bone or branch, followed by an agonizing pain through his lower leg and then nothing at all.

WILDER BLINKED BUT the world remained upside down. He tested his jaw. Not broken. His back ached while his left leg had a complete absence of feeling. Willing his rattled brains to come to order, he swung forward as silvery stars cascaded past his field of vision. Looked like he'd gotten strung up in a lodgepole pine. How long had he swung from his ropes like a pendulum, blood pooling in his head? He waited until the vertigo passed and took a shuddering breath. The main chute had tangled in the branches while his left leg was caught tight in the reserve's line, cutting circulation off below the knee. Not good.

The forest was silent except for the branch creaking under his weight. No one else was around for miles. He'd blown too far off course.

If he was going to escape then it was up to him—for once it would pay to be a stubborn S.O.B.

Getting down wasn't going to be a picnic, not with a headfirst, ten-foot plummet to anticipate. No choice though, especially not when the ridgeline above exploded in an avalanche of flame.

Aw shit.

His whole body reacted against the impending doom. A pulse ticked in his throat as cold sweat sheened his chest. He hadn't survived the fall to be roasted alive. *No. No. No.* His thoughts screamed until he realized it was his own voice chanting the single word.

No man in his sound mind longed for death, but he'd idly hoped for a car accident or disease when his time came. Even a gunshot or poison.

Anything but fucking fire.

Wilder fumbled for the compact utility knife clipped to his Kevlar jumpsuit and after a few clumsy attempts, his trembling fingers popped open the blade. There were a shitload of cords and he ground his wrist hard, sawing back and forth, going through one after another.

"Come on, come on," he muttered. The initial fall's impact left him with as much strength as a baby. "Stay in control." Hard to believe the pep talk given the pathetic rasp undercutting his voice. The forest thickened with choking smoke.

After he cut some ten cords, he dropped an inch, two more and then a foot while embers drifted past, devilish fairies, bright with hypnotic beauty. He couldn't afford to screw up this landing because in another minute it was going to be out of the frying pan and into the—damn it—he recoiled from the explosion as the fire jumped from the ground to the tree canopy with a noise like a freight train taking a corner too fast.

His blade popped through the final filaments and he plummeted to the pine needle duff with a muffled thud, automatically rolling away from the encroaching blaze. He pushed to his feet and keeled over. Something was wonky with his left leg, the one still wound tight in the reserve parachute line. He lurched up and fell again, panting. A few large scattered boulders ahead where the trees thinned. A clearing.

The Lost Moose Gulch landslide.

He exhaled, a jolt of purpose shooting through his core, open space meant a shot at survival.

If he could crawl, there might be a chance.

His radio crackled from his backpack. "Kane, are you there? Fucking copy, man."

McDonald.

A crash. Wilder froze as a doe and fawn hauled ass through the underbrush. They each had four working legs to their advantage. The air was devoid of birdsong, even the radio's static couldn't compete with the roar—the same nightmarish sound that haunted his dreams for over twenty years.

Fire had always held a strange sort of destructive beauty, dazzling in its doom. He learned that lesson as a six-year-old, while his little brothers, Sawyer and Archer, clung to his hands, whimpering while their family home transformed into an inferno, trapping Mommy and Dad inside.

The two younger boys had cried when the roof caved, after the police and firefighters arrived too late to do anything but sort through the smoldering rubble. They sobbed until Grandma Kane had showed up in her flannel pajamas, hair tightly rolled in pink curlers, offering stiff but heartfelt hugs.

Wilder hadn't said a word. He didn't have the right to tears.

Not when everything was all his fault.

This job, this life, was a way to atone.

But he came from a long line of gamblers, and every debt must eventually be paid, right?

Wrong. The fire wouldn't win. Not today.

He tore open his backpack and grabbed the radio. "Copy, McDonald, I'm here, but things are getting hot."

"What are your coordinates, over?"

The embers lit the underbrush around him, a dozen

tiny spot fires stood between him and the clearing. Time was almost out. He scrambled faster.

"Can't check the GPS," Wilder panted. "Got to deploy the fire blanket pronto. My location is the southern perimeter of the Lost Moose Gulch landslide, over."

The heat was all consuming. It was too much. Too far. He heaved onto his back, to glimpse a last patch of blue, a final shred of sky, but nothing remained except for an ashy haze.

Death would come quick and there was a certain mercy in that knowledge. Maybe on the other side his parents waited, and he could finally say sorry.

Or he might burn forever.

Either way he'd soon find out.

The sound of mad thrashing grabbed his attention and he turned, raising his head. The baby deer from earlier had run headlong into a thicket on the rockslide's edge, trapping itself among the bramble in its panic, abandoned by a terrified mother.

The pitiful sight forced him to gather the dregs of his nonexistent strength. *Just a little farther.* Hand over hand, ignoring the coals branding his palms, the sweat stinging his eyes, he reached the fawn. It struggled for a moment before stilling, as if understanding this was the only choice.

Wilder couldn't feel the thorns, not through the red-hot pain radiating across his palms and shooting up his arms. "Go," he growled at the fawn, ripping down the branches and slapping its spindly leg. "Get out of here." He tugged the fire blanket from his backpack. Survival odds were statistically nil. The blanket might protect him from the fire's caress but the heat could easily scald his lungs, incinerating from the inside out.

The young deer didn't budge, instead it stared transfixed by the approaching horror.

With a muffled curse, Wilder seized the delicate, trembling body tight, somehow tugging the blanket over them as the fire's edge passed like a vengeful angel of death. He angled his face down toward the rocks, running water bubbled only feet below, the cool damp temperature making it possible to breathe.

After a few seconds, minutes, or hours, the roar subdued to a crackle, and the deer stirred, hopping to shaky legs and tearing out from under the blanket toward the west without a backward glance.

Wilder coughed and wiped his mouth, ignoring the blood staining his blistered hand.

Bright blue fireworks shot across his peripheral vision as the womp-womp-womp sound of a helicopter closed in. More time passed and then a deep voice called his name.

He couldn't answer.

Couldn't sit.

Couldn't do a damn thing but slump under the blanket, suspended in this numb semiconscious state, teetering on the edge of oblivion.

THE WORLD HAD gone white. Was this the other side—whatever came next? No. Not unless the afterlife was full of dull, throbbing pain, that peculiar hospital disinfectant smell, and voices refusing to ever shut up.

"Wilder? Wilder?"

"Did you see his eyelids twitch?" Another deep voice chimed in. "See? There they go again."

"Come on, man." The first male voice increased in intensity. "Wake up."

You've got to be shitting me. His brothers were here. Sawyer. Archer. He hadn't seen these two in years. Couldn't bear their presence. Not when he'd ruined their lives.

He dragged his lids open, no small effort when each must weigh a few hundred pounds.

"Hey, you." Archer bent down, trying and failing to execute his trademark permagrin. "Good to see those bright eyes. You've been scaring us all shitless."

Wilder cracked his mouth open but no sounds emerged except for a groggy jumble of consonants, like his tongue had transformed into a cotton ball. *Christ.* What happened? His hands were wrapped in thick gauze, the fingertips an angry red. Last he remembered, the fire somehow left him alive. Then there was a helicopter, right? Clearly the cavalry had come.

But everything since was a black hole.

The mattress creaked as he shifted, trying to shield his eyes from the fluorescent light. Why did his body feel off? Something wasn't right. He contracted his abdominal muscles, raised himself to half-sitting before Sawyer braced his back. "Hey, come on now, go easy."

Wilder gaped at the lump under the sheet, the stump

that ended where his left calf and foot used to be. "Where the hell is my leg?" Talk about five words he never expected to say.

Sawyer spoke slowly, getting down to business. "After the accident, you lost circulation for too long, and with the fire, the helicopter had a hard time Life Flighting you to the hospital. Coupled with a shattered leg, the lack of blood flow meant that necrosis set in and the tissue damage was irreversible."

Wilder couldn't focus on the words. They made too much sense and this situation had taken a wrong turn to the land of fucking insane. His windpipe went on lockdown. He pushed to the edge of the bed, toppling an IV tower.

"Let's call the doctor in," Archer said, glancing to the door.

"Wilder. Listen to me. You can't stand up," Sawyer ordered. "Take it easy, we're going to sort this out. You'll get a prosthetic soon and with some work and time, you'll be able to resume most activities no problem. It's amazing you've survived given what—"

"Stop. Stop talking." Wilder buried his face in his hands. He could kiss his career goodbye. Jumping was out of the question. His only way to cope had gone up in flames.

"This has to be a helluva shock." Archer rapped his knuckles on the side of the bed. "But don't forget one thing—we're family. No matter what happens, Sawyer and I have got your back. Always have, always will. We're not giving up."

"Look at me." Wilder signaled to the empty space in disgust. "I'm half a fucking man."

"I don't make a habit of judging a book by its cover and neither should you," Sawyer said quietly. "We're here to help—"

"Help. You want to help?" Wilder growled, fighting for equilibrium but losing the battle to vertigo. He might be the oldest brother, but right now he felt ancient.

Sawyer's chiseled features froze a moment before he gave a small smile. "Anything. Say the word and it's as good as done."

Wilder used the last of his reserve strength to lift his head, struggling to bring their faces into focus and level a hard stare. He'd reached the end of his rope and was in a free fall to hell.

"Get me a gun or get out."

Chapter Two

Four Months Later . . .

THE *LES MIZ* soundtrack tested the limits of the bookstore's rinky-dink boom box. No customers were around so Quinn Higsby joined in, belting out along with Fantine and her broken dreams. Big, fat snowflakes spiraled past the plate glass window, ferried along by the strengthening wind as a looming cloud wall replaced the normally heart-stopping view of rugged Eastern Sierras's peaks. Right at the crescendo, the phone's shrill ring cut in, ruining the moment. She turned down the volume, cleared her throat, and answered, "Good afternoon, A Novel Experience, the place where you can read yourself interesting."

"Hey, honey, it's me. Listen, I'm not going to be able to get into the store in time for close. The Weather Channel is saying tonight's storm will be a doozy." Quinn's boss,

Natalie, was visiting her new boyfriend up in South Lake Tahoe.

"That's okay, the store's been deserted all afternoon. Book club got canceled. You just worry about keeping snug and warm."

"Oh, I don't think that will be any problem." Natalie let out a mischievous giggle. She was fifty years young and had found real happiness with a blackjack dealer and Johnny Depp look-alike ten years her junior.

"You're so bad." Quinn glanced down at her solitaire game on the counter, grinning from ear to ear. Her former job had made it hard to believe any decent people remained in the state. This assistant bookseller position might pay peanuts and lack glamor, but she was happier than she'd ever been in Hollywood.

"Bad is the new good—you've got my permission to stick that on one of your t-shirts."

In addition to her faith in humanity, Quinn had also left behind high fashion in Los Angeles in favor of vintage denim and funny slogan shirts. Today's choice was a grey hoodie that read, "I love to party, and by party I mean read books."

Which was the actual truth, no shame. She had a thing for older men—*much* older men to be exact. Mr. Darcy, Mr. Knightley, and Captain Wentworth were all excellent boyfriend material, and the magic of literature meant it didn't matter if they clocked in at well over one hundred years old. Those guys still had it going on.

"Quinn, are you listening to a word I'm saying?"

She snapped to ramrod straight posture. "Of course."

"You've drifted off with the fairies again, haven't you?" Natalie said fondly. "I said that you should leave early too, beat the storm. Oh, and shoot, there's that package to mail, I meant to—"

"Stop. Breathe. Think about your blood pressure. I'll handle it no problem." After all, handling was what Quinn did best, at least until that unfortunate night in Beverly Hills a few months ago when her career as a celebrity handler came to a fast and furious end—fired for having a pretty face and a lecherous client. She flipped her ponytail over her shoulder, smoothing the ends. "Now listen, I want you to get back and enjoy, er, whatever dirty deeds you are enjoying."

"I love you, peaches." Natalie planted a loud, affectionate smooch on her receiver.

"You must be getting treated right in that love nest." Quinn chuckled. "Remember how just last week you called me a pinecone after I advised that one customer where to find a title online rather than offering to order it into the shop. Which, for the record, was totally boneheaded of me."

"Pshaw. That was my hot flash talking. You know how I adore you."

"Yeah, I do actually." And Quinn did. Natalie didn't have children of her own so she mothered everyone. Unlike Quinn's own mom who was far more interested in a quixotic quest for the Fountain of Youth with her endless mud baths, antioxidant facials, and plastic surgery appointments down in Palm Springs. "Hey, real quick, before you get your jiggy back on, want to hear this week's mystery order?"

"Always."

"Let me see." Quinn peered into the cardboard box beside her feet. "We have *The Curious Incident of the Dog in the Night-Time*, *Breakfast at Tiffany's*, *The Sound and the Fury*, *Frankenstein*, and *Fun with Whittling*."

"*Fun with Whittling*?" Natalie hooted. "Oh, jeez. Eclectic as always."

"Next week might be *Duct Tape Art* or *Tapophilia 101*."

"Tapo-what?"

"You know, gravestone rubbings—with charcoal and butcher paper?" Quinn shook her head—useless information took up way too much grey matter real estate. "Anyway, we should try and predict the order."

"Ha, we'll lose."

"No doubt." The snow fell in earnest now, making it hard to see across Brightwater's Main Street. She had to leave soon to hit the post office before checking in on Dad. "Hey, I should get moving. Have yourself a great night."

"Of course, I'll be in when we open again, day after tomorrow. Black Friday means green for us. And thank you, sweetie. I won't do anything that you wouldn't do."

Quinn laughed. Mostly because she didn't *do* anything. Hadn't in well over a year. She hung up the phone and grabbed a marker and packing tape. Sealing the package shut, she printed across the top in big black letters:

W. Kane
405 Castle Falls Lane
Brightwater, California 96104

"W. Kane." She tapped the initials. The mysterious W. Kane started emailing orders right after she moved to town and landed this job. A Novel Experience didn't have a digital store; instead this person just sent requests and monthly checks. Each week was the same, a curtly worded request for four or five wildly different titles to be posted to the Castle Falls address. Last week was Virginia Woolf, Shakespeare, Dr. Seuss, and Nora Roberts. Odd combo and strange in the day and age of online shopping but, hey—no complaints if someone wanted to buy local.

Quinn shrugged into her white puffy coat, the marshmallow-looking one that seemed like overkill when she purchased it during a SoCal summer sale but now appeared totally sensible. Brightwater's autumn had been mild but as soon as mid-November struck it was as if the weather gods were issued a green light to let the elements rip. Temperatures plummeted and everyone in the checkout line at the Save-U-More suddenly discussed nothing but snowfall predictions and when the ski hills would open.

Quinn struggled with walking in a straight line while chewing gum, so the idea of careening down a steep slope on a pair of glorified sticks held little appeal. Plus, as much as she was happy to leave her sunny beach life behind, she and winter weren't going to be besties.

Grabbing the store keys, she hefted the book box under her arm and flicked off the light. The shop had been quiet today, most of autumn actually, except for the Chicklits, the book club that met Wednesday mornings. But Natalie reassured her that things would pick up once the snow bunnies flocked to the mountains. Summer was also apparently boom time with all the newcomers flooding in to build their second, third, or even fourth vacation homes.

"Enjoy the quiet, it won't last," Natalie often said from her ancient red velvet chair that was perpetually stationed by the window, nose buried in a book. Sometimes Quinn wondered if Natalie had used her parents' inheritance to start a bookshop in order to justify reading all day. But then it did seem like a perfectly reasonable way to spend both money and time.

She stepped outside, lungs constricting from the sharp cold. Holy heck, if it wasn't even December yet, what would official winter-winter feel like?

Scary thought.

Fumbling with the big brass door key, she finally got it locked and, turning, collided with a body, a big, hard masculine body. The type that could play NFL football and was topped by the sort of face often seen on a Disney hero, unquestionably handsome but almost cartoonish with an oversized jaw and deep canyon chin cleft. Thick blond hair protruded from underneath his navy blue "Brightwater Volunteer Firefighter" ball cap.

"Garret, what a . . . surprise."

"A good one, I hope?" Garret King's toothy grin matched the snow. No. Scratch that, those stark white incisors outshined the swirling flakes. Some women no doubt swooned for his type, but that muscleman build, stylishly disheveled hair, and sexy-and-I-know-it attitude left her decidedly unintoxicated.

"Cold day." She checked her coat's zipper and steered the subject straight to Boring Town. Garret was the exact type of person she'd hoped to leave behind in Hollywood. Figured that she'd flee across half the state to a small mountain town only to collide with someone whose ego rivaled any multimillion-dollar overentitled action star's.

"We're going to The Dirty Shame," he said, blocking her path.

"We?"

"You. Me. A few IPAs." Sunglasses were required to withstand those luminescent chompers.

She tried not to let her annoyance show. "Sounds like a blast, but I'm pretty busy."

"Busy?" His smile dimmed to a lower watt. "With what?" As if how could anything be more important than fawning over him?

Good grief, she'd rather watch paint dry in one hundred percent relative humidity.

"I have to run to the post office to send off this package to a customer and then duck around to check on my dad."

"Oh yeah, how is Crazy ol' Higsby these days?" Lenny, Garret's friend, sprouted like a surprise mushroom behind his best buddy's elbow. His snub nose was a mottled red and dripped before he could wipe it on his fleece sleeve. "Did you know the last time I saw him out and about was at the Save-U-More? He growled at someone in the meat department. Growled! As if the butcher would give him a bone or something."

Even Garret looked shocked.

"What the heck is wrong with you?" Quinn snapped,

any patience evaporating in a flash. "My father is a sick man. That's not justifiable cause for mocking him."

"Of course not." Garret sent Lenny reeling with a sharp elbow jab. "Hey, don't be an asshole, dude," he ordered.

"Yeah, well, have a good evening, fellas." When would icicles be hanging from the rafters? She'd love to clock the pair of them over their thick insensitive heads.

"Wait, hold up, I'll walk with you," Garret said, brushing past Lenny. "Keep you safe."

She fought a hard eye roll while regarding the empty sidewalk. "Oh, spare me," she muttered.

"What was that?" Garret leaned in. "You want my phone number? No need to mumble. You only have to ask."

"Thanks but that won't be necessary." She sidestepped him and dodged Lenny, increasing her pace. Throughout the autumn, she had put out every polite "no way in hell" signal that she could think of. Did she emit some sort of jerk-magnet pheromone? Douche Bag No. 5?

Because if she was a superhero, her power would be attracting assholes.

"What about tonight?" Garret asked, hot on her heels. "Need help keeping extra warm?"

"I'll be reading." Was there enough snow on the ground to make a snowball? Throw it in his face?

He frowned. "A book?"

"Yep, one with an actual cover and pages. Taking a break from my e-reader for the week." She tapped her glasses. "Eye strain, the struggle is real."

"Wouldn't you rather—"

"Oh look, here we are!" Quinn chirped, booking it toward the historic post office. She tightened her grip on the box in her arms. Garret did a double-take at the address and frowned.

"W. Kane, huh? You friends with that guy?"

Guy? Her heart rate increased. So W. was a guy—at least now she knew that much.

And he was a man of few words. Case in point, his email from this morning. She had asked for a clarification. "We have the original publication of Faulkner's *The Sound and the Fury* but also this reprint edition with a new cover—I don't know, maybe trying to appeal to a younger audience—and I wasn't sure if you wanted the classic or the reprint. Or maybe you want both? I know I love owning my favorites in all their iterations. Anyway, thank you for your order. I'll process it after you get back to me about the Faulkner."

His reply? "Classic edition."

That terseness could mean shy or asshole.

She'd seen a few cute and friendly-seeming guys around town, but they were all taken. Sawyer and Archer Kane, for example. Nice guys with sweet girlfriends, the postcard-perfect pictures of love and contentment. For some people fairy tales existed. Not her. But hey, life wasn't one big lemon either. Not all happy endings had to come between the sheets. She had hers every night between the pages of a good book.

Wait a small-town second. Sawyer Kane? Archer Kane?

W. Kane must be a relation. Hopefully an intro-verted, eccentric bookworm cousin—someone a little on the short side, wiry, adorned with Pendleton sweaters, dreamy eyes, and black Converse. An artist, musician, or writer? Better yet, all three—her exactly perfect type.

Nah, probably the drunk uncle who shows up at family picnics and never quits yammering about politics.

Safer to trade real life for a fictional lord. At least they inherently understood the importance of devilish charm. Garret seemed to have grasped only the concepts of sleaze and ball, breeding them together into a hybrid baby of teeth-clenching annoyance.

"We're not friends," she said, adjusting the box's weight. "He orders special delivery books from the shop. Do you know him?"

"Yeah and word to the wise, stay far away from him." His face lost its fleeting, troubled expression and dialed up the charm. "Anyway, I don't want to waste any more time discussing W. Kane." Even now Garret braced his big hand on the metal railing, blocking her path, unwilling or unable to take a hint. "I'm more interested in our plans—"

"Yeah, about that. I really have to run." She ducked under his arm, not exactly easy with her height, but she hadn't won limbo contest after limbo contest during that long ago spring break Caribbean cruise for nothing. He could stoop low, but she could go lower.

"Quinn—"

"Bye now." She straightened and spun on her boot

heel, the black knee-high ones with the big silver buckles that were quite badass if she said so herself.

The post office was quiet. Wanda Higsby, who was either her great aunt or third cousin once removed, gave a chipper wave from behind the counter. It was strange to be a Higsby in Brightwater. Her family had migrated west on the first wagon train and been settlers in this valley for as long as the Kanes or Carsons, but Quinn's dad had moved to L.A. in his twenties to make it as an electrician with a film studio. He didn't like big city living, but stayed long enough to land the part of Jacqueline Forest's second husband and father of her first and only child. The marriage was short-lived, so much so that Quinn couldn't remember a time when her parents were actually together.

After Dad split and moved back to Brightwater to start his own business, Quinn saw him for Christmas when he came and escorted her on their yearly trip to Disneyland and over summers during the hedonistic Julys she spent in Brightwater.

"How is your daddy doing?" Wanda didn't add "the poor thing" to the end of her sentence but it hung there unspoken like an invisible haze of sympathy.

Quinn automatically clasped the thin silver chain around her neck, the one with the bee charm she hadn't taken off since her thirteenth birthday. When you are in your early twenties, mortality should seem like a concept to be saved for the far distant future. And so it had been until her father got sick. First came the little signs.

They'd be having their usual Sunday night phone catch up and everything would be going along merrily. Well, at least normal. Dad wasn't a talker, more the strong silent type.

No big surprise why Mom went blue-collar. He had those old-fashioned Western movie star looks, all craggy features and a stare that swung to the horizon. He spoke easily enough about the weather, the Giants, how the 49ers were doing, and that was about it.

But these short, predictable, and fine, sometimes forced conversations began to turn into slow rambles where he'd introduce topics that didn't quite make sense. A story about a missing dog without a resolution. Or forgetting his pet name for her, Bizzy, a play on *busy bee* because she was always up to something.

A few sober hospital trips confirmed a diagnosis that Quinn couldn't help him with, no matter how much she wanted to. Early-onset Alzheimer's, which affects people under sixty-five, was rare but not unheard of.

As life fell apart in SoCal, she knew what she had to do. Move to Brightwater and be closer to Dad. His condition rapidly deteriorated to where he wasn't able to live on his own anymore but Quinn visited his assisted living facility every morning for breakfast and every night after work.

"Dad's good—he's on a new medication," she blurted after realizing Wanda still waited for an answer. The medication wasn't doing much to slow the rapidly advancing symptoms, but one could hope.

When faced with an incurable situation it was either

hope or fall apart. And falling apart wasn't an option when you were an only child, your mom was on lucky husband number seven, and your dad had been a perpetual bachelor.

There was no one else to count on. So she sold his house and hoped the selling price would be enough to keep him at Mountain View Village.

"I'm bringing over *Caddyshack* tonight. He loves Bill Murray." Funny how the brain worked. Dad often woke not knowing where he was, but could quote lines verbatim from random eighties movies. Not funny, actually. Terrifying. And with her own predictive test for early-onset familial Alzheimer's disease set for Friday, the last few months of agonizing doubt would be laid to rest. The genetic genie would be let out of the bottle to predict her future, good or bad.

"He was a good guy, your dad." Wanda heaved a heavy sigh while reorganizing the pens on the counter. "Did you know that he used to come around and clean out my gutters every October after my Raymond passed away?"

Wanda wasn't the only one who sang Dad's praises. Kind. Quiet but earnest. Always ready to lend a helping hand and needing little in the way of thanks. He was one of the good ones.

Crap, now even she was thinking of Dad in the past tense.

Not was, is.

Why do bad things always happen to the good ones? It wasn't fair.

Tears prickled and she blinked, willing them into submission.

"Tell him I said hello," Wanda said kindly, turning away to give Quinn the privacy to wipe her eyes.

Quinn bit back the reply that Wanda could always visit him herself but that wasn't fair. A lot of people couldn't bear to see Dad at the facility, as if personal tragedy was contagious. Instead they offered her sympathetic smiles and kind words. Everyone meant well, could do nothing, and she tried to bear it.

At least if her turn came, no one would have to carry the load.

Her cell played the tune "Defying Gravity" from the musical *Wicked*. "Excuse me," she said to Wanda, passing over W. Kane's package. "Can you please pop this box in the mail? I should take the call."

Her phone didn't ring much these days. Old friends fell away after she was fired. Guess they weren't such good pals after she lost her professional connections and VIP passes. Good riddance. They'd have never stuck around if the test confirmed that she . . . if she . . .

Just wait and see what will happen.

She answered the phone with a forceful "Hello?"

"Quinn? Is that you? Thank goodness you picked up." The frazzled female voice sounded vaguely familiar. "This is Denise over at Mountain View Village."

Quinn's blood chilled. The facility Dad was at.

"What's happened?"

"Your father. He's gone missing."

"Excuse me?"

"Well, as you know, he's taken to wandering of late and today we had him off the unit for a routine physical. Another resident fell in the waiting room, diverting the nurse's attention. We have reason to believe that he left the facility during the ensuing chaos."

Quinn's hand flew to her mouth as her stomach dropped. "What?"

"I'm so sorry." Denise spoke fast. "Nothing like this has ever happened here before. Your father is so young and all, the new front desk girl didn't suspect a thing when he walked on by."

"Have you called the police yet?"

"I'm just about to but wanted you to be notified first."

"Never mind. Let me handle this. I'm right across the street from the sheriff's office now." She'd manage the disaster personally. "Please arrange a search party, the weather is bad and getting worse by the minute." Her voice held a shrill, almost hysterical note. Who cared? Dad was lost, possibly hurt.

"I know. I know." Denise sounded on the verge of tears herself. Not reassuring. Quinn needed to believe that her father would be found. That nothing bad would happen to him.

Wanda leaned across the counter, her broad face puckered with concern. "Is everything okay?"

"No," Quinn snapped, for once admitting the truth as she tore to the door. "Not by a long shot."

She pushed outside and gasped. The temperature had

dropped at least ten degrees in the last few minutes and the gale-force gusts pushed her back against the building. A tear froze to her cheek.

Dad was outside wandering alone in these conditions? What would happen to him?

Chapter Three

WILDER WALKED AGAINST the wind, head down, jaw
clenched. The new rhythm defined each impatient step.
Cane. Foot. Foot. Cane. Foot. Foot. Cane. Foot. Foot.

The doctor said that if he persisted with his regime of
ambulatory and endurance exercises eventually he could
say sayonara to the cane, but adjusting to a prosthetic took
time. "The good news is that the amputation occurred
below the knee, saving you a great deal of mobility." The
doctor had grinned as if he'd dished up a plate of good
news, like losing your leg in a freak parachute accident,
having your career go up in flames, and returning to the
town you had long fled was cause for fucking optimism.

"Hey, at least you're alive," Archer had muttered
midway through the silent flight from Montana.

Wilder hadn't replied—couldn't find the right words.
The only people capable of looking on the bright side
were those who still saw the light.

These days, Archer had it pretty damn good. He ran Hidden Rock Ranch, lived in the big house with his pretty fiancée, Edie, and together they took care of Grandma Kane who struggled with mobility issues after breaking her hip mid-summer. In his own, more understated way, his other brother, Sawyer, appeared just as content. He served as Brightwater's sheriff and settled into a comfortable life in his hand-built cabin with his old flame, Annie Carson, helping to raise her young son. Family life suited him and it was only a matter of time before either of the two guys tied the knot.

Wilder didn't begrudge his brothers a single ounce of their hard-won happiness. How could he when he single-handedly destroyed their childhood? Wilder swiped the snow from his face. Almost home.

Home.

He couldn't restrain a snort. Returning to Brightwater had come with one non-negotiable condition: His brothers must let him live alone. They agreed with a caveat of their own, saying if that was the case, he needed to stick with physical therapy, get out and about. Figure out a plan. A new career.

Easy for them to say with their loves and lives.

All Wilder had was a cane and ghosts.

A deer stumbled up the ravine wall, sending down a small cascade of snow and soil. It was going to be a hard winter. All the old-timer signs pointed to it; squirrels were busy, leaves fell late, halos kept appearing around the moon. He could pick up some cracked corn from Higsby Hardware to help supplement the deers' diet, but it might not make a difference. The wind keened, seemed to carry his mother's voice, her oft-repeated refrain, "No act of kindness, however small, is ever wasted."

His next step was a stumble.

Forget about the deer. Focus on not face-planting.

He purchased a small cabin near Castle Falls for a song. Even with property prices booming in the Brightwater Valley, the fastest growing real-estate market west of the Rockies, Castle Falls was steeped in long-time fear and superstition. Stories went around about the gulch, whispers suggested that the place was haunted. Cursed. People kept their distance.

It was a perfect place to become a hermit.

"Why, this old place does have a certain charm, what with these cobblestone walls and, look, the floorboards are genuine redwood planks." Edie Banks, Archer's fiancée, had announced during his move-in day. "They don't build houses with this type of craftsmanship anymore."

Archer had managed to hold his tongue for once and Wilder knew why. Edie might look at the cabin through rose-colored glasses, but this faded hovel held all the cheer of a mausoleum, and that's exactly what it would be—a tomb for Wilder to bury away any future hope or ambitions. He'd kidded himself into thinking Montana would be a fresh start.

Brightwater was his penance.

The wind picked up in ferocity, tossing him forward. The stick, cane, or whatever, broke through a puddle. Thin frost sheened the surface, ice that hadn't been there an hour ago. Sawyer had given him the simple hand-carved oak walking stick as a welcome-home gift, replacing the one better suited for a man three times his age. "A cane for a Kane," he'd said, his mouth quirking even as his eyes stayed serious.

All the Kanes shared the same bright green eyes, but Sawyer's gaze searched out your soul. A useful skill in law enforcement.

Too bad Wilder didn't have one.

He peered through the snow. Someone hunched in front of the mailbox at the end of his driveway. Maybe his latest book order had come in.

No. He wiped his eyes clear. This wasn't Fred, the local postman. The guy was middle-aged, dressed in a pair of grey and green camo pants and a tucked-in plaid shirt, the same kind a lumberjack might wear. Red and black, thick wool, but in this weather the guy must be freezing his ass off.

What reason in hell did he have for poking around in his mailbox?

"Can I help you?" Even with the wind, his words carried. Wilder knew how to project his voice, had years of practice yelling out commands over the noise of the jump plane or a fire's roar. A skill he wouldn't need anymore.

Can't be a smoke jumper without a leg.

The stranger didn't hear him though. Or ignored him. Wilder tried to pick up his pace but shit, he couldn't move quick.

"Hey!" Wilder shouted as he approached. "Hey, you there."

Nothing.

A chill shot down Wilder's spine that had nothing to do with the windchill or snow. Something wasn't right.

He settled a hand on the man's wide shoulder and the guy half-turned. Black hair hung over his forehead and he had a trimmed mustache. The guy was big. Not as big as Wilder but also vaguely familiar. He knew the face but couldn't place the name. He'd been out of Brightwater for over a decade but could still recognize a local.

The gaze was what got him, staring into space, eyes slightly unfocused, even as his cheeks were bone white and slack lips almost bloodless. His pants were streaked with moss and his tennis shoes were mud-caked. Wilder turned and picked out a few faint footprints leading to the hill across the street. Castle Falls was below the main part of town. Where'd he come from? The silent stranger wasn't out on a random pleasure stroll. The bluffs were steep, riddled with small cliffs and dense prickly black-berry thickets.

The man mumbled a few words, tapping his fingers against his chest in an erratic pattern. There was some-thing wrong with him, cognitively speaking.

"Come on then," Wilder said gruffly. He didn't want company but he'd be damned if he'd leave a confused man alone on a night like this.

SAWYER KANE, BRIGHTWATER's sheriff, hung up the phone and stood, hooking a hand over the back of his neck. "Well, that's the shortest unsolved mystery in Brightwater's history."

Quinn's shoulders slumped in relief. She'd only been in the sheriff's office a few minutes but panic had clawed her insides to shreds. "Someone found him?"

A troubled look passed over Sawyer's ruggedly handsome features, gone so fast Quinn wasn't sure it had ever been there at all. "My brother of all people. Your dad was cold and confused, but he'll be okay."

"Archer found him up by Hidden Rock Ranch? But that's miles away."

"No." Sawyer took off his hat and tossed it on the edge of his desk. "My other brother, Wilder. He's recently back in town, been living in Montana for years."

"Must be great having more family close," Quinn said, distractedly. "If I could just get his address, I'll get out of your hair and—"

"You sit tight," Sawyer said, grabbing his jacket. "I can collect him just fine."

"No, no." She jumped to her feet. "It's no trouble, I'm anxious to see him."

There was that mystifying look again. "My brother isn't great with strangers."

"Oh." Quinn didn't know how to process that information, but there wasn't time to ponder. "I won't stay long. In and out. I'll grab Dad and hit the road, keep ahead of the blizzard. I need to figure out what happened at his facility. This situation can't be repeated."

Sawyer hesitated and she froze, feeling scrutinized—

but why? Whatever the reason, the sheriff gave an almost imperceptible nod, coming to some private decision. "You know what? You're right. You should go. My brother is gruff but he's a good guy deep down."

"I'm sure he's wonderful."

Sawyer cocked a brow and jotted something on a notepad, tearing it off to hand to her. "Here's his address. It's not far."

She swallowed a gasp. "Castle Falls Lane?"

Wilder Kane. *The great and mysterious W. Kane.*

A lick of heat shot up her spine. Too bad she hadn't solved the mystery under better circumstances, but still. At last she'd made a definitive crack in the case of W. Kane and his eclectic book selections, so many titles that were her own personal favorites.

She left the sheriff's office and strode to her parking spot behind A Novel Experience. Her stomach muscles gave an aching twinge as the silver Tacoma pickup came into view. This had been her dad's truck, his baby. She remembered sitting in his front yard during warm Brightwater summer days, sinking her fingers into the lush grass, tilting her face to meet the sun's kiss as cool air blew down from the mountains while he waxed and washed it in the driveway.

These days, he didn't even remember that he owned a truck.

She started the engine and it sprang to life despite the temperatures. After this storm passed, she'd take Dad for a drive along the country back roads. Let him listen to all his classic rock favorites without a single eye roll. Heck, she'd even sing along.

Right after she raised holy hell with his facility. How could Mountain View have been so careless as to allow him to escape and wander? Yes, he was around twenty or thirty years younger than the average resident but still.

Thank God, Wilder Kane found him.

At the town outskirts she turned left and then hooked a hard right past the crooked road sign that said "Castle Falls Lane." She had never come down this way. Once she'd asked Dad about it because she wanted to see a waterfall so close to town, but Dad shook his head with a vague, "Not today, honey."

Or any day, it turned out. No one ever went to Castle Falls and eventually she sort of forgot about the place. There were so many other things to do while visiting Dad: four-wheeling, going for long day hikes in the John Muir Wilderness, or trout fishing. Activities that would never occur to Mom to do in five squillion billion years.

Things Quinn loved.

The truck radio started playing "White Christmas" and she hummed over the potholes. She loved musicals and adored Christmas. The holidays would be bittersweet this year but no shame in clinging to the simple comforts of the season.

"401 . . ." She peered at what appeared to be a rusted trailer. "403" was a burned out foundation surrounded by thorns. "Cheese and rice," she mumbled. Brightwater was such a cute, charming old Western town. Castle Falls Lane was like a dark and dirty secret.

405. There was a black mailbox and a long winding

driveway enclosed in a dark tunnel of pines. Ominous. She swallowed but her throat remained thick.

"Stop being silly." There was nothing creepy here. Just the textbook definition of a dark and stormy night, the clichéd backdrop triggering her subconscious.

She parked her car in front of a stone cabin trimmed with forest green shutters and a dark green tin roof. Her headlights illuminated two black windows in the front, but smoke spiraled from the chimney. Someone must be home.

She stepped outside, slammed the door and tendrils of hair whipped from her loose ponytail, slapping at her cheeks as she trudged to the house. Imagine Dad out in this weather? He must have been scared to death. Fresh tears threatened. Yes. Thank baby guardian angels for Wilder Kane. Who cared if he lived in a creepy place? She'd bake him a pie as a thank-you, actually scratch that, she could barely boil water. She'd buy a large bourbon pecan one at Haute Coffee. Her boots skidded on black ice and she caught herself, just.

Throw the bakery's new pumpkin spice latte pie into the mix as well.

Right after giving Dad the biggest hug.

She kicked snow off her boots on the top step before crossing the small porch. As she raised her hand to knock, the door swung open, the space filled by a man's enormous silhouette. She was in two-inch heeled boots and he still towered over her. So much for the wiry hipster of her imagination. This hulk read *Little House on the Prairie* and *The Great Gatsby*?

Does not compute.

"Hello there, quite a night, hey?" she said, sticking out a hand in greeting while grappling for her brightest tone. It wouldn't do to sound scared or suspicious. "I'm Quinn. Quinn Higsby from the emails? I mean, from A Novel Experience. We email a little. About books. Obviously." She cleared her throat. "Anyway, um, thanks so much for rescuing my father. You're a real hero."

"Where's Sawyer?" he snapped, ignoring her offer of a handshake. His voice was rough like someone had enthusiastically sandpapered the edges.

"The sheriff?" She blinked, lowering her palm and wiping the sudden sweat on her denim-encased thigh. "Your brother? I—I—why, I told him I'd come instead. You did find my father, right?"

He folded his arms. "You shouldn't have left him alone, he isn't a well man."

"I know that." Nerves had frayed away her manners. If he wanted to parry, she'd bring an axe to the sword fight. "This wasn't intentional."

He didn't move.

"So may I come in?"

"Inside?" He pronounced the word as if it were a tricky piece of foreign language.

She rubbed her hands over her arms. "I'm sort of freezing out here. Blizzard and all."

"Right. Yeah. Sure." He half-shook his head and raked a big hand through shaggy disordered hair. She couldn't discern much from his features, only harsh lines; a tough, angular, and scruffy jaw; one seriously craggy brow; and an unrelenting gaze. Somehow those severe eyes of his were oddly brilliant, catching light, but from where? The interior was dark except for the small fire burning in the hearth. It looked cheery enough despite the chill he projected, a cold that could rival the wind lashing the back of her neck. She stepped forward and he flinched as if she were a repellant magnetic force.

She hesitated. Maybe Sawyer was right.

What if coming here had been a mistake?

Chapter Four

WILDER FLATTENED HIS back against the wall as the stranger barged past in a cloud of cherry mint lip balm and flowery shampoo. Hold up. This was the woman who'd been sending all those overly friendly emails from the bookshop? Not even the cottage's gloomy interior could dim her loveliness. He should never have let her in. But the way she shivered hadn't left him with any choice.

Damned if I do, damned if I don't.

He turned and gestured mockingly at the cramped combined kitchen and dining room. " 'Fraid I can't offer you much in the way of a tour." The wildfire's smoke had damaged his voice box, made his words sound like a growl no matter his mood. When he pointed to the open door leading into the spare bedroom, there was no way to hide the scars on his hand. "Your father's in there."

She gasped and he resisted balling his fingers into a fist. Despite his ruined body, his ears remained in fine working order. This rush of frustration wasn't fair. It wasn't her fault that she reminded him of all the beautiful things in the world, a beauty denied to him.

"You've been hurt?" she whispered, eyes wide.

He gritted his teeth as wariness brimmed in his veins, ready to breach, flood his body, sweep away any semblance of calm. Better to ignore the question. "Your father has been resting for about a half hour." He set his cane against the small circular kitchen table and sank into a chair, picking up his knife and the chess piece he'd been carving before her arrival. When Sawyer first suggested the hobby, Wilder considered it another tedious way to pass away the time, but he'd grown addicted to the simple action, the slow creativity involved in paring back wood to reveal shape and structure. "Is he always that combative?"

"Oh no." She pinched the bridge of her nose. "What happened? Did he try to hit you?"

"Only about a dozen or so times."

Quinn's father might be out of it, but he was big and strong, confused at being led into an unfamiliar house by a man he didn't recognize. Wilder couldn't say he blamed him. Nor did he resent the right-hook to his gut even though his abs still stung.

"It's called Alzheimer's aggression."

He strained to hear her softened voice over the wind howling through the eaves.

"No one is really sure why it happens. He was never the least bit violent before getting sick. I think the symptoms come on most strongly when he's scared or frustrated. Please don't take it personally." Her words came out matter-of-factly but the way she addressed the room's corner, rather than his face, made him suspect deeper undercurrents ran beneath her calm exterior.

That or he repulsed her.

He dug his knife into the wood. "I gave him some stew and decaf coffee. He settled quickly after that. Snored a few times so I know he's out."

"Thank you," she said. "For taking him in."

"Wasn't more than anyone else would do for a man in his situation."

"Maybe. Maybe not. But to have him fall asleep means you made him comfortable."

The house shook as the wind redoubled its assault.

"It's getting wild out there." She glanced to the ceiling. "I should wake him up and get out of your hair."

He opened his mouth to agree, but one look out the window made him bite his tongue. The day's light was almost completely gone, the surrounding woods eclipsed by a total whiteout.

He didn't want this woman to stay but hell if he'd let her venture out in these treacherous conditions.

"You can't drive in this storm."

"It's fine." She adjusted her glasses. "I know how to handle a truck."

He didn't doubt it. Her face might hold an intense fragility but there was no missing the athletic long lines of her body or determination in her expression. This was a take-charge woman.

"You have snow chains?"

That lowered her stubborn chin a fraction. She bit the corner of her lip, worrying it a little. "No, but I don't see why—"

"Even if the visibility was good enough that you could back out of my driveway, there's no way in hell you're getting up the lane's steep grade."

"The truck—"

"Doesn't have the guts."

"Says who?" she snapped, hands flying to her hips.

"Me. It's not a four-wheel drive." Her feistiness drew him in for some reason. How long had it been since anyone tried to put him in his place? Everyone was always tiptoeing around his moods or forcing good cheer as if he didn't know the difference between a real and a fake smile. He knew his brothers and their partners cared about him, but it was hard when he didn't care about himself. Or much of anything.

And now there was this argumentative woman, and suddenly he found himself curious, and that was the first step to caring.

Hell, maybe she should go, foul weather or not.

A loud tearing creak, followed by a crash and breaking glass, reverberated from outside.

"What was that?" she gasped, flying to the front door before he had managed to grab his cane. He limped after, wondering what had happened to inspire such rapid-fire cursing. Jesus, this woman was spitting out choice phrases on the porch that would make a pirate blush.

He paused behind her. A fat Douglas fir limb had been shorn from its trunk, smashed onto her truck, shattering the windshield. That sealed the deal. She wasn't going anywhere tonight.

"Guess this is the part where you say 'I told you so,'" she muttered.

"Not after you took the words out of my mouth," he grumbled back.

"Could you drive—"

"Can't." He knocked his cane against his left leg and she glanced down at the hollow reverberation. "Not allowed. My Jeep's a manual and I haven't been given the all clear to get behind the wheel. Not enough coordination to work the clutch yet."

Sawyer had said if he got a new vehicle with an automatic transmission it would be fine, but he loved that old Jeep and balked at more lifestyle changes. "Guess you're stuck with me."

"Can I bother you for a tarp?" Her expression was guarded. "I'd like to get the window covered, otherwise my cab will fill with snow."

"I'll do it. Get inside. There's still warm stew on the stovetop. Nothing fancy, just Dinty Moore." Something told him this woman was pure trouble.

She shook her head. "I can't ask you to stay outside in these conditions."

"Why?" His gaze scoured the sky. "Because I'm a cripple?"

"What? No! Because this is my responsibility."

She started rambling about her father, how she'd barged in, inconvenienced him, but he stopped listening. He knew the real reason.

She'd glimpsed his hand burns, knew about his leg, and now thought him good for nothing, a half-man who couldn't even secure a tarp over a truck.

He hobbled down the step, stepped into a knee-deep drift, and tipped forward.

A light touch gripped his elbow, steadied him. "Stop, wait—"

"I said go inside," he snarled. This was his new reality. He used to be able to hike twenty miles carrying a hundred-pound pack and barely break a sweat. Now even getting to the shed was akin to *Mission: Impossible*.

"Do you hear yourself? It's a near blizzard." Her brown eyes narrowed, eyes that were sharply intelligent behind her glasses.

"It's an actual blizzard," he muttered, struggling forward. He'd make it to the shed or die trying. He didn't know if she stared or quietly slipped back inside. Damned if he'd turn around to check.

FOR THE NEXT ten minutes Quinn lurked by the window above the sink, peering into the swirling snow and gathering gloom. "Stubborn donkey," she repeated for the tenth time. Why wouldn't Wilder accept her offer of help? Must be some sort of manly display, a depressing notion when she'd been so fascinated by him for months. And when she mentioned the book orders he had skimmed over her statement as if they meant nothing.

Now he was out in a blizzard, slipping and swearing, doing a job she could have easily finished by now.

If she had one pet peeve in this world, it was a macho man.

From the spare room, her father gave a wet snort and a few lip smacks followed by a lengthy snore. There it came again, that niggling pang of guilt. As much as she was annoyed by the present situation, she was also undeniably grateful. Wilder Kane might be gruff and surly as heck, but he'd given her father refuge, and what's more, calmed and fed him. Dad actually fell asleep, something she couldn't even manage when he started to get agitated.

At last the front door blew open and the heavy limping sound came down the narrow, short hallway.

"All good?" She propped a hand on the mantel above the hearth as if she hadn't been checking on him.

He gave a curt nod, slinging his jacket on the back of a dining chair. "I didn't need a babysitter."

Darn. He'd totally busted her spying. She crossed to the table and picked up the small wooden horsehead that he'd been whittling. "This is nice."

"It's nothing." He shrugged, brushing snow from his thick, glossy hair.

Another object lay on the table. A half-finished castle. "Are these all chess pieces?"

"Yeah."

"*Fun with Whittling*." She tried for her best smile. "I got that order in the mail for you today. Didn't know I'd be paying you a house call or I could have saved you some postage."

He moved to the oven and stared into a pot. "You didn't eat any stew."

"Not hungry, thanks. I'm a snacker, low blood sugar and all. I nibble on dry cereal throughout the day, pack sandwich bags of Corn Pops and Fruity Pebbles. My taste buds haven't graduated from the third grade, it's a problem. Anyway, why do you place book orders if you live this close to town? Why not come into the store? Won't one of your brothers take you? How do you shop?"

His brows contracted at her game of twenty questions. "Don't like charity. Sawyer brings groceries in once a week. Otherwise, I keep to myself."

"You have a dog?"

"No." He sounded wary.

"Cat?"

"No."

"Hamster?"

"Nothing." Exasperation laced the word.

"Not even a houseplant?" She threw up her hands. "A Christmas cactus or a couple of philodendrons could go a long way to cheering things up around here. Don't you ever get lonely?"

He looked as if he was about to answer in the affirmative before turning away to frown at the fire. "Do you ever stop talking?"

"Sorry, I'm sort of a Chatty Cathy." Especially when nervous.

He rubbed the back of his neck. While he was big, grumpy, and unsmiling, Wilder wasn't unattractive. Not at all. In fact he was rather good-looking. His profile was strong, ruthless, as if he was a Caesar of old. Bold and brutish. Maybe not the type she normally went for, but somehow appealing.

Quite appealing actually.

He turned, unexpectedly meeting her gaze, and she fumbled, the castle slipping through her fingers and clattering on the tabletop.

What was wrong with her? He wasn't even nice. She was nice. At least most of the time. Friendly and a natural extrovert. She liked people and people seemed to like her.

Unless they were married to a randy celebrity who had tried to proposition her.

Or sported the initials W. K.

"Would you mind sitting down?" She drilled her fingers on the table. "You're making me a little edgy with all that looming. Hence the gab."

He looked startled, as if he never considered that, and leaned against the far wall, as far away from her as he could get in the small space. His body tensed as if preparing for a fight rather than a little pass-the-time small talk. "I'd rather stand if that's all right by you. More comfortable."

Couldn't argue with that. The silence continued until her teeth were set on edge. No point beating around the bush. Might as well satisfy her curiosity. "So you're a reader?"

He nodded with a touch of impatience. "You know the answer."

"I've wondered about who you were over the last few months because your choices are always so diverse. Most people like to read similar stuff. Occasionally they might get in the mood for something different, but you are impossible to pin down. Every genre. Big authors, almost undiscovered ones. Kid-lit to poetry."

He mumbled something that sounded like "the list."

"What list?"

He tilted his head, regarding her for a moment, before grabbing a notebook off the mantel. Flipping it open, he removed a newspaper clipping. "The list," he repeated, limping over to lay it on the table.

She glanced down. " '1001 Books to Read before You Die'? That was the big mystery?" What a simple explanation. She didn't know whether to laugh or be disappointed.

"I have a lot of time on my hands so am working my way down title by title. Wasn't ever meant to be mysterious. It's just a by-product of boredom." He sounded defensive, his features set in a scowl.

She cocked her head. "You know, you can drop the sullen, gruff act anytime. You don't scare me."

"No?" He had a gaze that cut through her flesh, straight to the bone.

Maybe he'd be better off doing scrimshaw than whittling.

She feigned calm. Something did scare her about him and it wasn't his glower. It was the way her heart picked up a few extra beats, the pressure building in her thighs. It was all she could do to keep from trembling. How long had it been since she responded with this sort of physicality to a guy? A long time.

And never this quickly.

She had worked in a town that peddled fantasy. Everyone had their celebrity crushes, would argue over so-and-so hot guy versus so-and-so hot guy. And that's fine, but nothing she could ever get into. She didn't fangirl over faces or have stargasms. She always went for a guy who could make her laugh. Sitcom screenwriters and the like.

This guy? She wasn't laughing with Wilder, not by a long shot. Instead every molecule in her body was hyperaware and her stomach warmed with a happy, soft feeling. The whole thing was so cliché and probably not even real. These weird bodily sensations probably wouldn't be happening if he had fluorescent kitchen lights. Anything seemed possible by flickering firelight.

She cleared her throat. "Are you sure you don't want to sit?"

"I sat for a long time this year. I'd be happy to never sit down again."

"So this is new for you, the leg?"

He took a moment to reply, long enough she wondered if he'd ignore the question. "Lost it in late July."

"I'm sorry."

"Me too. I was rather attached to it."

An inward jolt struck her core at his unexpected and fleeting smile. He'd made a joke. Oh God, he could be funny too?

Then he really was dangerous.

Chapter Five

QUINN UNZIPPED HER jacket, pausing halfway. "You don't mind, do you? Seeing as I'm staying, at least for a while."

"No." *Yes.* Because the minute she slid out of that white, puffy coat her breathtaking body was on full display. Those snug-fitting jeans weren't overtly sexy but the way the denim contoured the slight flare of her narrow thighs as she sat down made him swallow. Hard.

It had been a while since he'd been in the company of any woman who wasn't a medical professional or intimately involved with his brothers. Also, as much as he didn't want to admit it, he had a type and this forward, strong-looking woman fit it right down to that thick wavy brown hair pulled back at the nape of her long sexy neck.

Necks were underrated female geography. He loved how they tasted when he kissed them there, how they smelled as he nuzzled.

Equally fascinating was her lush mouth, how the corner remained quirked on one side despite the natural pout, as if in perpetual secret amusement.

This woman was bright, spunky, and happy, despite her father's miserable situation. His heart sank. He had nothing to offer someone like her, not when his whole world had burned to a cinder.

He shook himself inwardly, not moving a muscle. No point succumbing to the ugly truth, however true. Maybe he could pretend to be a normal guy for the night. Normal except for the scars, the missing leg, and the fact he hadn't spoken to a living soul since Sawyer dropped off his groceries six days ago, and was tongue-tied around strangers at the best of times.

Shit.

What would Archer do? His younger brother was good with people, especially the ladies. He'd navigate this situation like a pro.

She gave him a tentative smile, probably because he was staring at her like a loon.

Compliments. Women like compliments.

"Your teeth are real white," Wilder blurted. Goddamn it, the words hung over them like a comic strip balloon. He wished for a string to grab on to, so he could stuff the idiocy back into his mouth, swallow it down.

"Excuse me?" Her shoulders jerked as her lips clamped, clearly not anticipating the awkward flattery.

At least he hadn't said how much he liked her neck. Yet.

Damn, this was a mistake. He wasn't good with people. Didn't like people. Didn't need people.

Quinn set her chin in her hand. "Did you just pay me a compliment?"

"No." He answered quickly.

She peered at him, clearly unwilling to let this go. "Yes, you did. I heard you. Or maybe you need to send my dentist a fan letter."

He ignored her joking tone. "Forget it."

"I . . . it's okay . . . it just surprised me."

He snorted. "You don't look like someone who is short on compliments." If anything, he guessed the opposite was the case. A woman like Quinn didn't exist in the world for men to ignore, not with that face, that body.

She shrugged.

"You telling me you don't get attention?"

"Attention? I guess I get"—she frowned, as if searching for the right word—"lines."

"Lines?"

"You know, like 'did you sit on a pile of sugar, because you have a sweet ass?' or 'Hey, baby, I'm not staring at your rack, I'm looking at your heart,' or, oh, here's a good one, 'Let me have your picture so I can show Santa what I want for Christmas.' "

He knitted his brow, his stomach muscles getting tight. "Guys have seriously said all that stuff to you?"

"Yep." Her matter-of-fact tone didn't mask a twinge of annoyance. "And those are the ones that are at least a little bit funny."

He gritted his teeth. "Dumbasses."

"Yeah. Guys can be that all right." She shrugged

before glancing up quickly. "Present company excluded though."

Yeah sure.

Hard to believe her encouragement given the way he bungled through their conversations. He sank into the antique rocking chair beside the fire, the one Annie, Sawyer's girlfriend, brought over from her farmhouse. It was well-made and a well-intentioned gift but still made him feel like a thirty-one-year-old geriatric.

"So." She crossed her legs, idly smoothing a hand over her knee.

"So." A dull ache spread through his chest. He was used to phantom pains in his missing leg, but apparently the same phenomenon could happen to your heart.

"You read and whittle. Plus start fires."

"What?" His voice came out a harsh bark. She looked perceptive but how could she—

"Hey, that's a darn good fire." She flicked a thumb toward the hearth before giving him an odd, lingering look.

"Hrmph." He had nothing else of use to offer the conversation. Going from a hermit to a human in polite company was jarring. "I put fires out or used to."

She flashed a smile, tucking a loose strand of hair behind her ear. "Literally or metaphorically speaking? Because I used to put out fires too." She grabbed the tendril back and began looping it around her finger. "But they were things like how my boss didn't want to be asked if he wore shoe inserts in his last movie to appear taller or had Botox done. The answers to both were yes by the way. I worked for a PR company in Hollywood and handled stars. One in particular. Tim Beckett."

"The guy from all the *Fatal Night* movies?"

She shot him an indecipherable look. "You a fan?"

"Not really."

"Really?" Her shoulders dropped a fraction. "Most guys seem to like big explosions, car chases, spy rings."

He shrugged. "Guess I'm not like most guys."

There came that appraising stare again. "Guess not. And by the way, I'm going to make a deduction that you fought actual fires."

He spared her a covert glance. The fire illuminated her sweet features, the nervous way her tongue darted to tap her top lip. "What tipped you off?"

"The hands for one."

Those lingering looks she kept casting in his direction were just his imagination. No doubt she found him repulsive. Couldn't help but stare. He affected an indifferent shrug. "You mean my scars."

"Do they hurt?"

"Not anymore." He glanced down at his crooked fingers. "Did at the time though. Third degree. Required grafting. Surgery. It's why I took that up." He nodded at the whittling. "Part of my therapy. Helps with regaining dexterity."

"What about sensation?"

He swallowed. "Most of the nerve endings were destroyed." He'd never be able to gather all that long luscious hair and revel in the texture of soft strands slipping through his fingers.

"You can't feel anything with your hands?"

"Very little."

"And this was the same accident that cost you the leg?"

"More or less." He swallowed, throat thick. "Parachute accident followed by a wildfire."

"Oh my God." Her voice rose an octave. "That's unlucky."

"Don't ask me to pick a lotto ticket number."

She made a strange sound, almost as if she wanted to chuckle but choked it back.

"Go on, laugh. It was a joke."

"I thought so, but got to say, you don't seem like the jovial sort."

There was a cough from the spare bedroom, followed by a long low moan.

"My dad! He's waking up." She jumped to her feet. "Mind if I get a glass of water? I have some of his Ativan in my bag. He's going to be anxious waking in a strange place. Best if I can keep him subdued, comfortable, and sleeping until morning."

Wilder gestured to the four glasses lined up on the shelf. "Help yourself. Whatever you need." He clamped his mouth before starting in on some "mi casa es su casa" crap and eyed his watch. His entire body prickled with awareness. The night hadn't even properly settled and he wasn't sure how he'd survive it.

QUINN PRETENDED SHE didn't notice Wilder's covert watch check, but that didn't fool her heart. The uneven lurch was a stupid physiological reaction because it wasn't as if he had requested her company in the first place. She grabbed a glass and ran it under the tap, resisting the urge to splash her face and cool down. Good thing the room was dark because a hot flush had permanently stamped itself on her cheeks.

She walked out of the kitchen space without another glance at the big male body slouched by the fire, and she entered the bedroom without a knock. Maybe Dad had just stirred in his sleep. Maybe he'd . . .

"Who are you?" he yelled, sitting straight up in bed.

"Hi, Dad. It's Bizzy. Quinn. Your daughter."

He didn't answer with more than a grunt. He'd forgotten her name last of all. Maybe that fact should make her happier.

He thrashed with the comforter. "Get me the hell out of here."

"Hear that wind?" She pointed to the roof. "There's a heck of a big winter storm outside. Lots of snow. We can't go anywhere. Have a glass of water and these pills and try to get more rest. You've had quite the adventure today." She held the glass to his mouth and exhaled when he swallowed in compliance. Took the pills without complaint.

"Are you hungry?"

His snort meant no.

Thank goodness Wilder had fed him earlier. The hot meal in his belly would help keep him comfortable and comfortable meant calm.

"How about you get up and use the bathroom before going back to bed?"

Dad muttered something else unintelligible but grasped her hand as she led him out of bed, shuffling beside her in his strange, stooped posture.

"Excuse me," she called to where Wilder was sitting. Or had been sitting. The rocking chair was empty.

"Yeah?"

He stood in the hall, behind her. Close enough she could smell pine, shaving cream, and the faint scent of honey. She fought the temptation to turn and burrow her face into his broad chest, sniffing deep and long. Instead, she refocused her grip on Dad's hand.

"I need to take him into your bathroom."

"I heard. I came to take him myself."

"You don't have to do that."

"Your dad might not know what's happening, but trust me, he'd rather not have his daughter watching him take a leak. It's no big deal. The bathroom is off the back. He'll be out in a minute."

She released Dad and he smiled at Wilder, offering his hand, looking so much like a trusting boy that it was almost impossible to swallow the knot in her throat.

Dad never went to a new person willingly.

Wilder must send out some sort of good vibe, some wavelength Dad picked up on. Or she'd spent way too much time on the California coast. Good vibes? Wavelengths?

"What's so funny?" Wilder asked, back again with all his faint yet distracting manly smells. He stood, shoulders relaxed, casual, as if the two of them in a dark narrow hallway was no big deal.

And it wasn't a big deal.

It wasn't.

"Hey." She cleared her throat, hearing Dad opening the door. "Do you have a book I can borrow? My dad likes me to read to him before bed. It might settle him down."

"You know I have books."

"I mean, may I use one for an hour or so. I don't want to presume—"

"Shelves are through there." He pointed. "My bedroom."

She froze. "You stash books in your bedroom?"

"That's where I read them so . . ."

Good lord, the man liked to read in bed too? The idea of his bare chest bathed in lamplight while he furrowed that strong brow over a hardcover created a flurry of butterflies that transformed into water buffalo, trammeling her insides to mush.

Come on, this is so not fair, fate. Really not fair.

"Light is on your left," he called.

"Got it." She walked through the door and ran her hand over the wall to find the switch, flicking it on. If she hoped to discover any clues about the mysterious man, this room wasn't yielding answers. There was a full-sized four-poster bed covered with a plain green down comforter, a framed poster of Mount Whitney, a bedside table with a half-full glass of water. And then . . . oh. Okay. *Now we are talking.*

Two large pine bookshelves bracketed either side of the window, stuffed with books. Many she recognized. Many she had sent herself.

Never in a million years did she expect to ever see them again.

As she stood, staring at the titles, she became aware of something else. The room smelled good.

It smelled like *him*.

"See anything you like?" With the light on, his face was clear for the first time that night. None of those rough features could ever be described as handsome. But he had that quality, the elusive and indefinable spark that made you look a second time, everything an interesting paradox. Wide brutal lips, but at the same time, the idea of them fastened to her skin made her dizzy. His hair tumbled in every direction, thick, dark, and shaggy, grazing his shirt's collar, and yet the texture invited touch, and those eyes held a magnetic longing, as if compelling her to give . . . what?

Good God, get it together, woman. He'd notice her legs shaking in another second, rattling the floorboard. "Anything I like? Um . . . yes . . . this." She grabbed blindly, realizing it was *Grimm's Fairy Tales*. Good enough.

"Interesting choice," he rumbled. "Those stories were darker than I expected."

It had been a long time since she had read any Grimm, but vague recollections hung over her. "They are pretty macabre, huh? Death. Doom. Old ladies snacking on young children, etcetera." She rubbed the front cover to avoid his intense scrutiny. The book seemed oddly perfect, like of course she'd read a fairy tale on such a windblown wintry night, hunkered in a little lost cabin down a strange lane, haunted by a brooding man who—

Dad coughed from the kitchen as a flood of guilt doused her warm heart in a cold splash of realism. What was she doing? Romantic thoughts had no place in her real world.

Not when she had to take care of Dad, handle his affairs. Not to mention that her own brain might be a ticking time bomb.

Better to keep her dreams confined to imagination. Live vicariously through plucky bluestockings and dashing dukes or wolf shifters or alpha tycoons. Those men might be dangerous on the page, but they were safe for a bookworm like her.

"You okay?" His deep voice broke up her train of thought.

She snapped up her head. "Huh?"

"I asked if you were okay. You made a face."

"What kind?"

"A thinking one." A note of amusement clung to his words.

She squashed her brows together, readjusting her glasses. Was he making fun of her? "Newsflash, I do have a brain."

"I wasn't hinting you were a scarecrow."

She stared, lost.

He scanned the shelf and plucked another title, holding it up while arching a brow. *The Wizard of Oz*.

"Oh. Right. If I only had a brain." Duh. "I'm not really winning any Mensa awards tonight."

"You're tired and worried." He shelved the book. "Go take care of your dad and then think about getting some shut-eye yourself. You look as if you could use it. My bed is free."

If she was befuddled before, now her brain turned to mashed potatoes. "Your bed?"

"Not with me." He tripped over his words in haste and coughed into his fist. "I'll settle out by the fire. You take my bed. It's more comfortable."

"I can't do that."

"Where else will you sleep?"

"The floor next to Dad."

His expression turned stony. "You really think that I'll let you curl up on the frigid floorboards?"

"I don't think you are going to *let* me do anything," she snapped, hackles up at his tone. "I make decisions for myself."

"You will sleep in my bed." He stepped forward, his flat tone suggesting the debate was over.

He clearly didn't know who he was up against.

"I wouldn't sleep in your bed in a million years." He flinched at her riled-up response. *Shiznits.* She hadn't meant the words as a personal insult, only as hyperbole. If truth were to be told, under vastly different circumstances, she'd be interested in sleeping in that bed all right—just not alone. No, she didn't want to sleep on the ground, listening to Dad's snoring but she also didn't want to kick a guy out of his own room. Especially this tall, broody, Byronic stranger whom she'd already inconvenienced and who was dealing with a score of physical injuries.

"You're as stubborn as a Missouri mule." It didn't sound like he offered the line as a compliment.

She bit the inside of her cheek. "Takes one to know one." Good lord, this guy really brought out her sass.

He glowered down at her. She was tall but he was taller still. Made her five-foot-nine feel dainty, petite, which never happened.

She marched past him into the spare room where Dad stood next to the bed. "In you get," she said, throwing back the sheets.

He responded easy as a child. Easier actually. The meds must be kicking in, coupled by exhaustion.

"You've had a big day, haven't you?" She smoothed back his hair, feeling not for the first time like the parent rather than the child.

He nodded, probably not because he comprehended, but because she ended the sentence on an upward inflection. He answered every question with some sort of yes. She liked to take that as a sign of innate optimism.

"And look what we have here." She held up the *Grimm's Fairy Tales* for inspection as if she were a sommelier at a wine bar. This time there was no nod, only more staring. She turned to a story in the middle, "The Frog Prince," and began to read about a beautiful young princess who lost her golden ball down the well. A frog promised to recover it if she would grant his wishes—let him sleep on her pillow and eat off her plate. She desperately agreed and he returned the ball. Afterward, the girl had no intention of keeping her promise, but the king shamed her into keeping the bargain, which she did with resentment in her heart. After three nights, poof—the frog became a handsome prince. Cue the happy ever after.

"Oh spare me." She frowned at the page before glancing up, startled by Dad's snore. The princess was mean and awful. Why did she deserve to win? Why did the prince love her?

Quinn stared at her father's sleeping form.

She hadn't meant to be prickly in Wilder's room. It wasn't his fault that she couldn't afford to be attracted to anyone right now. She should go apologize. Yes. That's it. Right now.

She rose slowly, tiptoeing into the adjacent room.

"Hey," she called in a loud whisper. "I'm sorry about the way I acted."

Wilder didn't budge in the rocking chair.

"I was rude in your room and that's inexcusable. Sometimes I say things without thinking."

Still no answer. *Tough crowd.*

She crept forward and that's when she realized his eyes were closed and his breathing was deep and rhythmic. He had dozed off, angled ever so slightly toward the direction of the spare room. Had he been listening to the bedtime story too?

She leaned forward, crossing her eyes and sticking out her tongue in case he was kidding around.

He didn't flinch. In sleep, his features held something gentle, an innocence, as if you could see the boy he once was, long ago. All dark hair and long lashes. A face you wanted to touch. Instead, she balled her hand into a fist before it got any funny ideas and padded into his room, plucking up the blanket folded on the edge of the bed. She couldn't bear to wake him when he looked so peaceful in front of the dying fire—warm, safe, and content.

She lifted the afghan and placed it over his lap. That didn't seem like enough so she lifted it to his shoulders, hesitating when he made a soft noise, almost a sigh of contentment, as if suggesting this minor act of kindness was something more.

Maybe that's the way with all little gestures. So small and yet they can hold strange power.

She smiled at her capacity for silliness. The fairy tales must have really gotten under her skin.

The cottage was quiet with two sleeping men. What to do now? Because sleeping on the floor at this point would seem like an insult.

Instead, she went into his room, unzipped her boots and gingerly crawled into his bed. His smell lingered on the pillows, that shaving cream and pine blend mixed with the faint honey salve scent. After a few deep breaths, she relaxed, drifting to a fathomless sleep, and dreams where a man waited in a dark wood with strange longing in his eyes.

Chapter Six

WILDER WOKE WITH a start. It was the ache that took him from troubled dreams of a low, husky laugh and lean lines of a body out of reach. This wasn't a phantom pain but a throb where the prosthetic rubbed against him. The fire had long since burned itself to coals, but here and there, a bright orange glowed beneath the ruined logs, a hidden menace, beautiful in its terribleness. He glanced down. The afghan from his bed lay draped over his chest. Quinn had done this, an unexpectedly kind gesture, and now he couldn't curse her for haunting his sleep.

Outside the window, the dawn light was dim but growing in strength. The trees were blanketed but no more snowflakes fell from the steely skies. The heart of the storm had passed. Quinn would soon take her father and leave.

Good. That was good. Better she go before he started to like her presence around here—the scent of cherry mint ChapStick, the questions, the chatter.

But for now, for these next few quiet minutes, she was in his bed. Her skin under his sheets, her long hair spanning his pillow. Would she leave that flowery shampoo scent behind? Or the one she carried on her skin, the deeper secret that must linger beneath the shampoo and body wash. He hadn't gotten close enough to her to catch it.

Correction. He'd never get that close.

Time to wrap up those inclinations and stuff them in a box, tie the damn thing up in a big bow of yellow "Caution: Do Not Enter" tape. Then stuff it in a locker and toss it off a bridge into a flooded river for good measure.

Quinn was like a flame. Something he was drawn to despite the fact that he knew the danger. He learned a long time ago, in the worst way possible, that it wasn't a game. And then got a damn good refresher course last summer.

He reached into his pocket for his beeswax hand salve, opened the tin, and rubbed it over his scars. You don't play with fire unless you want to lose everything.

He clung to what little remained. Which was what? One good leg. Two eyes that could still read. A pair of burned but functional hands.

Whoop-dee-fucking-doo.

Better to accept reality. The facts were cold, hard. They didn't fuck around. He wasn't the guy who'd get the girl.

Not now. Not like this. Not ever.

WHEN QUINN CAME out of Wilder's room, rubbing her eyes, he was seated at the kitchen table, halfway through a cup of black coffee. A saucer smattered with toast crumbs was set off to one side.

"Morning." She put her glasses on as her stomach audibly rumbled. She hadn't eaten dinner last night. Bread and that pot of raspberry jam sounded mighty good.

He pointed to a pot on the counter. "Coffee?"

"Always." She waved. "Hi, my name is Quinn Higsby and I am a caffeine addict."

"Good." He nodded as if her words somehow pleased him. "Folks who don't drink coffee can't be trusted."

"There's a wise life rule." She selected a pale blue ceramic mug from the cup rack and filled it near to the brim, trying to ignore the heat radiating up her spine at the idea of being included in this man's circle of trust.

"You take anything in that?" He eyed her cup.

She was tempted to answer straight black, same as him. It sounded sexier for some reason. Mysterious. She wanted to be that woman who drank her coffee thick and dark while staring into space with a hint of world weariness. But she opted for the unsexy truth. "Milk and one sugar. Okay, two sugars."

"Milk in the fridge and as for sugar . . ." He frowned slightly. "I don't have any."

"You are lacking in sweetness, Mr. Kane." She opened the fridge door.

"Tell me something I don't know."

Her answering giggle faded. Perched on the fridge shelves were half a dozen eggs, some questionable-looking deli meat, a couple of oranges, a six-pack of dark beer, and an empty bottle of hot sauce. That was it. "I thought you said your brothers were looking after you? Is this all you have to eat?"

"That's because today is usually . . ." A loud knock cut him off. "Shopping Thursday."

"Hello? Good morning." The front door opened. "You up, brother?"

The sheriff. Quinn wished she could fall through the floorboards.

"In here," Wilder responded, straightening his flannel collar.

She wondered if she shared the same "busted" expression and took a big gulp of coffee, searing her tongue. Last Sawyer knew, she was off to collect her dad, not pay his big brother an overnight visit.

Someone pass the awkward sauce.

Sawyer entered the kitchen, removing his Stetson. "That your truck out there?" he asked, as if it wasn't at all strange to find her here for this unexpected breakfast date.

She gave a hesitant nod, tugging down the corner of her shirt and trying to think of a suitable explanatory ice-breaker.

"Looks like it has itself one hell of a tree problem," he deadpanned.

She allowed herself one small, relieved sigh. He wasn't going to demand any excuses. Apparently the crushed truck served as perfectly adequate explanation for her presence.

"You'll need a tow out of here. The weather is clearer than I expected and road crews are making good progress with the plows. I'll put in a call to Don's Auto and have those boys out here in a flash. They are good people, family owned, and won't give you a runaround on the repair costs."

"That would be great, thank you." A good, honest mechanic was worth their weight in gold.

That's when she noticed how neither brother was looking in her direction. Instead, they stared each other down, engaged in a drawn out and silent conversation.

Finally, Sawyer glanced back over, clearing his throat. "And your dad? He's—"

"Fine," she answered quickly. "Better than fine. He slept like a log, which is a funny expression when you think about it because logs don't sleep, right? They roll which is . . ."

It was too ridiculously easy to babble when two identical pairs of bright green eyes focused on her, eyes set in two vastly different faces. Sawyer was handsome, no denying it, with those classic good looks that never go out of style. Wilder wasn't a style at all, more of a statement, bold and a little savage. He pushed his chair back. "I'm going to go wash up," he announced, rising.

Sawyer turned and instinctively reached out a steadying hand. One Wilder clearly didn't need.

Quinn had a flash of understanding. People wanted to help Wilder but he resisted charity. He was a proud man. And strong. He didn't need to be treated with kid gloves, but he also shouldn't be allowed to rampage around acting rude, sullen, and downright hostile.

Except, when was the last time she graciously accepted

assistance? Oh God, she was some sort of help rejector too. People kept asking what she or Dad needed and she'd just smile and chirp, "I've got it handled."

She couldn't ignore the blatant curiosity in Sawyer's gaze once Wilder shut the bathroom door. Deciphering the meaning was the tricky part. Was it her overactive imagination or was he passing some sort of judgment after all?

She took another sip of coffee, annoyance combining with the dark roast to flood her mouth with a bitter taste. After all, how could he have left Wilder with hardly any food?

"Have you seen your brother's fridge?" she said slowly. "He can't be left without food and no transport."

A muscle in Sawyer's jaw flexed. "You spent the night with him, right?"

"Yes. Well, no. I mean, yes, but not . . ." Her cheeks burned. "I slept in his room, he slept on the rocking chair out here."

Sawyer kneaded his forehead. "You're both adults and it's not any of my damn business where you choose to sleep, or not sleep as the case may be. But if you've spent a few minutes in my big brother's company, you're bound to notice he's not exactly gracious about receiving help."

"But that's no reason to—"

"He hasn't opened the door to me all week. That's why I'm barging in so early, seeing if I could catch him bleary-eyed and docile. But I'm not taking him to do any shopping right now because tonight he'll have that entire fridge crammed with turkey and cranberry leftovers."

"Of course." Quinn resisted the urge to face palm. Today was Thanksgiving.

Wilder entered the room with an audible groan. "I said I didn't want to—"

"You're coming," Sawyer answered with a tinge of weariness as if they'd gone around and around with this conversation.

"I forgot today was a holiday," Quinn said. "I'm so discombobulated."

"Wish I could forget," Wilder murmured.

Sawyer said nothing, but gave a slight flinch, as if the words hit a secret mark.

"Hey now," Quinn chastised Wilder as he huffed back toward the table, looking and sounding like a grizzly fresh out of hibernation. "I know it's early and I kept you from your bed, but that doesn't mean that you can behave like a bear with a bee up its butt," Quinn said.

Wilder's head snapped up, gaze furious even as Sawyer burst out laughing.

"Hey, what are you doing this evening?" Sawyer asked after his chuckles subsided. "Want to join us Kanes for dinner? I can't speak for this big lug, but the rest of us don't bite."

She waved him off. "Oh, that's okay. I couldn't impose."

"Course you can," Sawyer said even though Wilder's folded-arm posture communicated otherwise.

Why was his dark and broody act so darn appealing? Never had she been such a cliché, all twitterpated for a mysterious guy. But like it or not, she was intrigued. What were his secrets? He either had one doozy of a story or she had the world's most overactive imagination.

"You have plans for dinner?" Wilder asked at last.

"I . . ." *No.* She had planned to spend lunch with Dad. Mountain View Village was going to host their own midday food fest. *Say yes, say you're busy.*

"Let me guess, you have a thing against turkey too?" Sawyer asked.

"Too?"

"My girlfriend, Annie, is a vegetarian. She's making Tofurky, whatever that is."

"No. I'm not a veggie," Quinn said with a little shiver. "Mad respect to our plant-eating friends but I love my meat." If it wasn't for her fear of rickets she'd subsist on the stuff. "But that's okay, I hate imposing . . ."

"Imposing? You know my other brother's fiancée, Edie, owns the bakery in town, right? Word on the street is that she's bringing five desserts. Five. Tell me how we could eat all that?"

She didn't want to barge in on a holiday family dinner, but Sawyer was being insistent.

Wilder scowled like a gargoyle. Except the effect was sort of sexy. Which shouldn't work because weren't gargoyles monstrous? Confused frustration swirled through her stomach. Why did this guy tie knots in her mental circuits?

"She doesn't have plans," he rumbled. "But isn't sure if she should accept."

"Grandma will appreciate fresh blood at the table," Sawyer cajoled.

"That's cruel, man," Wilder said.

"Grandma?" Quinn raised her brows. "Fresh blood? What, is she a scary vampire?"

"Scarier," both men answered at the same time.

Quinn stared in disbelief. These were two of the more attractive and powerful-looking men she'd ever come across and she had worked for an action superstar. Who could strike fear in their hearts? "I've seen your grandma at the Chicklits book club but we've never spoken. What on earth is she like at home? Pointy ears. Sharp claws. Fangs that only pop out at night?"

Wilder smoothed a hand over what appeared to be an unwilling smile. "Come and see for yourself."

"She doesn't have fangs," Sawyer said.

"Nah, she'd rather gnaw through your jugular," Wilder added.

"Wow, you two really know how to tempt a girl."

"Just want you to have the facts." Wilder slouched back in his seat.

"Remember I don't have a working truck at the moment," she said.

"We can arrange a ride," Sawyer answered firmly.

She eyeballed Wilder but he was busy turning a wooden chess piece over in his big hand, a knight from the looks of the horse. Wilder scraped the nose with a blade. Soon it was going to look like a donkey.

"I—"

"You're doing me a favor," Sawyer pushed. "Annie and Edie will kick my ass to the doghouse if they hear you spent Thanksgiving alone."

"I don't even know them." She'd seen both women around town and they seemed nice enough and ran thick as thieves. Sometimes she'd walk over to Haute Coffee and see them sitting at the counter sharing a coffee and laughing and she'd keep going because their easy friendship made her jealous, and she hated feeling jealous. After all, she had Natalie, and her books, and Dad.

But Natalie had her boyfriend, the book relationship was a little one-sided, and Dad, well, God, he *needed* her, but didn't even know it.

Didn't know her, not anymore.

She disliked having negative feelings, the ones that leaked out whenever she was in the shower, face turned to the spray as if they could be washed away before she noticed.

"Darn allergies," she'd mutter while toweling off. Allergies that struck in late autumn when most plants were dead or dormant, allergies that had never appeared until now.

Hey, it could happen.

Or maybe she was just allergic to the pressure resting on her shoulders, threatening to bow her spine. The pressure to . . . that was the problem . . . she didn't even know. It was like there was pressure just to survive, make it through each day. Stress, depression, and burnout from Dad's condition nipped at her heels. Plus the fear. The always nagging fear. What if Dad's condition is hereditary? What if . . .

No. Not now.

"Sure, I'll go," she said. "If it's not a nuisance. There's

a luncheon at Dad's place so I need to be there for that, but later I'll be alone." God, could she sound any more pathetic?

"If you're crazy enough to want to eat with our family then you're welcome to it," Wilder muttered, his hand slipping slightly. The blade sliced his thumb, a line of red welled up. He swore softly, ripped a handkerchief out of his back pocket and pressed it to the small wound.

Looking up, his gaze was frustrated, a challenge, as if "Yeah, I'm just a guy okay, cut me and I bleed."

"Do you want a Band-Aid for that?" She realized he expected her to ignore him.

He blinked. "Don't have any."

"Never fear. I do." She walked to her bag, grabbed a small bandage from the box, and passed it over. "No point carrying around a purse as big as my head if I don't keep it well stocked for anything from a zombie apocalypse to a small kitchen accident."

Sawyer's phone rang. "Sorry, this is work, got to take it. I'll step outside." He walked away, taking away the ease of the conversation with him.

Wilder glanced at her and then away. Wordlessly, he undid the wrapper and wrapped the Band-Aid around his finger.

She wanted to tell him she didn't have to go to Thanksgiving. That she didn't mean to barge into his whatever-this-was life he had going on in a haunted gulch at the end of town. But that would mean letting him know that he had gotten under her skin, was circulating through her system, the confusing feelings multiplying at an alarming rate.

She wished he'd just say no. Or yes. Anything but ignore her. Every silent second was a form of intense but addictive torture.

He wasn't carving, rather poking the wood with his knife, these useless little stabbing motions, and it dawned on her.

He doesn't know what to do about this thing between them either.

This thing.

What else was there to call it?

"Any requests?" she asked, shifting her weight, wincing at the telltale creak.

That drew his gaze back.

"For dinner," she clarified. "What are you bringing?"

He shrugged. "Napkins."

"What? Really."

"Yeah," he ruefully admitted. "They left me in charge of the important stuff."

"Do you have any favorite recipes?"

He set down his knife. "You cook?" He sounded surprised.

Better to get the truth out there as fast as possible. "No actually. I'm terrible."

"Well, Archer is doing the turkey with Grandma, Edie will bake bread and probably five different cakes, Annie is doing her Tofurky and probably other granola stuff that no one will touch but Sawyer because he's under obligation."

"Okay. So . . ."

"Rice Krispies Treats," he said suddenly.

"What about them?"

"My mom used to make them for every holiday." His gaze turned wistful. "She let me lick the spoon. You'd have liked her. She had a laugh sort of like yours, loud but in a good way that made everyone feel good."

She hugged herself, as if it would be possible to hang on to the warm feelings he'd given. "Hot dogs," she said. "That's the taste of my childhood. I used to spend summers out here with my dad as a kid. Every Fourth of July we'd go to the rodeo grounds and he'd buy me a hot dog. I can't see one without thinking of him." She scrubbed her face, willing away the tightening in her throat. "But no point moping. If he ever saw me sad he'd say 'No use crying over baked beans.' Which doesn't even make sense come to think of it."

Wilder raised his head, blinking as his leg slammed against a table leg.

He turned away, but without even seeing his face she knew. Something had shifted—but what?

He drew a harsh, rattling breath. "Have we met before?"

"I don't think so." She swallowed. The comfortable exchange had taken a sharp turn. She tried to think but her brain didn't work right, not when she was locked in that forceful gaze. "But maybe? I mostly spent my time here with Dad, going camping, riding his four-wheeler, hiking, and stuff like that. Sometimes I played with other kids during town events though. But I'm twenty-five and you're . . ." He was older than her, hard to say by how much.

"Thirty-one."

"Sorry to get us going, but we got to get going." Sawyer came back in, face grim. "I got you a tow organized but I'm going to have to head in to work. I'll be back for you around lunch," he told Wilder.

"What's up?" Wilder asked.

"Fire." Sawyer shook his head. "On one of the new properties. No one was home, thank God. The owner lives somewhere out on the east coast, but the damage is extensive."

Quinn didn't miss the long look the brothers exchanged before both cleared their throats and went back about their business. She went to get Dad up and going, trying to ignore the unnerving feeling Wilder induced. Just when she had him pegged as gruff and bad tempered, he surprised her with some sort of awkwardly endearing interaction. And it scared her.

It scared her how much she liked it.

Chapter Seven

WILDER HUNCHED IN the big leather chair as the cheerful sounds of Thanksgiving preparations hummed throughout Sawyer's cabin. Quinn hadn't arrived and already his stomach muscles clenched. It wasn't just her gorgeous face or that infectious laugh that set him on edge. No, it was when she said, "No use crying over baked beans." As soon as those words left her mouth, that one bad memory, long shoved into the "never think about again" mental file sprang front and center.

A dimly lit stall. The earthy, rich smell of hay. A small hand settling on the small of his back. "Why are you crying?"

No. Impossible. That couldn't have been her.

He glanced at his watch for the fourth time in ten minutes. Maybe she reconsidered coming. Then again, Archer had just mentioned that Kit, a second cousin and his youngest brother's best friend, was giving her a ride out to the ranch.

Good for Kit and his two long strong legs and the SUV he could drive without any problem. What did Wilder care? He took another swig of beer. He didn't.

Why are you crying?

He cleared his throat. Across the coffee table, Annie's son, Atticus, making engine sounds with his mouth, drove Matchbox cars between the stacks of *Astronomy Today* and *Vegan Life* magazines. The kid kept sneaking a not-so-subtle stare at his legs.

Finally Wilder couldn't bear it.

He didn't feel like playing patty-cake at the moment. "Got something to say, pal?" He growled, leveling his best junkyard dog expression. "Spit it out why don't you?"

But Atticus didn't scamper off; instead he took the question as an invitation and crawled over. "Is it true?" The kid's eyes were wide. "That you're a pirate?"

Wilder snorted. "What would make you say that?"

Atticus glanced around, making sure the coast was clear before leaning in and whispering, "Mama said you had a fake leg. I thought only pirates have wooden legs but you don't have a patch."

"Or a ship."

The kid grinned. "Or a parrot."

"Guess I'm not a pirate then."

Atticus looked crestfallen for half a second before perking back up. "Can I see it?"

"My leg?"

"Yeah."

Everyone was busy bustling around in the kitchen. Outside came the rhythmic thud of an axe as Sawyer chopped kindling. He'd just gotten in a few minutes ago but looked strained. Something must have happened with the fire.

Atticus waited patiently. He had the look of his mother about him, sweet, kind, and a little wild with all that natural trust. The two of them were so open, always hugging, saying "I love you."

That wasn't Grandma Kane's way. She held court in the kitchen like a dowager queen bee, perched in a chair beside the oven, apparently willing to let Archer take over cooking the turkey but not without her eagle eye supervision, as if her mere presence would keep the meat from getting too dry.

"Time to baste again," she announced.

Archer had been sneaking up on his fiancée, Edie, who was halfway through frosting a very large, very delicious-looking chocolate cake. "Grandma." His youngest brother turned with a mock exasperated sigh. "I did that five minutes ago, and five minutes before that."

"I don't want a dried-out bird," she barked.

Archer advanced on her slowly, arms outstretched like a zombie, groaning in the back of his throat.

"What are you doing, boy?" Unwilling amusement creeping into her voice.

"This. Is. My. Turkey." He did a deep monster voice. "I. Hunted. The. Turkey. I. Am. Cooking. This. Turkey."

"Are you out of your ever-loving mind?" Grandma yelped, warding him off with two hands.

He broke from zombie mode to duck and present his cheek before her puckered expression. "I am waaaaaaiting."

"For what?"

"Don't you have a kiss for the cook?"

Grandma laughed, once, short, and sharp before swallowing it back down. But she did give him a quick, frosty peck. "Good lord, I've said it once, but I'll say it a hundred times. Archer James, you could charm the habit off a nun."

He gave a little bow. "Pity there's no convent for hundreds of miles."

"Yeah," Edie said, giving him a mock-stern expression over one shoulder. "A national tragedy."

"And what about you, Freckles?" Archer sprang toward her, wrapping his arms around her waist. "Surely that pretty mouth has got a kiss for the cook too?"

"Cook?" Edie stuck her finger in the frosting and swiped a dab on the tip of his nose. "Who's a cook? You fussed over that bird all morning. Annie and I were the ones who made the salad—"

"Mashed the potatoes," Annie said, stirring gravy on the stove. "Candied the yams. Cranned the berries."

"Put together the icky cream-of-mushroom green bean casserole you insisted on." Edie crinkled her nose. "Fried onions smell gross."

"Now hold up, ladies. That dish is the best part of Thanksgiving." Archer hooked his thumbs in his belt loops and puffed out his chest. "Except for my damn fine turkey."

Edie wrapped her arms around his neck and gave him a short but enthusiastic kiss. "*You* are a damn fine turkey."

Everyone burst out laughing as he wiped his nose clean.

Grandma caught Wilder's watchful gaze and allowed a tight-lipped smile.

Something had happened to his family. These antics weren't what he had known. Somehow while he was gone, laughter and lightness crept in. Even Grandma wasn't as ornery.

It was as if everyone had moved toward a brighter future. Everyone except for him.

"So can I?" Atticus repeated. "See your leg?"

Shit, he'd forgotten the rug rat was lurking down there.

"It's not all that interesting but sure." He reached over and hiked up his 501s to reveal the prosthetic's smooth plastic.

"Whoa! That's so cool," Atticus murmured in admiration. "You're like half robot."

More than half, junior. A tin man without a heart.

The door banged open as Kit barreled in with two six-packs of beer. "Happy Turkey Day," he boomed.

And there she was, Quinn, looking a little shy and clutching a glass pan. She turned in his direction as if by instinct and another shudder of recognition ran through him.

Those big brown eyes, full of kindness and humor. She couldn't be that long-ago girl—the one who saved him when he was on the brink.

And there he was, sitting in a chair like an invalid, with his fake leg out for the world to see.

The room fell silent except for the Bing Crosby CD warbling from the stereo, the one Annie had insisted on for holiday atmosphere.

"Hey, guys, did you know Uncle Wilder is half robot?" Atticus said, completely missing the awkwardness. "He's like a super cool superhero."

Everyone broke into uncertain laughter.

"Yeah, a regular Iron Man," Archer said, suddenly fiddling with the oven setting.

Sawyer entered the room with his arms loaded with wood. "Figure this should last the night."

"Good lord," Annie said, wiping her hands on her calico apron, "that should keep us warm for a week."

"What can I say, I like my fire hot." He gave her an eyebrow waggle as she giggled and blushed.

Jesus. Wilder rocked his head against the chair. Somewhere hell was freezing over and Satan was figure skating. Even stoic, sensible Sawyer had guzzled the contentment Kool-Aid. He'd finished rolling down his jeans when a pair of green leather ankle boots came to rest on the edge of his field of vision, boots that capped off a long pair, a hell of a long and lovely pair, of legs.

That connected to a most interesting set of hips.

An hourglass waist.

Leading to . . .

Shit, he stared like an idiot.

Quinn peered over the top of her glasses. The modern frames suited her, bold and colorful. "So I brought your favorite."

His mouth dried. Her jacket was unzipped and the t-shirt inside said, "Reading Is Awesome." He couldn't disagree, but even more awesome was the way the fitted cotton hugged her—

"I'm referring to the Rice Krispies . . ." Her lip quirked in one corner as he went red. "Jeez, you should really see your expression right now."

He couldn't believe it, but a damn blush had crept up the back of his neck, marched toward his ears. He scratched the scruff on his jaw, painfully aware his hand had a slight tremble.

"You made these?"

"Just for you. I didn't bring a spoon for you to lick but hopefully it passes muster." She waved the pan under his nose. "It was supposed to be easy, recipe.com said. A fool-proof recipe. Except apparently I am a fool with a talent for burning butter and scalding marshmallows. But I got there in the end. Barely."

"Thank you," he said gruffly. He didn't know how else to convey how much this simple gesture meant to him. "I haven't had one of these since . . . well . . . in a long time."

"I'll go set them in the kitchen," she said gently, as if sensing he was fraying down to some sort of invisible breaking point. "Oh, hey, I also forgot my purse at your cabin. I realized when I got home. Can I swing by after dinner? I feel naked without it."

He gave a nod, watching her walk away. *Don't think about her naked.*

Something, or someone, tugged his jeans. The rug rat again.

"She likes you," Atticus said.

"No one likes me," he replied. "I'm scary."

Atticus blinked before shaking his head. "Nah. You're not scary. Just sad."

"I won't be able to eat another bite for the rest of the year," Annie said, nudging the yams toward Quinn. "Can you finish off this last little bit?"

Quinn shook her head with a rueful laugh. "My mouth says yes, but my stomach says, 'Hey, what about all those pies and cakes over there?'" She pushed back her seat. "Let me give you a hand washing up." The table groaned under the weight of the biggest Thanksgiving meal she'd ever seen.

"No way." Annie held up a hand, looking surprisingly intimidating for a tiny, blond-haired woman. "Kit Kane is the dish dog. He lost a bet and this is his punishment."

"Woof," Kit said good-humoredly, rising to collect the dirty plates.

"You're gambling? Looks like we Kanes are rubbing off on you yet, Annie Carson," Archer said, sliding his arm over the back of Edie's chair and giving his flat stomach a contented pat.

"If Kit is so foolish as to stake dozens of dirty dishes on a taste test and lose, far be it from me to stop him." Annie shot back.

"What's this all about?" Edie asked with a giggle.

"You'll read about it next week. It's part of an article I wrote for the *Brightwater Bugle* comparing vegetarian meat products to the real thing. Kit volunteered as my tough-talking taste tester. He assured me he'd pick the "real" meat dish every time. Bet Thanksgiving-dinner dishes on the outcome. Let's just say he failed. Miserably."

Kit threw up his hands. "Turns out I like Fakin' Bacon."

Archer mock gagged as Annie smugly set her hands on her hips. "Looks like Carson won this round, Cowboy."

Good-natured banter flew around the table except in one corner, down at the end where Grandma (Quinn tried to call her Mrs. Kane but that went down like a lead balloon. The older woman frostily claimed that she'd earned the title along with her grey hair.) and Wilder watched in silence. Quinn's heart gave a little pang. They both had the air of people who wanted to join in, to laugh and joke around, but didn't quite know how to start. And what was going on between them?

Quinn dabbed her mouth and resmoothed Annie's sweet hand-embroidered napkin back across her lap. This was a far cry from her earlier meal. The one at Mountain View Village where Dad barely touched his plate. He had been less responsive than usual, probably tired and out of sorts from yesterday's misadventure. She'd had a few lukewarm invites to go around to dinner at different Higsby homes tonight, but this was better, even with the strangeness that existed between her and Wilder.

Her relatives would be full of questions about Dad, about his prognosis and whether or not she'd take that test.

Somehow it leaked that Dad's condition was genetic, traced from his mother's side. Grandma married into the Higsby clan but had died too young, in her early fifties. People muttered that she'd been acting strangely before she had the car accident. Testing had confirmed the genetic Alzheimer's.

Now Quinn had a choice—to test or not. The trouble

was, she didn't know which was worse . . . confirming that a terrible fate awaited you, or not knowing and hoping for the best.

It was a fifty-fifty chance. Maybe the gene was heads and she was tails.

But she didn't want to think about it. Not now.

Annie and Edie couldn't convince her to stay seated when it came time to serve dessert. Annie had baked a pumpkin pie from an heirloom Sugar Pie variety that grew in her garden, plus oatmeal cookies. Edie made pecan pie, the chocolate cherry cake, and a snickerdoodle cobbler that made Quinn's eyes bug out of her head. Her own Rice Krispies Treats looked elementary in comparison.

"Oh, great choice. So classic," Edie said with an encouraging smile.

"I . . ." Quinn wasn't sure what to say. It seemed strange to say Wilder mentioned them.

"Your ma used to make those," Grandma said, her voice unreadable.

Everyone paused for a moment.

"Did she?" Archer said, midway to snagging a cookie. "I can't remember."

"I do," Wilder said shortly.

"Well, I just want to take the opportunity to thank everyone for making me feel so welcome." Quinn finished cutting a Rice Krispies Treat, set it on a plate, and walked it down to Wilder.

"Can I get you one?" she asked Grandma.

"Not me." Grandma sniffed. "Too sweet for my taste."

"You're full of sugar is why," Archer said, breaking the tension, and everyone returned to the serious business of eating dessert.

Edie's snickerdoodle cobbler was absolutely delicious but it was hard to chew under Sawyer's continued scrutiny. He kept watching her. But why? It was like she'd done something illegal. Having lusty thoughts about his big brother wasn't a crime, right?

Right?

"Fire get sorted out?" Wilder asked abruptly, wiping his mouth.

"Fire?" Grandma's fork clattered next to the pumpkin pie.

"Yes," Sawyer said, speaking carefully. "One of the volunteer firemen was nearby, saw the flames early and called it in. House is pretty damn well destroyed. They had to put lots of wet stuff on the red stuff. Looks like it started in the garage, which is strange because it was empty. The owners hadn't moved in yet. Must have been electrical."

Wilder frowned, eyes narrowed. "But it's a new house, right?"

"Yep." Sawyer nodded. "Just finished the permitting process. Electrician is going to have a lot to answer for."

"Nothing was recovered?" Wilder pressed.

"Only part of a dirty old sock." Sawyer shrugged. "Probably left by one of the builders."

"Well, all's well that ends well," Grandma interjected with uncharacteristic shakiness.

"That's right," Edie said. "And I just want to say how

happy I am to spend this Thanksgiving with all of you. I've dreamt of having a holiday like this for a long time. I am so thankful you are making my dreams come true." She wiped her bright shining eyes and turned to beam at Archer.

"Aw, hell," Archer said softly. "I'm thankful for each of those freckles."

"Get a room, you two," Kit hollered from the sink. "I'm thankful for the game tonight. Enough of all this hugging and kissing."

"We like hugs and kisses," Atticus piped up. "I'm thankful for my puppy, Orion. And for my mom. And Sawyer."

"Oh, honey, me too." Annie pressed a hand over her heart.

"I'm thankful for both of you," Sawyer said, rumpling Atticus's hair with one hand while tightening his grip on Annie's hand with the other. "My life is better with you in it."

"What about you, Grandma?" Atticus asked. "What are you thankful for?"

"Well . . . I'm, let's see now . . ." She fiddled with her dessert plate.

"How about having your three handsome and most favorite grandsons back together under one roof?" Archer's smile was easy but his eyes seemed to ask for something.

"Yes," she muttered. "Took the words right out of my mouth."

"What about you, Wilder?" Quinn asked right when it

looked like conversation would resume. How was it that they were all so frightened of him? It was as if they hosted a wild bear in the corner and no one wanted to poke it with a stick.

His head snapped up and he stared at her impassively. "Books. I'm thankful for books."

"Good answer." She smiled. "I hope from now on you come down each week and place your order with me directly."

"What's that all about? You've been reading, brother?" Sawyer asked curiously, glancing between them.

"Yep." Wilder's one word answer hung across the table for a moment.

"He's one of the most well-read people I've come across," Quinn said.

Kit burst out laughing at the sink. "Now that's a surprise."

"Why?" Quinn asked.

"You weren't exactly valedictorian material in school, were you, cuz?"

"Nope." Wilder responded, not looking at anyone.

"What sort of material were you?" Quinn asked, determined to keep him engaged in the conversation. "Athlete?"

"That was Sawyer." Wilder's lips turned into an uneven smile.

"Oh. It must have been all that charm. Prom King for sure."

Archer covered up a laugh with a mock cough.

"That would have been Archer," Wilder said tightly.

"What was your skill then?" she asked.

"Suspensions," Grandma snapped. "He was gifted in getting kicked out of school."

"Kicked out of school." Atticus's eyes grew wide. "By the principal? For what?"

"Being bad." Wilder tipped an invisible hat at Quinn. "For being a real bad guy."

Chapter Eight

IT WAS QUIET on the drive home. The truck lights shined over high packed snowbanks and an empty road. Kit listened to talk radio and Quinn was acutely aware of Wilder's silent presence in the backseat. Why did he have such a rift with his lovely family? Despite being in the center of a warm and affectionate crowd, he'd looked alone all through dinner and then during the football game. And no one seemed to know how to bridge the gulf. The loneliness that surrounded him made her throat tighten.

"Don't forget to go by Wilder's place first." She cleared her throat as Kit turned onto Main Street.

"Yep, got the memo." Kit shot her a quick sideways glance. "Not a problem."

She looked out the window at the closed storefronts. "It's nice living in such a small place. While my truck is getting fixed I can walk everywhere. That would never happen in L.A."

Kit coughed into his fist. "You like your place?"

"It's a cute rental, bright and cheerful. Looks like the flowerbeds will be amazing come spring. I think the owner is traveling overseas."

"Yeah. Marigold." Kit said the name like it cost him something. "Goldie is off gallivanting around the world. Finding herself or something, probably doing yoga in India as we speak."

"I'd love to go to Europe someday. Her adventures sound great."

"Peachy keen," he muttered, turning down the narrow steep grade of Castle Lane while Wilder said nothing at all.

Kit parked the truck in front of the cabin and Quinn jumped out, grateful to escape the sudden awkward silence. She'd put her foot in it with Kit but wasn't sure what "it" was. She waited for Wilder to emerge and followed him toward the porch. Even though they walked a foot apart, their shadows merged in the high beams. There was a quiet jingle as he dug his keychain out of his coat pocket.

She kicked the snow off her boots. "I had a nice time tonight."

He froze, holding the door open. "I did too, surprisingly."

She stepped into the dark, narrow hall. He flicked the overhead light on and she turned, gasping, not expecting to find him near enough that she could make an in-depth study on why his irises were such a perfect green.

"What are you lookin' at?" he asked hoarsely.

"I think your eyes are the same shade as my ring." He

flinched when she set her palm against his scruffy cheek, comparing. "Yep. A near perfect match." This nervous inner jumpy feeling was going to give her a stomachache. "My birth stone is a peridot. I was born at the end of August. Virgo alert, sorry."

His thick brows knit. "What's that mean?"

"Apparently I should be a clean-freak perfectionist." She shrugged. "Except I'm an outlier because *ew* sums up my feelings on the subject of chores. I hate doing dishes and forget about folding laundry. But then again I do like to color code and alphabetize my bookshelves and arrange my comic collection by year so maybe there's something to it after all."

He shrugged out of his jacket and hung it on a chair. "Didn't peg you for a comic fan."

He wasn't cute or charming, just bluntly honest. After all those bullshit years in Hollywood, it was refreshing to speak plainly. "I wouldn't say I'm your average fan, more like a champion of the underdog. See, my collection consists solely of failed superheroes."

He was silent. If he breathed she couldn't see the physical evidence.

"Everyone loves Batman, Spider-Man, Superman, The Avengers. But what about Ashtray, who kills villains with second-hand smoke?"

He dipped his chin, peering at her. "Ashtray?"

Her cheeks flushed. The only way to end this conversation was to cease talking but the brakes were off. "There's also Echo Boy, the skilled mime, and the Incredible Spork, and don't forget Captain Canada. He fought for truth and justice, but also socialized medicine and—"

There was a sound of a truck engine starting, wheels backing up.

They both exchanged surprised glances.

"Where the hell is he going?" Wilder's thick hand-knit wool sweater made a scratching sound as he slid past her down jacket. He yanked open the door and the cold air was welcome relief against her hot cheeks. "Kit's gone."

"Oh no." She hugged herself. "I wasn't taking too long, was I? I know I have a tendency to talk a lot but—"

He shut the door, keeping his hand pressed against the wood. "My guess? This was a con job between him and my brother."

"I'm not following."

Wilder turned, pushing a hand through his hair. "He and Archer probably got it into their thick heads to play matchmaker. It's exactly the kind of stunt they'd pull."

She straightened her glasses. "You think Kit purposefully left me to . . ."

His Adam's apple bobbed. "Force us to spend the night together."

A zap of electricity coursed through the valley between her breasts. There wasn't room in this tight space to think or inhale or do anything but stand here with this crazy desire to reach out and splay her hands across his broad chest, clutch his sweater and drag him closer.

Apparently she wasn't as into funny wisecracking hipsters as big brooding alphas. For years she'd been doing it all wrong.

"I'll call Sawyer and he'll come fetch you." He made a low frustrated grumble deep in his throat. "I hate being so fucking useless."

"Stop that right now," she said quickly. "First, I don't want Sawyer to drive all the way out here—his cabin is miles away. Second, you are far from fucking useless."

"I can't drive."

"Neither can I tonight and I'm not unusable." His gaze shot to her face and she had to work for her next breath. "But walking in the dark is a little scary. Do you mind if we build up the fire, make tea and figure out what to do?"

"You think I'd let you set foot outside by yourself tonight? But I don't have tea, Trouble." His eyes gleamed and, God help her, she liked it. She was like a rabbit prancing under a hungry wolf's snout with a placard that read, "Eat me! I'm delicious!"

She exhaled lightly. "Well, you have a pot that can boil water, right? My purse just so happens to contain my backup tea stash." She sensed his question before he had a chance to ask. "Never know when a girl might need a quick cup of Egyptian licorice or peppermint or chamomile—but you seem like you might be a rooibos type of guy—"

His mouth covered hers. There wasn't a warning. The rest of her babble hummed into his mouth, turning into a soft sigh. Oh, thank the lord, he felt it too then, this inexplicable connection between them.

"I should push you away, but can't seem to get close enough." He had her up against the wall, bracing his weight against either side of her head and she grabbed two handfuls of sweater and the thick wool felt as thick, masculine, and sexy as she hoped. As for the muscles beneath it . . . oh . . .

Oh yeah.

He slid his tongue against hers again with a husky moan. "This is a bad idea."

"Stopping would be a worse one." She broke the kiss to fasten her lips to the side of his powerful neck between thick cords of tendon, his stubble rough on her lips. He tasted like soap, salt, and man. His pulse increased when she reached to tangle her fingers in the bristly waves dusting his collar.

"What the fuck are we doing?" His fingers found her jacket's zipper, grinding it open.

"What feels good?" She arched her back. "I want to forget everything for a night, don't you?"

"I need more, that okay?"

"Yes. More." She pressed her hips closer. "Good idea."

His big hands slipped under the hem of her shirt, unapologetic and forthright, the warm calloused pads of his fingers rough against her cool stomach, as if his body temperature ran a few degrees higher than normal.

He took his time, exhibiting absolute control while all she could do was hang on for dear life, her face buried in his neck, writhing while his hands moved over her ribs, one at a time, as if climbing a ladder. She wanted to be against him in bed, to take his hand and slide it where her nipples were peaked, aching to be rolled between his thumb and forefinger. She wanted it rough and fast and urgent. But then, as much as it made her twist and moan, it was nice for him to take his time.

He was there soon enough, at the base of her bra, tracing the outline to her underwire, teasing the satin.

She bucked a little, urging him on. She needed to be in this moment, jam-pack every second with life. Tomorrow she took the test and soon her world might spin off its axis. Everyone had a clock, but hers might be ticking faster.

She took his face between her hands and his jaw flexed against her palms. "You are being too careful. If we do this, I don't want to think. I want to feel." This was a night to forget fear, to live without regret, to let go, be in the moment.

He didn't answer.

"Wilder. Please, I want it rough." To heck with being coy or flirtatious. She desperately needed this man to take her.

He leaned close, his hands sliding to the top of her bra, over the soft swell of sensitive flesh. "And you think that's what I am?" His whisper was a challenge, spreading a tantalizing heat through the shell of her ear, a heat that ignited another flame, lower and brighter between her legs.

"I want to find out." She shifted her weight, the seam of her jeans pressing through the thin lace of her panties, not quite relief, but a subtle caress.

He reached her bra straps, holding her steady with an authoritative grasp. In the shadows he looked enormous.

He sucked her lobe with just enough pressure to make her eyes roll back in her head.

"Then we do it my way." His voice was strained. "Get on my bed. Now."

One of her least favorite parts about her Hollywood job was being bossed around. Told what to do as if she were some sort of robot that lived only to serve at her master's pleasure. It wasn't her thing.

Apparently unless she wanted the order.

Unless she craved the order.

There was a scrape of wood on the floorboards. The cane. She had forgotten his injury. His leg. Even his scarred hands. All she knew was the core of the man awoke something in her, primal, wild as his name.

Tomorrow the world could burn. Tonight was theirs.

She slid free, feeling him release her with tangible regret. Walking to the bedroom, she climbed on the mattress, running her hand up a bedpost. Soon she'd run her hand up him and the idea of his shaft against her palm made her clamp her knees together—the anticipation almost too intense to bear.

He took his time approaching. When he was close enough, he set the cane against the wall and limped closer, covering her hand on the post for a moment before reaching out to grab her wrist. There was a sense he marked his territory, staked his claim before reaching down to shove open his jeans.

"Want you to kneel."

Goose bumps broke out along the base of her spine. This was happening fast, but that's what she wanted, right? What she asked for. Rough anonymous sex. Or mostly anonymous. Except for the fact she had just spent the night with his whole family. That she knew the intimate details of his bookshelf. That she'd slept in his bed last night and could still remember the scent on the pillowcase. Clouds must have moved because moonlight appeared—suddenly she could see a little more, she could see . . . him.

He froze as if sensing her hesitancy.

It was like her body split into two, one part urging, "Go on, hurry up and do it already," while the other took a step backward, whispering, "Hang on, what if there is more going on here? More than sex, more than tonight?"

The two opposing parts broke into a furious wrestling match, clawing, gnawing, biting, and generally rattling her brain loose.

"Something changed," he said gently.

She flinched. "I'm not sure if I'm a one-night-stand sort of person after all." The "do it" part of her brain shook a fist, howling, "Good God, woman, we'd be getting pleasured by a hot-as-hell badass if it wasn't for you and your meddling morals."

She pressed her knees to her chest, setting her chin down at the place they met. "I'm sorry." Her heart pounded in her ears. "I'm not sure what I want to do here."

"No." He fixed himself, zipping his pants with a wince. "I should be the one to apologize. It's been . . . a while. Guess I got carried away."

Her gaze jerked to his. "No, really, I pushed."

"I started it."

She closed her eyes briefly. "Are we having some sort of guilt-off competition?"

He grunted, not without a trace of humor. "It's a specialty of mine."

"Well, consider yourself up against a grand master," she said with a rueful laugh. "I will meet your apology with a shirt-wrenching, teeth-gnashing plea for forgiveness."

"You don't strike me as the kind of person who lives with a lot of regret."

"Really, that's your impression of me?"

He ran a hand up her arm in a light, gentle touch. "A bright spark. Beautiful. Happy. Confident."

Maybe she picked the wrong job in Hollywood. "Smoke and mirrors."

"Hrumph. Maybe I should borrow a little for myself."

"Would you do something for me?" She inched closer.

"What's that?"

She patted the side of the bed. "Come here. Be next to me. We don't have to sleep together to sleep together. Maybe I'm not ready to go whole hog, but what about cuddling?"

"Cuddling?" His breath sounded labored.

"Don't be so dismissive."

"I'm not, it's just that . . . no one has ever asked me to before. I don't exactly have a reputation as the warm and cuddly type."

"Or no one's ever bothered to look close enough."

He froze before sitting on the edge of the bed, the mattress creaking from his weight.

"There we go, that's a start," she said encouragingly.

"Now what?"

"Now we both lie back on your pillows, get under the blankets."

"What about shoes?"

"Right. Shoes. Very practical. Glad one of us handles the details. See? This is what makes me a terrible Virgo."

"You nervous?" He slowly undid the zipper to her ankle boot, easing it off, giving her toes a squeeze before proceeding to the next boot. Her stomach muscles clenched. This guy would give amazing foot rubs; she knew it.

"A little, but in a good way."

He considered her. "You're strange."

"And you are terrible at giving compliments."

He chuckled at that, tossing her boots on the floor and pulling back the blankets, tucking her in.

"Aren't you getting in too?"

"For my sanity, I'd rather have this as a barrier." He tugged on the thick comforter, "Otherwise, I'll never fall asleep."

"Am I that hard to resist?" She batted her lashes with a faux-seductive voice.

"Woman, you drive me crazy." But he sounded happy or at least not angry, which was a change. And for not being a cuddler, he had an excellent way of putting his arm around the hollow of her waist and spooning her against him. Was the rumbling sound the blood still racing through her veins, or even his veins?

"What is that noise?" she asked.

"The falls. Castle Falls."

"You live that close to them?"

He gave a single nod.

"Will you take me to see them?"

He smoothed back her hair. "How about tomorrow?"

The warmth of his suggestion cooled under a dose of reality. "Tomorrow I have to do something, but soon."

"It's a date."

Something about the way he said the word made her thighs clench. "A date?" She turned and traced a small circle on the end of his nose. "I'd like that."

"You would?" He pretended to bite her finger.

She cupped his cheek and kissed the tip of his nose. "Don't sound so shocked that a person might like you, Wilder Kane."

Chapter Nine

WILDER COULDN'T SLEEP. Quinn gave another cute little sigh but he couldn't drift away with the prosthetic on. He needed to take it and the stump's shrinker sock off. If she glimpsed his body, she would pity him. He'd faced enough—no point breaking the last spindly straw of his pride. As much as he hated leaving her, it was better if he crashed in the guest room. That way he could set his alarm early, be showered and dressed before she woke. Before she could see.

He pulled away, jaw clenching as she let out an unconscious whimper of protest. How many people had ever missed him when he'd left their beds? No one. That had always been his goal with women. Use them and let them use him in turn. A physical release was fine. Emotions? Hell no.

He sat and, in the distance, the waterfall laughed. Go ahead, let the water have its fucking snigger. It wasn't as if it would get to run wild and free to the ocean. Soon it would be rerouted, sucked into some aqueduct to feed the insatiable, thirsty millions in Southern California. In a week this water would be irrigating a rich man's putting green, then who'd be laughing?

He scrubbed his face.

Is this how hermit madness began? Talking to inanimate objects?

He fumbled for his cane, wincing as it scraped the floorboards, but Quinn must be a sound sleeper. A good thing because it wasn't as if he could tiptoe. At first he'd balked at the idea of a two-bedroom cottage, thought one room would suit him plenty. He didn't plan on having company and didn't want to give Archer or Sawyer any excuse to stick around and play nursemaid.

But it came in useful tonight.

He got to the spare room, turned on the lamp and stripped off his sweater, t-shirt, and jeans. His cock poked like a hard and insistent bastard against his boxer briefs but he wasn't going to be able to get any relief with his own poor hand tonight. Loneliness took hold, made it hard to breathe. For once, he didn't crave release. What he wanted was connection.

He'd gotten the prosthetic and compression sock off when the floorboards creaked. Quinn had ten toes perfect for quiet movement.

"What are you doing?" he snarled at her outline in the doorway, acutely aware he was exposed, his stump on display to ruin everything.

"I rolled over and you were gone," she whispered. Her

eyes weren't fixated on his leg. For some reason she stared at his chest.

His back muscles tightened as his ears grew hot. "Go away."

Instead she came closer.

"Dear God, do you bench press sequoia logs or something?"

"Huh?"

"Seriously." She licked her lips. "How do you have such an amazing body? You're like a statue or something. I used to keep a D encyclopedia under my bed, to check out Michelangelo's *David* and—"

"Please, go. I can't stand it." He sank his hands into the blanket, a freight train running through his head.

"You are beautifully made, don't you know that?" She bent, bracing her hands on his thighs and lowering herself down to her knees.

He made himself well acquainted with the area where the opposite wall met the ceiling. "You've got a sweet-looking mouth for a liar."

"I speak the truth. I don't want a one night stand," she said, "but I also can't deny that I want you. Badly."

His muscles coiled as tightly as springs.

"Can you please look at me?" she whispered.

"Can't." It was all he could say with his throat in a vise.

She was quiet a moment. From this room he couldn't hear the falls, but the memory of the laughing water echoed in his skull. "What are you so afraid of?"

"I'm not afraid."

"Wilder. You're trembling."

Shit. He was. Toss another log on the pyre. Tonight this woman was going to burn him alive and he didn't mind a bit.

"Is it this?"

He jerked as she touched his leg, stump, whatever you wanted to call the useless appendage.

"Your injury isn't an issue for me," she murmured. "You survived a terrible accident. I'm sorry for what you suffered. But that doesn't subtract anything from who you are, the man I see."

He snorted. "Man? I'm not a man anymore."

She reached, her fingers tracing his chest hair. "You look plenty manly from where I sit, just saying."

Her damn hand kept moving, down over his chest, his gut tightening as she reached his navel, the place where the hair began again, the thick arrow, an unsubtle guide-post.

She reached the elastic of his boxers and stopped. "I won't go further unless you say it's okay."

"Isn't that supposed to be my line?"

"Right now I feel like the seducer."

He seized her with a groan, lifting her easily, falling back on the mattress and carrying her with him. It was short work to get off her shirt. Her jeans were a little trickier. They were tight, which was good and meant she had to shimmy her hips to get them lower, which was better.

He groaned and clasped her ass, the little scrap of lace doing not much more than framing the high perfect swell of her ass.

"I don't have a condom," he rasped.

"I'm on birth control." She kissed him again. "But we're barely acquainted."

"Never mind, I can make you feel good in other ways." He ran his thumb down the center of her panties. No hiding the wetness. No hiding anything. Her entire body was a live wire. She trembled against him and he shuddered once.

"Wait." She jerked up, shoving hair from her face. "I forgot. I have a condom in my purse. For emergencies."

"Emergencies?"

"I was a Girl Scout—always come prepared. It's stashed in my first-aid kit. I have a pocket-sized one."

"In case you get a cut, need a Band-Aid and then a fuck to make things better?"

She narrowed her gaze in mock ferocity. "Listen, buddy, I saw this whole survival show on cable. Condoms can hold water. You can even make slingshots."

"Slingshots?"

"Or a blow-up friend if you're stranded. Draw a face on it, you know, like Tom Hanks did with Wilson during that one island movie."

"Jesus Christ." He groaned. "Now I'm hard and thinking about Tom Hanks with that beard."

"Hey now." She gave his chest a shove. "He was pretty great in *The Shawshank Redemption*."

"You mean *The Green Mile*?"

"Yeah, yeah." She waved her hand as if flapping away pesky details. "Still a movie about prison and sads, right?"

"They are nothing alike."

"I'm really messing this up, huh?" She scrubbed her face. "We're supposed to be having hot monkey sex and instead I've got us discussing Tom Hanks. Need to share any deep thoughts on *Big*? *Splash*?"

"When you get back . . ." He gave her a long lingering kiss. "We're talking less, deal?"

"Got it."

Another kiss, short this time, but deeper. "Not that I don't like talking to you."

"No, no. Right, I get it. I like talking to you too. But this is about getting down." She waggled her brows. "Got a one-way ticket to dirty town."

He picked her up and deposited her onto the ground, giving the side of her ass a playful slap. "Go on, trouble-maker."

"Going, going." She fled the room.

Fuck. He was laughing. When had he ever laughed? Especially with a woman?

His dick throbbed. He was more turned on than he'd ever been and as much as it was disturbing, it also felt disturbingly right.

She came back and looked around. "Is it gone?"

"What?"

"The mood."

"I'm not sure what we had could be classified as mood."

"Atmosphere?" She jutted her hip.

His cock twitched. "Let's get you out of what's left of those clothes and see how much oxygen is left over."

She climbed up on the bed, passing him the condom. "Want to know a secret? You're sort of fun."

He clapped a hand over her mouth. "Don't tell anyone else."

"I'm glad Kit stranded me," she said through his fingers.

"We can send him a dozen roses." His eyes rolled back in his head when she skillfully sucked his finger.

She took one more down before pulling back and biting her lower lip.

He tore open the foil and sheathed himself. "I haven't done this in a while. And not since . . ."

"Hey." She settled a hand on his bicep and squeezed. "Hey, be with me. Right now all I see is your face. And all I feel is this." Her other hand encircled him at the root, guided him home.

He didn't even have to push. She was more than ready and, fuck, so was he. Too ready. One thrust and he had to close his eyes, stop, and breathe. "Need a second."

"Take your time," she gasped, rocking a little from side to side. "You're a lot more than what I'm used to."

He had a fleeting moment of hating anyone who'd ever been there before, touched this woman, heard her make this same gasp. But then she leaned up, her soft lips brushing his, and nothing more mattered because for once he existed fully in the present. No past. No future. He wasn't even a fucking hermit. He was here buried inside this gorgeous woman and while it was a little awkward and his balance needed some adjustment, his arms were strong and he could keep his weight off her to concentrate on the in-and-out slide. She clenched those long legs around his waist and it was like a little slice of heaven was served with a fucking cherry on the top.

Her fingers raked down his back and he jerked, plunging deeper, spreading those long legs wider. Shit. The world was dissolving to this single point of contact, the hard rhythmic breaths. Their gazes locked and he was lost, hypnotized. He dragged his tongue over her neck, the pulse echoing in his cock. It had never been this way, rough yet soft. Tender even. Shit, he was going to get there too fast. He ground against her mons and she bowed too. Thank God. He wouldn't go alone. He did it again, increasing the friction. "Like that?"

She didn't answer but the way her jaw tightened, that low shallow whimper, told him she did.

"Say yes."

"Yes." She moaned the word.

His balls squeezed with hot, tight pleasure, edging him closer. "Say my name."

"Yes, Wilder. I love it."

The pleasure sharpened, took on a dark edge, and she began to contract around him, pulsing, milking, and everything was too good. Fuck it, incredible. His abs flexed, ass clenched, and with a primal groan and one last mad kiss, he joined her on the other side.

Afterward, he rolled onto his side, clasping her close, not wanting to sever the lust-drunk connection, not when everything felt exactly right. "Jesus, I didn't even have enough time to bust out any big moves."

"Wait. You've got bigger moves than that?" She cocked a brow, pushing a damp lock of hair off her forehead. "I guess the rest of you is big but whoa. Go on, pray, share your big move."

"What I really want is to go down on you, savor every goddamn glorious inch." Even as he said it his mouth watered. She'd taste amazing, strong, bright, and tangibly addictive as the rest of her.

She traced a bead of sweat trickling down his chest.

He cupped her cheek. "You aren't impressed?"

"Don't get me wrong." She rolled, nestling closer with a grin. "I'm sure I'd like it, correction—love it. One teensy problem though, I'm not sure if I'm in a great position to get into a relationship with anyone."

Despite her words, she still threaded her fingers through his hair and drew him in for another kiss, one that started to harden his exhausted cock. Her tongue was sweet but tasted of falsehoods.

"That's good," he muttered before deepening the kiss. "Because I don't do relationships myself."

At last she broke away, breathing faster than she had a few minutes ago. She pressed her cheek against his and gave a tentative grin. "This is a big mistake, isn't it?"

"Huge." One that felt like it could change his whole world, and just maybe for the better.

Chapter Ten

TWO THOUGHTS COLLIDED in Quinn's head the moment she woke up: (1) It felt damn good to be wrapped in Wilder's big strong arms and (2) the fact they had used up her one emergency condom was a national tragedy because she wanted more, more, more, like Susan Sarandon in *The Rocky Horror Picture Show*. How could she ever get enough of this man?

She stretched her legs, smiling at the delicious soreness radiating between her legs before a third thought wandered in, late to the party.

Today is test day.

Great. Thanks, third thought. Way to ruin the moment.

Stupid brain.

She had to get to the hospital lab by nine-thirty for a blood draw, the one that would reveal if she too would develop Alzheimer's at a young age, just like Dad. Fifty-

fifty odds meant she didn't know where to place the bet. All red? All black?

It wasn't mandatory. She didn't have to find out. But the Virgo in her wanted to plan, needed to know because even if this was a worst case scenario, maybe she could live her life to the fullest without being plagued by nagging uncertainty. The exhausting what-ifs that slithered in when she was almost asleep or relaxing under a hot stream of water in the shower or brewing a pot of morning coffee.

Wilder responded to her stirring by nuzzling the side of her neck, his stubble prickling her flesh in a pleasant way. God, he felt good, but her instincts last night were right. This was a mistake. She was set to sail off into an uncharted ocean and no one else deserved to go along on that voyage.

"Morning," she said, lifting his arm and wiggling away to freedom.

"Morning."

Her feet hit the cold floor as her stomach sank at his stiff tone. There was a wall between them again. As much as she hated that it was there, this screw-and-scram behavior no doubt gave him ample cause to ramp up his defenses. Her throat tightened but no matter how fabulous last night was, leaving was for the best. Chalk this encounter up to a little one-time fling that helped provide much needed distraction.

"So I have to get going," she said, tugging on yesterday's clothes. Yeah, it was dodgy as heck to avoid his eyes, but if she didn't, he'd see in her gaze that leaving was the last thing she wanted. Last night she rambled about making a Wilson condom and he still wanted to have monkey sex. If she let him in, they might spend the morning doing sock puppet shows interspersed with fellatio. Then he might go ahead and bust out that big move he kept alluding to and she'd never want to do anything but live life with her legs wrapped around his shoulders.

Better to stick to black and white though. Grey wasn't really her color.

"I realized it's not far to walk back into town." She reached for her purse.

"Less than a mile."

"You don't have to do that." Sullenness dulled his gaze. "My keys are—"

"Truth circle? I want to get some exercise and clear my head a little. The last couple days have been out of the ordinary. And then all this." She waved her hand at the empty space between them, plus the disordered bed sheets and tangled comforter. "I wasn't looking for anything like this."

He was a master of the humorless smirk. "So you keep saying."

"Look, I know you weren't either. We're like two people walking fast with our heads down who ended up smacking into each other."

"What we did felt a hell of a lot better than that." He yanked on his own shirt and all those beautiful muscles were covered back up, but somehow that didn't make it easier to bear because now she knew they were there. She knew what they felt like. God help her, what they tasted like.

"I have an appointment that I can't miss in a few hours." She buttoned and zipped her jeans, having to try twice because of her dang trembling fingers.

He gave her a closer look. "Are you okay?"

"Yeah, of course."

"Sorry, honey." The lines bracketing his mouth deepened. "I'm calling bullshit."

She tied her hair into a quick ponytail. If she was going to leave with post-sex bedhead, she owed him the truth. "Fine. Actually, no. I'm not okay. I'm not even orbiting in okay's solar system. But I also don't want to talk about it right now."

He paused, eyes darkening, before giving a single nod. "Fine."

"See you around then." She turned to leave.

"Wait." His tone was ragged.

She closed her eyes and grimaced. Why was it so hard to go? "Mm-hmm?"

"I'd like to see you again." How did he make that voice, all rough and snarling, have such a tender bite?

She tried to arch an eyebrow, go for casual, even as her mouth dried. "It's a small town. I don't have a Magic 8 Ball on me but your outlook is good."

He shook his head, ignoring her lighthearted tone. "You know that's not what I mean, Trouble." His smile was dry, but hey, it was a start.

"Trouble?" He'd called her that before.

"That's your new name. You're welcome."

"Good trouble or bad?"

"Depends on the situation." That wolfish look he gave

her. God, she was ready to drop her drawers again. Time to run before she sent her better judgment packing for a one-way vacation on a remote tropical island.

He cleared his throat. "I had a real good time with you."

Those weren't words of poetry, anything romantic, poignant, or even memorable. But the absolute sincerity in the words weakened her knees. Surely her better judgment would enjoy a mai tai and beach cabana.

The thought was dangerously tempting. This cottage did make a perfect love shack and—*no! Retreat. Now. Don't drag him into your medical drama-rama.*

Sigh. Too true. Being a responsible adult was no fun but those were the apples.

"Me too. Okay. I'll show myself out." She patted her hair. The ponytail felt like a wild rat's nest. She must look absolutely feral. "Goodbye, Wilder." There wasn't a clock in sight but she must have grabbed her coat and purse and been out the door in a world record time.

She walked up Castle Lane, her breath coming out in small white clouds as she puffed up the steepest bit. Add getting regular cardio to her "to do" list as well. Maybe a kettle ball. Or Zumba?

Or tantric sex?

After ten minutes she hit the stop sign at the top of the hill, where the freshly shoveled sidewalk began next to the *Welcome to Brightwater* sign. It was there that she finally allowed herself the luxury of two tears, one escaping out each eye before she swiped the rest away. No need to overspend her sorrow allowance. Time to pull the plug on the pity party. She didn't want to medal in the Pain Olympics.

But really? Really, universe? She finally met someone she connected to, finally felt that indefinable spark she'd read about her whole entire life, and it was right now, when her life was a veritable shit storm.

"No fair!" She kicked a snowdrift, wincing as a cold wash of snow slipped into the top of her ankle boot.

Temper tantrums were pointless, especially as she might be unable to recall any of this in a few short years. She could forget all about this man, what he did, how she felt when near him. And suddenly that scared her more than anything.

WILDER GRIPPED HIS phone, pacing across the kitchen. Sawyer answered on the third ring.

"Kane." His younger brother sounded distracted.

Wilder coughed into his fist. Maybe this was a bad idea. He wasn't a guy known to give in to impulse. "It's me. You busy?"

"What? No," Sawyer said quickly. "I'm always here for you, man, just a bit sidetracked is all. There was another fire this morning at dawn."

"Shit." Wilder froze. "Where?"

"New place set up the hill from the old depot on the edge of town." Sawyer didn't elaborate but there was no denying this was a troubling development.

"Want to talk it out later?"

A pause. "You're freely offering to have a conversation?" Incredulity crept into Sawyer's stoic voice.

"Yeah, guess I am." He cleared his throat. "And there's another thing, the reason I called in the first place."

"Shoot."

"I want to go buy a new vehicle. An automatic. I'm sick of being stuck. I need to get out more." After Quinn left this morning, he went out and chopped as much firewood as he could pile into the kitchen. Then he tried whittling and cut himself four times before he tossed the knife across the table, cursing his distraction. Something had shifted in him during the night. He didn't know what, not exactly, but suddenly the four walls of this cottage felt too damn confining by half.

He wanted to get out in the world a little. It seemed like there was a hell of a lot that he might be missing.

"That's good news, great." Sawyer caught himself, tried to sound a little less eager. "About damn time."

Wilder's mouth quirked. "Don't get any big ideas about hugging me or anything."

"Course not. But this is me saying that I'm proud of you, big brother."

"Hanging up now." His cheeks flexed. Where had this full-blown smile come from? Quinn. Forty-eight hours ago he had nothing and now . . . what? As quick as it came, his beam faded.

Facts were still facts, stubborn bastards. This morning she couldn't leave fast enough. You could almost hear the sound of burning rubber as she fled his house. But one thing niggled at him despite all his attempts at distraction: the look in her eyes the moment before she bolted, more regret than relief.

He should know. He'd seen that particular expression staring back in the mirror enough.

His features twisted into a glower as another thought whispered. *Or was it pity?*

"Fuck." He tilted back his head and exhaled a drawn-out breath that came out closer to a growl. His guts were tied in an impossible knot.

Maybe he should tell Sawyer to forget it. Bid the memory of Quinn good riddance. Still, another stubborn part of him couldn't deny the pleasurable chill he got every time Quinn so much as glanced in his direction.

Shit. He was in trouble, big trouble over this woman, but his instincts wavered between flight and fight.

But fight for what?

And how did she feel?

When did life get so damn confusing?

The tangled, mixed-up feelings remained well into the afternoon, even after he paid for a new 4Runner SUV, trading in the Jeep.

"Your ride handles well," Sawyer said as they pulled out of the dealership. "Got to love that new car smell."

"Yup." Wilder turned onto the road, easing into traffic. There were three cars on the road, which meant it was busy out.

"Hungry?" Sawyer rested his elbow on the armrest. "Want to go grab a beer and burger at The Dirty Shame?"

"Don't you have to get on home?" Annie and Atticus

were no doubt waiting for him. He didn't want to keep his brother from his new family.

"No one's there. They went to San Francisco to visit Annie's sister and do some holiday shopping."

"Gotcha." Wilder wasn't all that hungry. Confusion killed his appetite. "How about you take me by the site of the morning's fire?" Work would refocus him. It always did.

"Sure thing." Sawyer fired off a few quick directions. "Same situation as last time. Empty place, but new, only built last summer. One of those McMansions, a five bedroom, three bathroom job."

Wilder didn't respond, just tightened his grip on the wheel. "You have a lot of unexplained fires in town?"

"Not really. These have been the first in a while. Why?"

"No reason." Wilder stared straight ahead, ignoring Sawyer's probing gaze.

"You're not the sort to say anything without a reason."

"Let's have a look, then we'll see what I have to say." Wilder flicked on a country station, so music filled the cab and drowned out the silence.

They parked halfway up the driveway. The air still smelled of smoke even though the fire was out. The house was gutted. Wilder and Sawyer slammed the truck doors and walked the property line perimeter. Wilder left his stick in the car. The snow wasn't too deep and he wanted the practice. His limp was pronounced but he managed to stay mobile and upright.

Small victories but he'd take them for once.

"This the garage?" he called out. Sawyer had stopped

to survey the mountains. Place had a hell of a view, positioned to catch sunrise and sunset.

"Yes—a three-car deal. Owner said the place was empty. Think it could be faulty wiring again?"

"Nope." Wilder walked forward, scanning the ground, kicking here and there at bits of char. Shit. There it was. His heart sank. "Come over here and take a look at this."

Sawyer walked over. "What's that?"

"Part of a sock." Wilder brushed a light dusting of new-fallen snow from the perimeter. "That's where the fire started. Didn't the guys do a check?"

"The volunteers got it under control fast. I didn't quiz them."

"Should have." He pointed. "See, someone started this, probably poured gasoline into a milk jug. Check out that bit of melted plastic too. The sock helped ignite it, burned like a wick."

Sawyer squatted and whistled low. "Shit. You're thinking arson."

He mashed his lips together and thought a moment. "Yeah. I'd say the likelihood is pretty fucking good."

"I'll call the boys at ATF."

"Good thinking. It's not going to be easy to catch him. It's usually a him by the way. But they'll be of use helping to build a profile. We've had a couple arson cases in Montana over the years. A few were arrested but most eluded justice."

"I'll brief Leroy and Kit," Sawyer said, referring to his deputies. "Request they keep a sharp eye out for any suspicious activity during their patrols."

"Could be anyone." Wilder hooked a hand over the back of his neck, rubbing the thick cords of tight muscle. "Don't want it to be a place with people inside next time. Also, you might want to see if the gas station and Save-U-More will help keep track of who is buying two-gallon milk jugs."

"Be like searching for a needle in a haystack."

"True, but it's a start at least. Could be a loner. Or someone seeking attention."

They stared at the fresh cinder and ash. "You ever think about that one night?"

Wilder didn't have to ask which night his brother referred to. He knew. The worst night of his life.

"I don't remember any of it," Sawyer said. "Weird, isn't it? Like I should recollect something."

"No," Wilder replied firmly. "Consider it a very good thing."

"Do you remember?"

Wilder shrugged, unable to face him.

"Shit, you do, don't you?"

He wasn't going to say he could still hear the deafening groan from when the roof caved in. The crash cutting off the scream. Their mother's scream. He remembered the thick smoke cloud, clogging his lungs, burning his eyes. He remembered more too, from earlier in the night. How he couldn't sleep because Dad had his weekly poker game, all the men were laughing too loud, drinking lots of beer. His brothers both fell asleep fast, but he'd tiptoed down the hall, peeked into his parents' bedroom and saw Mom reading by lamplight.

He almost went in. She always went to bed with a book and didn't mind giving him a snuggle. She'd rub his back, call him "my big beautiful boy." She smelled like rose water and baby powder. But tonight he was curious about the men so kept going down the hall, perched on the top stair, listening to crass jokes he didn't understand, followed by loud booming laughter.

Eventually, Mom turned off the light and the guys began to leave. He waited for Dad to stumble upstairs, scoop him up, tuck him in.

But he didn't come.

So Wilder decided to find him.

"Hey, man." Sawyer clasped his shoulder. "You look like you've seen a ghost."

"Let's get out of here," Wilder said, turning. That far-off night something happened to his soul. For a long time he thought it was burned away but the last few days revealed little shots of green in the black barren wasteland. But what if he didn't have the right to regrowth? Hadn't he lost the right to most everything good in this world?

He took Sawyer back to the station, dropped him off with a tense handshake. Next, he found himself driving slowly past A Novel Experience as if that might be a way to curb this restless sensation in his gut. Maybe he was a damn fool, but he couldn't extinguish the small light inside him, fragile as candlelight that murmured, "Maybe."

A woman walked by the bookshop window but it wasn't Quinn. She was older, had long black hair, parted down the middle, and wore a flowing silk outfit that seemed to fit into the new Brightwater. Not so much the old. Things were changing around here. This wasn't the hardscrabble Western town of his youth.

But he wasn't sure if he fit in back then, and he sure as hell didn't now.

What was he going to do?

Kit and Archer's trucks were parked out in front of The Dirty Shame. He didn't want a beer or to go shoot the shit over a game of darts or pool, and hell if he wanted to go home to an empty house. He didn't even have Quinn's number or know where she lived. Instead, he parked and went into Higsby Hardware to buy cracked corn for the deer. On the way out he stared at a few tulip bulbs. They might come up pretty in spring.

Hell, now he was thinking about flowers? What was going on?

On his way back to his parking spot, he paused, peering into Haute Coffee's big plate glass window. Edie's bakery shop. He'd never gone in but right now, on this cold, grey late-autumn day, the warm and cozy atmosphere called out to him.

The bells rang as he walked in. The tables were mostly empty as closing time approached. Shit. No chance of anonymity. He turned to beat it when Edie appeared behind the counter, gave him a double-take followed by an enthusiastic wave.

Trapped.

"Howdy, stranger." Edie's hair was caught up in a bun and there was a dusting of flour on the tip of her freckled nose. Archer, the playboy of Brightwater, had finally settled down and it didn't surprise Wilder one bit. Edie was marriage material: beautiful, smart, and could cook in the kitchen like she was conducting an orchestra, a symphony for the taste buds.

"Can I get you a cup of coffee on the house? And how about a muffin. No, wait . . ." She gave him an appraising once-over. "I know just what you'd like. Take a seat. Any seat."

He did as he was told, not minding getting Mom'd around when she had such a kind smile. Plus he was starving. He glanced out the window. A few snowflakes fell.

If he concentrated hard enough maybe Quinn might walk by.

How pathetic could you be?

"Penny for your thoughts," Edie said, returning with a piping hot cup of coffee and a giant bear claw.

"Jesus, look at the size of that thing." He eyed the plate. "That pastry could go toe-to-toe with a polar bear."

She smiled. "I got caught up listening to a podcast and made this one a little too big, wasn't sure what I'd do with it. But then you came in and, hey . . . got to love serendipity."

He picked up the flaky, buttery bread and bit down, sugar and almonds flooding his taste buds. Impossible not to moan.

"Oh yay." Edie clapped her hands. "You like it!"

"Good." It was all he could say while shoving another bite in his face.

She sat down across from him, staring out the window.

"This will be my first winter in Brightwater. I'm excited. It will be a real Christmas this year."

"You don't miss the big city life?" Archer had mentioned she came from New York.

"Oh, sometimes. Mostly the little things, like getting salted caramel macarons delivered to my apartment door, that iconic skyline, or the lit-up marquees along Broadway. But mostly, no. Turns out I'm a small town girl at heart." She propped her chin in her hand. "And what about you?"

"What about me?"

"It's been a long time since you've been back home, huh?"

"Over a decade."

"Your brothers missed you, you know. And while she might not say it, your grandma did too."

"If that's a joke, I'm having a hard time laughing." He took a long bitter swig of coffee, letting it burn his inner cheeks.

She gave him a searching look. "I'm serious."

He set down the mug and sought out his gruffest tone. "Look. Here's a free piece of advice. You don't know anything about me. I'm not the sort of guy people miss. I'm more the 'good riddance' type."

"Well, I do know one thing." She sat back in her chair. The smile playing around her mouth showed his brusqueness had no effect. "You and Quinn Higsby."

He tried to keep his face implacable and knew he failed. "What about her?"

Her eyes softened. "I saw how she looked at you during

Thanksgiving dinner and how you looked back. You two had more chemistry going on than the inside of a mad scientist's laboratory. Pretty darn explosive."

What was with this damn blush creeping up his neck, spreading to his ears?

Edie didn't point it out; instead she doubled down like a bird dog during duck season. "You'll need to take her on a first date, something where you wow her a bit but can still be yourself. What does she like?"

He knew what Quinn liked when he was pumping inside her, how she responded to a grinding rhythm, but outside of the bedroom? He cleared his throat. "She, uh, likes books."

Edie gave a thoughtful nod. "That's good. You'll always know what to buy her for a gift. Plus, she probably likes to stay up late." She winked. Winked? In that moment he saw how she and Archer made sense. She might be a little refined but was like chocolate laced with chili, all that sweetness came packed with a helluva bite.

"Just be yourself," Edie advised.

That's the problem. He was a grump, putting it mildly. Some would say asshole and he wouldn't dispute it. The two women at the corner table, former teachers from Brightwater High, kept bobbling their necks in his direction. They must remember him from when he had been a student, at least in name. In truth he'd spent more time hanging behind the bleachers smoking unfiltered cigarettes and kicking ass than he ever did attending class. How could he focus on algebra or economics when that old restless anger took hold? Throwing or taking a punch was the only thing that kept him from climbing out of his own skin before he started smoke jumping.

But he didn't want to return to those old fighting days, at least not with his fists. He'd rather fight a way back to himself, see if there was anything left of the man his mother would have been proud to call her son. Reaching out to his brother and getting a better-suited truck was a start. But he needed to go further. Be the guy who could try again, risk his pride and hermit life on an unpredictable and captivating woman named Quinn.

The faint light inside him burned a little brighter, heating his chest.

"Hey, I have to go see about a few things," he said to Edie. "But thanks for the coffee, pastry, and kick in the ass."

"I have some solid experience kicking Kane butt." She smiled. "I'm at least a green belt by now."

He pulled out two twenties. "You see those ladies over there?"

Edie glanced in their direction. "Beryl and Donna? Sure, they come in here all the time. They're in that Chicklits book club with your grandma."

"Cover their bill for me, will you?"

Edie eyed the money. "But this is way too much. All they had was a shared banana nut muffin and two—"

"Then load them up with a few extra treats. I used to be one of their students and owe them one."

She smiled up at him. "Wilder Kane, you are a nice man."

"Don't let the secret out, okay?" Wilder rose, keeping

a safe distance. Edie seemed like the sort who might do something crazy like go in for a hug. He might be turning over a new leaf, but there wasn't a way to paint stripes over all his spots. Hugging wasn't in his vocabulary.

Although cuddling was, with the right girl.

He stepped outside, shoved his black knit beanie on, and paused. The sun had come out while he had been stuffing his face. The mountains stood out in stark relief, rugged and wild. He'd lived in Montana for years but this was home. He took a deep breath, the clean, cold air filled his lungs, filling him with renewed purpose. Nature was its own kind of therapy.

A ray of light cut through the cloud, illuminating the new-fallen snow swathing the side of Mount Oh-Be-Joyful. He might be a physical mess, and together they were oddballs, but there was no doubt Quinn was a special snowflake.

He began to walk, slowly and with a limp up Main Street toward his 4Runner. A few cars might have slowed, but he didn't look over.

Wilder Kane was back in town.

But maybe, just maybe, the black sheep would surprise them all.

Chapter Eleven

QUINN BLEW SOAP suds off her forearm with an irritated huff. She'd filled the claw-foot bath to the brim with hot water and jasmine scented bubble bath. The trip to the lab had been short, methodical, easy even, except for the fact the needle made her a little lightheaded. After they drew her blood, she'd had to sit in a chair and drink a disposable cup of orange juice. But since she got home, her plans to relax had revealed themselves to be rather ambitious.

She'd brewed three separate cups of tea and forgotten each one until they'd grown cold on the kitchen counter. Then downloaded an app onto her phone, some sort of meditation guide, but had been unable to focus. When the calm woman's voice announced it was time to scan her thoughts, all she could do was visualize them sliding through a sieve, disappearing.

Her blood work was being sent off to a diagnostic lab

in the city and the results should arrive back just in time for Christmas. She'd either be getting the best present ever or a lump of coal in the form of a positive Alzheimer's prognosis.

This bubble bath coupled with the glass of pinot grigio on the window ledge was supposed to be her Hail Mary "feel better" pass. It might not quite be five here but it was somewhere in the world.

She sank under the water, holding her breath, hearing her pulse in her ears, seeing if she could make it to sixty. Once she'd held her breath that long down in the Brightwater River and Dad called her a mermaid.

There came a muffled bang. Someone pounded at the front door. She sat up, gasping, wiping the suds from her eyes.

Who'd be stopping by? Probably one of the Higsbys. Dad's family was large, and God love them, they didn't see the value in calling before coming over. It was rare for one of the family to leave Brightwater, so since her arrival she'd been viewed with a certain level of fascination, especially with regards to her old job. They wanted to hear about which celebrities she had rubbed elbows with, having no idea that her boss's wife had essentially chased her out of town with a pitchfork.

She stepped out of the tub, wiped the fog from her glasses, and did a quick towel dry before slipping into her red silk bathrobe, the one that was fine in L.A. but, seeing as Brightwater wanted to give Narnia a run for its winter money, fell short of providing any meaningful warmth. She was freezing cold halfway down the hall.

"Coming!" she called through chattering teeth.

It was only then that it occurred to her that she didn't have to answer at all. But she was programmed to respond. To people please. Even now. The thought grated her. Today had sucked. She'd just politely tell whoever it was out there that she was busy, had a headache, or—even more potent—cramps. Yes, cramps, good. That would send anyone scurrying away. She'd even clutch her lower belly for added effect.

Wait, hmm, clutching was too dramatic. She'd worked with actors. Better to give a slight rub and rueful smile. *Perfect.*

She threw open the door and all thoughts of fictional periods disappeared at the sight of Wilder filling the doorway in a black jacket and a black knit cap low slung over his broad forehead, offsetting those bright eyes.

Oh.

Oh my.

"You're all wet," Wilder said.

"Yeah, I am." *God. Wait. No.* "Because of the bath."

"That's what I meant. What were you talking about?" His smile was slow, wolfish, and everything sexy.

Was this real life or had she drowned in the tub and heaven was all about ravishing brutish-looking men? The cold winter brushed her bare thighs and said, "Real life."

"Come in, come in," she stammered, closing the door behind him. Could he hear her heart going like a battering ram against her sternum? Despite every wish to the contrary, all she could do was remember him above her, hot, sweaty, and so hungry, the ravenous way he'd inhaled her.

Don't swoon. Keep it together. This wasn't a good idea.

"How did you know where I lived?" she squeaked.

He shrugged. "Small town hotline."

"You dial in and make a request to a busybody?"

"Basically. Or walk into The Dirty Shame and ask my cousin Kit because he picked you up for Thanksgiving yesterday. How was your appointment?"

"Oh, you know." She waved her hand, hoping the effect looked suitably casual. The last thing she wanted was to saddle him with her medical woes. That's why she'd run away this morning. But now he was here, and despite everything she couldn't deny the thrill. "Boring doctor stuff. Wait. How did you get here?"

"Drove."

"Huh?" She glanced out the bay window at the blue 4Runner parked in her driveway. "Wait. Is that yours?"

"Yeah. Got an automatic this afternoon. Easier for me to drive. See people. See you."

His gruff tone didn't offset the hint of underlying sweetness. She didn't bother resisting a grin. "That is so amazing." He looked so uncomfortable with the praise that she took pity and changed the subject. "And what's in the bag?"

He glanced down at the Save-U-More paper bag. "I wanted to take you on a date."

A date? That sounded like a big mistake. Huge. But she was intrigued. "A date in a bag?" She sat on the couch, checking that her robe didn't gape. She didn't want to flash him.

"I'm sort of improvising here. First off we've got . . ." He pulled out a box of cake mix. "Red velvet." Followed by a jar of chocolate frosting.

"This is already in my top ten percent of dates."

"I'd like to improve on that. There's more in here." He rolled the bag shut. "But I think we'll start with what we've got. You ran out today so maybe you don't want me here, but I thought I'd—"

"No. I am happy to see you." And that was the truth. She was tempted to run into the kitchen and execute a private happy dance. Instead, she flipped her hair out of her face. "You're going to bake for me?"

"Sure, you have a sweet tooth, don't you?"

"Try a whole mouthful."

She followed him into the kitchen, gave a few directions as to her pots-and-pans cupboard, and fumbled with the mixer. She ducked into her bedroom with reluctance to change into a pair of grey lounge pants and a long-sleeved cranberry colored top.

And maybe did a few steps of the cha-cha.

"Want a lick?" He was pouring the batter when she returned, and handed her the whisk. "My mom always let me do that."

"Yum. She had the right idea." She gripped the metal handle, her misgivings retreating the moment her tongue made contact with the sugary goodness. "You lost her a long time ago, didn't you?"

His eyes went flat. "When I was six."

She forced the swallow. "That must have been so hard."

He gave a single nod. "My brothers don't remember her or my dad. She used to take me to Castle Falls. No one ever went down there, said the place was haunted. But she would laugh at the idea. We'd sit at the top of the cascades, watching the water tumble over, and she'd say if the place was haunted, the ghosts were kind. And there were the fairy rings."

She set the whisk on the counter. "Fairy rings?"

"Flower circles. No one knows why they came up. It was part of the reason people were uneasy about the place."

"Sounds beautiful."

"It was." He moved his arms aimlessly as if not sure what to do with them. At last he folded them tight to his broad chest. "But Brightwater is a practical place. No one here has much use for magic."

"That's why you moved to Castle Lane," she said slowly, sinking into a chair. A few puzzle pieces clicked together. "Not because you wanted to get away from everyone. It's because you wanted to be close to a good memory from your past."

He glanced out the window, averting his face. "Maybe both."

The sweet smell of cake infused the air as they sat in uncertain silence.

"It was sweet of you to come over." She paused for a beat. "I need to tell you something. The way I bolted from your bed, I wasn't sure if I spoiled everything."

"Don't mention it." He put the bowl in the sink with a little too much force.

"I'm serious. I had a hard morning and to have you come by, surprise me—"

"I'm serious. Don't mention it." He looked uncomfortable. What was it about this guy that seemed genuinely afraid of compliments, of kindness?

"There is a lot more to you than meets the eye." She approached him. "Underneath all these big muscles and grumbles is a soft center, isn't there?" She set her hands on his shoulders and rose on tiptoes, planting a kiss on the scruffy patch between his wide mouth and jaw, right on the hint of a frown line, a tattoo of sadness. How could she resist this man?

Oh yeah, she couldn't.

"I wouldn't be so sure."

She slid her tongue across his, slow, tentative, a stroke, but gentle, an introduction. "You taste pretty darn good."

"You do too."

She pulled him closer. He'd been lost for so long, was it too naïve to hope she could kiss him found?

He broke off, glanced at the kitchen table, and took her hand. "Come over here." He sat on a chair and pulled her down, positioning her legs so she straddled him, her pelvis nestled against his, grazing his hardness. She rocked closer, teasing, unable to get enough, wanting to fist his glossy hair with two hands. God, if she could, she'd inhale him. Her head spun. It could be low blood pressure after the bath, but more likely she'd gone woozy with wanting.

"What do you want?" He sucked on her neck, pulling from her a gasp. "From me?"

She dug her fingers into his shoulders. "To remember that there is still some good stuff out there in the world. What about you?"

His lips twitched against her skin. "I want to forget the bad."

"We're quite a pair, aren't we?"

His hands slid under her shirt, up her bare back, hungrily stroking the braless expanse of sensitive skin between her shoulders.

"We're something."

This time his kiss took control, the pleasure almost excruciating. He had the power to render her helpless, hungry, until she shamelessly humped against him, burrowing close, her body rebelling at any place that didn't make contact. Their teeth collided and they each tasted the other's moan. Then he dropped one hand, slid it into the elastic waistband of her pants, running his fingers over her soft curls. One slow finger stroked through her center, gathering wetness and bringing it right to the tip of her clit. For a big guy with thick, rough fingers he moved gently.

"Let me know if it's too hard," he muttered. "I—I don't have great sensation here."

"Wait." She grabbed his wrist. "You can't feel me?"

"I can a little." His glance fixated on her lap, not daring to rise to her eyes. "Not much with the burns."

"That's unfair." She refused to be sympathetic, it was a luxury he didn't want and she couldn't afford. Better to offer honesty. "I feel. You feel. That's the deal between us."

"I don't mind."

"I do." She peeled off her shirt, her bare breasts tightening in the cold air, nipples two tight peaks.

"Fuck, Trouble. You're gorgeous."

She stood and reset her glasses, checking the oven timer before offering her hand. "We have thirty-two more minutes before that alarm goes off. Think we can put it to good use?"

He laced his fingers with hers and rose. "Wager we can have a damn good half hour."

They got to her room and somehow her pants disappeared on the journey. She was naked while he was completely dressed. For some reason she liked it, though, loved the roughness of his wool and denim against her exposed skin.

They fell onto the bed. He grabbed her hips as she reached for the headboard.

"You want me to feel you?"

"So much."

He buried his face between her legs, inhaled deep, his lips fastening on her slick flesh as he gave a long, slow, suck. "Oh, yeah. I feel that."

She let out a whimper that would have to pass for "I do too."

He dragged his tongue around her clit, twirling over the hypersensitive nerve endings until she sank into a gyre that was nothing but his sucking, probing, and nibbling mouth.

"Let me see you watch what I'm doing," he rasped. "Want to see your face as you get there."

She glanced down, mouth drying as her heart accelerated. Her hips were inches off the bed as she greedily bucked against him for more. "I'm right there."

"Yeah? I'll bet you can go a little further."

Even though she was teetering on the edge, toes curling and pulse racing, he plunged onward.

Her legs locked tight against his head but he didn't seem to care about the pressure. Instead, he rolled back and forth between her thighs as if he'd never get close enough, like every lick, suck, and stroke was precious, to be savored. In the distance, an oven alarm went off. No way. He couldn't have been down there a half hour. No one had ever been down there a half hour. How the heck did he do this? Not allow her release, but kept leading her forward, out along a tightrope of almost painful desire.

It hurt not to be coming. Her entire body was reduced to a single clench. Finally, he eased a finger inside, no easy feat when she was this tight, this wound up, this—

"Oh. Oh God." He pressed up, mirroring the same action on the outside with the flat of his tongue. It ratcheted everything from merely "good" to "glorious and floating aloft on a cloud being serenaded by angels."

She didn't know it was possible to feel this much . . . everything. Still he took her deeper and deeper into her climax until her back bowed. She writhed, pinned against him. His hands braced her hips and he took her whole center in his mouth. She skyrocketed to sitting up, her brain waves going into a perfect flatline while every other body part trembled uncontrollably. White light pulsed in her peripheral vision and as it ebbed she floated like some sort of feather, wafting back to earth.

"Good?"

"Dear Lord, I'd give you a standing ovation if I could trust my knees to hold my weight." She could barely find the energy to move her lips. All she could think of doing was curling up like a kitten in the dappled evening light filtering into the bedroom.

He kissed one thigh and then the other, planting one last sensitive kiss at her apex, before resting his head on her lower belly.

She breathed deep, trying to rejoin her mind and body.

The alarm kept ringing.

"Better go grab that cake," he said at last.

"You do this and then feed me red velvet cake?"

"This is a date, right?"

"Best in history."

His smile took her breath. "You look happier than when I knocked on your door."

And she realized, impossible as it was given the morning's strain, that she was able to smile back with her whole self. Even if for the next few weeks she lived under the weight of an invisible axe, for this one moment maybe it was okay to believe that everything would be okay.

Whatever this was between them, was more than a fling. It was more everything. And that meant she'd have to tell him what might be waiting ahead for her. She'd never in a million years ask anyone to be part of her ticking time bomb. If she was going to go off like a grenade, best to limit the collateral damage. But she wouldn't run off again, sneak away like she did this morning. Time to hike up her big-girl panties and explain the grim situation.

She grabbed her yoga pants and hiked them over her hips. Then her shirt.

Wilder banged around in the kitchen. Not exactly a domestic sound. More like a bull in a china shop, but the idea that this big brutal man would make her something as simple and sweet as a cake melted the ice that she had around her heart. There was more to him than met the eye.

He came back in a few minutes, carrying a slice.

She took the plate and pressed a hand to her mouth. "You put sprinkles on it?"

"You seem the type to like a little sparkle."

That was it. Holding the plate, staring at a cake with rainbow sprinkles, she bent over and began to sob.

Chapter Twelve

THE SIGHT OF Quinn's tears cracked Wilder's granite heart, sank roots into the barren waste. The growing pains caused an ache but a good one that felt like living. For so long he'd kept himself from feeling anything except for what came easy. Anger, mostly. Or dogged determination. He'd learned to stop fighting others when he started to fight fire instead, reminding himself of the real enemy. Since he'd stopped working he'd turned the fight against himself, beating himself up night after night. But now he finally had a productive direction in which to channel his urges.

He wanted to fight for the woman in front of him. The one wiping her eyes and taking great shallow, sobbing gulps of air.

"You going to tell me what's going on here, Trouble?" he asked, lifting her chin.

Her eyes were haunted. "There isn't an easy way to say this."

"Take all the time you need."

That set her off on a fresh bout of crying. "Why are you so good to me?"

He caressed her hair, wishing he could feel every nuance of the soft, silky-looking texture. "You make me want to be a better man."

She took off her glasses, wiping the lenses with her sleeve. "Stupid things, they always fog up. But contacts make my eyes itch. My mother used to force me to wear them in high school. Always said, 'Quinn, no man wants to look at a four-eyes.'"

"Are you shitting me?" His voice went quiet, anger scraping his stomach hollow.

"Let's just say we aren't taking our mother-daughter duo act to Vegas or anything. I used to pull straight A's but all she cared about was how many guys asked to take me to prom. I haven't even told her about anything that's going on."

"Take it easy, Trouble." He kissed her warm brow, wondering what could have her so rattled. "You're hyper-ventilating."

She braced her hands on her knees and appeared to fight for a deep breath. "I've tried to handle everything, but it's like I'm so jam-packed that leaks are springing everywhere. I hate it."

"Go on and eat some of that cake. We can talk whatever it is out afterward."

QUINN OFFERED A prayer of gratitude that he was willing to give her space. "Okay."

"I'll be right back." He left, returning a few minutes later as she licked the frosting from her lips. Chocolate had a funny way of making bad or scary things seem better. Magical stuff indeed.

"What's all this?" she asked, looking at his laden tray.

He passed her a mug of warm milk. "My mom used to heat me a cup of moo juice whenever I got upset."

She cupped the ceramic mug between her hands, hoping the heat might loosen some of her body's tension, and took a tentative sip. "That's so sweet of you. Thank you."

He held up a book. "The other night, I noticed how you read to your dad, thought maybe you'd like someone to read to you for once?"

She stared at the woman in the Regency dress on the cover, her brain trying to register the image. "*Sense and Sensibility*? You want to read me Jane Austen?"

He set down the tray on the nightstand and picked up the book with a trace of uncertainty. "It was on my list, and when I went into your shop today after going to Haute Coffee, the woman working there said that you like this author."

"Jane is life. I love her."

His chest heaved a little bit. "This is good then?" He sat down on the bed, grabbed the soft throw blanket on the end, and shook it over her lap.

"A cup of warm milk on an almost winter's day? Cake in bed? A hot guy offering to read me Jane Austen after mind-blowing oral pleasure? I don't think good can hold a candle to what's inside me."

He opened the book and flipped through the soft, creamy paper, a shy smile tugging the corner of his mouth. He paused, but not for long. "Chapter One."

For the next hour he read in a low, methodical voice about the two sisters, Marianne and Elinor, and their life in Sussex and Devonshire.

Finally, he closed it and placed it on her nightstand. "We can do more in a bit."

A chill licked up her spine as the pleasantries of the eighteenth century receded. Reality could only be held at bay for so long. "You want to know what's going on with me, don't you?"

The silence between them grew taut, vibrating as if someone plucked an invisible string. "If you care to make it my business, maybe I can help in some way."

She shifted the dirty dishes to the night table and twisted her hair into a quick, messy braid. Her stomach muscles clenched as an unseen weight settled on her shoulders. "You know how my dad is sick?"

"Alzheimer's."

She nodded. "Exactly. Well, it looks like his mother might have had the same thing. I can't say for certain before that, but one of my great-grandparents must have too, and so on." She was afraid to squeeze her eyes shut but the idea of looking at him scared her half to death. "Do you see what I'm saying?"

He blinked. "Not quite."

"This disease is genetic," she whispered. "Early-onset Alzheimer's disease runs in families. There is a fifty-fifty chance of a child getting it from an affected parent."

He made an indecipherable noise. "So you're saying you might have it?"

"I took a blood test today that's going to tell me which way the chips are going to fall. I had to know. I really thought for a while I wouldn't want to, that whatever will be will be and all that, but that's not me. I needed to have certainty, one way or another."

A muscle ticked in his jaw. "When will you get the results?"

"In a few weeks. If I'm negative that's the end of the story. My kids won't carry it either. I'm my dad's only child so no other siblings would be at risk. If I am positive then . . . I'm twenty-five now, maybe I'll have another twenty-five good years to go before things unravel. And that's something, right? There are people who have a lot less than that."

She dug her fists into her eyes as tears prickled. "I'm sorry. I'm trying my best to look on the bright side and everything, but the truth is I'm scared out of my mind."

He put his arm around her shoulders, cradling her close. "You don't have to do this walk alone."

"Don't you see? I can't share this journey with anyone. If it goes bad, it's better if I'm the only one affected."

He looked a little sick. "Quinn, I—"

"Please." She laced her fingers with his. "If this doesn't go in my favor, please, promise me one thing."

"Anything." His words held a quiet intensity. This wasn't a man who made promises lightly.

"That you'll leave me alone."

He froze. "I can't do that."

"I'm serious," she persisted, suddenly too hot, too cold, too everything. "This isn't a pity party. I'm being entirely selfish. I'd rather have a memory of these few sweet stolen moments. One truly happy time. How many people get this lucky? Please, don't make me beg. It's what I want." She hoped the lie sounded convincing.

"I promise."

At least more convincing than his.

But she pretended to believe him, at least for now. "Thank you."

There was the sound of wheels disturbing the gravel in the driveway, and then a loud motorcycle engine cutting off. Quinn wrinkled her brow as someone knocked on the door. "I haven't had hardly any visitors since moving in, and now twice in one day."

She got up from bed, aware Wilder followed behind. She sensed she hurt him by extracting that promise but he was only just starting to get his life on track and she wouldn't ask for it to be destabilized because of her.

She opened the door and her heart dropped a good few inches. "Garret, what on earth are you doing here?"

"Surprise, surprise, pretty lady." He grinned, stepping in uninvited and raising a six-pack. His cocky smile slipped at the sight of Wilder lurking behind her.

"Kane? Got to say I didn't expect to see you."

"King." Wilder spit the word like a curse.

A mixture of feelings coursed over Garret's Ken-doll features. Everything from annoyance to anger to fear. He was a big guy, but Wilder still had an advantage.

"You two know each other, right?" Quinn asked with

forced cheer. She didn't want to become an unofficial ref in an amateur boxing match.

Garret tried to recover his easygoing attitude. "We went to school together, didn't we, buddy?"

Wilder said nothing.

"Graduated same year, at least I did. Not sure about this lug." Garret looked friendly enough but his words held a prodding note.

"Oh. Okay." It didn't take extra-honed Spidey senses to tell these two weren't the best of friends. They stared at each other with a subtle snarl to their gaze.

"I wasn't expecting you." Quinn wavered, unsure whether to move to the couches or remain standing. It was one thing to annoy her at work or around town. It was a whole other thing to show up unannounced on her front doorstep.

"What can I say, I like to amaze the ladies." He took advantage of her indecision and sprawled into her love seat. "Hey, grab a seat, man," he said to Wilder, gesturing to a chair across the room as if he had every right to be here. "Be good to catch up."

"Thanks, I'll stand."

"Bummer about the leg, huh? I heard about that shit in Montana." Before Wilder or she could say more, he'd barreled on. "Oh, and I hung with your brother's woman today. Kooky Carson's kid, Annie. She grew up to be pretty thing, didn't she? She's doing a story for the paper on the fires, wanted an interview."

"The fires?" Wilder echoed, soft but with an edge of menace.

Quinn glimpsed the other Wilder, the dangerously unpredictable one who made his brothers skittish, even as adults. The Wilder with a feral edge.

"Yeah, there've been a few lately. I and the volunteer force are on top of it. You'll see it in the Sunday paper. Big hero profile." He rubbed his chest in satisfaction.

"That's really something," she said, picking up his six-pack and handing it over. "Um. Thanks for stopping by but I've got some jobs to do."

"Oh. Sure. So what time can I pick you up tomorrow?"

Her brow knit. "For what?"

"Dinner." His smile was so wide he exposed a bunch of gum. "You promised me a date at The Dirty Shame."

From the corner of her eye she saw Wilder stiffen. "No, sorry, I did no such thing."

Wilder made a warning rumble in the back of his throat. "Sounds like she's pretty damn clear, Garret."

"Hey, hey, no need to get your panties in a bunch. We're just kidding around, Kane. Quinn and I are friends. *Good* friends." He gave her a wink and finally she'd had enough.

In her old job she tried to ignore it when her employer made lewd innuendos, little jokes. Figured she'd treat him like a child. If she gave him no reaction, he'd stop.

But he didn't and that's how she lost her job. One night he went too far, had too much cocaine washed down with champagne and decided that the best revenge for fighting with his wife was screwing his assistant. Whether she liked it or not was of little consequence. He was big but out of his mind, and Quinn fought him off. When his wife walked in, she thought that the woman would leap to her defense. But instead she called her a "home-wrecking whore."

Before Quinn could open her mouth to quit she was fired.

All her life her mom had told her to pluck her eyebrows, wear push up bras, and "smile pretty." She had even tried to for a while. Even when her job required her to babysit a grown man who threw a fit over the kind of bottled water served in the green room or because the media questioned him about whether or not he got Botox treatments.

Screw nice. She didn't want to smile.

"You and I don't have a date planned." She folded her arms. "And you're not welcome here in my home."

Wilder moved to the door and opened it. "Guess some things never change, do they, *buddy*? You still have a hard time knowing when to back off."

Garret finally lost his easy grin, rising to his feet. "You know what? Fuck this," he snapped, taking his time to look Quinn up and down. "You think you're a hot piece of ass but your shit stinks same as everyone else's."

"Say another word to her and your tongue will be in the front yard." Wilder's face didn't betray a single emotion and that made him utterly terrifying.

"Or what?" Apparently Garret didn't value self-preservation. "You going to clobber me with your peg leg." He turned to Quinn with a sneer. "Gimps do it for you? Please tell me he takes it off and you ride it like a fucked-up dildo—"

Wilder's punch came hard, fast, and unexpected, like a striking snake. All she registered was a flash, a wet smack, and then Garret's face was bleeding. Looked like his lip had split open.

Her hands flew to her mouth. "Oh my God."

"If you're not out the door in three seconds," Wilder said acidly, "you'll lose the tongue and be writing postcards to your front teeth."

"What the fuck, man?" Garret backed up.

"One . . ." Wilder held up a finger.

Garret eyed the door as if calculating how much time he had to scram if he left a parting shot. "Everyone was right—you are a fucking lunatic."

Wilder stepped forward, closing the distance. "Two . . ."

"I'm out. Watch your back, Kane."

"Three . . ."

Garret was down the front steps, jogging toward his motorcycle. Wilder slammed the door as the engine revved to life.

Quinn took his hand and squeezed it. "You didn't need to punch him for me."

"Sometimes a man needs hitting."

"Maybe that's true, but I could tell that doing it bothered you." She rubbed the inside of his palm with her thumb.

"It's who I am, Quinn." He was unable to keep the disgust from his voice. "At least who I used to be, and people never really change, do they?"

"I think we grow as time goes on. We get more life experience. Maybe we never lose the core of ourselves, but I think that we don't stay the same either."

He pulled her close and leaned in as if to nuzzle her

hair before averting his face. "I'm sorry you saw this part of me. I'm . . . not proud of that part."

She gripped his strong arms, holding him steady. "You used to get into a lot of fights. It sounds like you were angry."

Wilder shrugged.

"Why?"

He shrugged again.

"You can tell me anything. Seriously. I doubt it's more shocking than anything I disclosed today."

Wilder wavered, and for a moment she felt positive he'd open up about whatever it was that was burning inside him. Then he set his mouth and the guy who'd read her Jane Austen, made a cake, and gone down on her until she was dizzy vanished behind a stony wall.

"You aren't alone." She brushed her lips over the edge of his clenched jaw. "I know we just met, but I care about you, and your family cares about you."

He stiffened. "You don't have to worry about me."

"He got to you, didn't he? Oh no, Wilder—"

"You're quick to see the good in people, at least the good in me. And I'm not going to lie . . . I like it. But you're a good girl. That truth is plain on your face from a mile away, and me? I've done bad things. Things that would make you lock that front door, lock me out."

"Calm down, nothing you say is going to scare me off."

"Why not? You should be frightened." He raised his voice.

"Knock it off." She gave his chest a push. He didn't budge, but his expression did change to one of surprise. "This big act you are pulling?" She was really heating up.

"It's worked for you in the past, hasn't it? You yell, make your face get all mean . . . yeah . . . just like that. Ooh, I like how your nostrils flare, an excellent touch. You put on a show and everyone ducks for cover, don't they?"

He chewed the inside of his cheek.

"Well, guess what, that behavior isn't going to fly with me. You go on and on about the darkness, as if you're the only one who's ever had something go wrong. Here's a news flash. Everyone hurts. Everyone deals with life junk. So do us both a favor and cut the badass con. You're a man. But it's not your physical strength that impresses me. It's not that tough-as-nails attitude you throw around. It's your gentleness. The kindness that brought you over here in the first place with a paper bag full of cake mix, rainbow sprinkles, and Jane Austen."

He opened his mouth and closed it.

"You don't scare me, Wilder Kane. Waiting to learn if I can expect to develop early-onset Alzheimer's? That's the sort of thing that gives me the bad kind of goose bumps. But leave your bulldog behavior on the front porch before you ever think of coming to visit my house again, got it?"

Her chest heaved. Lack of sleep, a hot bath, an impending sugar crash, post-orgasm fatigue, and good old-fashioned annoyance had shaken loose her tongue. In short, unadorned sentences she stated exactly what had transpired during the last year, how the blood draw went today, and what she could expect to learn in the next few weeks.

Wilder's face was like a mirror to her words, it started out agitated, angry, turned to shock, and finally a mounting horror as comprehension sank in. He slouched over and rubbed his temples. "I'm sorry for starting crap with King. Garret and I have history."

"That much was crystal clear."

He looked at her then, his gaze oddly intense. "No use crying over baked beans."

"That's the weird saying of my dad's."

"What about you, have you ever used it?"

She shook her head, puzzled. "I'm twenty-five, not exactly ready to settle in with the folksy sayings."

"That same day I had a big fight with King, I had a blowout with Grandma and considered running away from Brightwater, from her and my brothers. Figured they'd do better without me. All I ever seemed to do was cause problems and it had gotten old. I didn't have my license yet, figured I'd start walking, thumb a ride, and head to a new place. I'd decided on Phoenix."

"Phoenix?"

His mouth crooked. "Rising from the ashes and all that."

"I'm surprised you didn't end up in Hollywood, put that flair for the dramatic to good use."

"There was a reason I stayed. A little girl kicked some sense into me."

"Wait." A glimmer came back to her, faint but growing stronger by the second. A horse stall. A big boy who'd been crying. "Wait a second." She pressed a hand to her mouth.

He gave an almost imperceptible nod. "That was you, wasn't it? The kid with the cotton candy."

Chapter Thirteen

WILDER'S PHONE BUZZED. He didn't answer. This was important.

Quinn stood up and came over, sitting beside him. "You? You were that boy in the stable during the fair?"

"Yeah, I was—" His phone rang again. "Sorry, I don't know why but my family is harassing me. They're the only ones with this number. Hang on a second."

He clicked answer and Edie was talking before he could say "I'm busy."

"Wilder. Thank goodness you picked up. There was a fire at the bakery and—"

"Wait. Are you okay?"

"I wasn't there. I'm halfway home and just got the call. Archer is going to pick me up because I'm too upset to drive, then we're going to go back and see what happened. Apparently they caught it before it could do too much damage but . . ." She broke off, sniffling.

Wilder's jaw set. If someone had done something to purposefully harm this sweet, well-meaning woman he wouldn't be responsible for his actions. "What can I do to help?"

"It's Grandma Kane. We can't have her up at the house by herself. Sawyer is on duty and Annie is in San Francisco. Can you please go to Hidden Rock and stay with her?"

"Yeah." He closed his eyes briefly. "I'm on it."

"Oh thank you." She acted like he'd just bestowed her with a bag of leprechaun gold.

"It's not a big deal. I'll leave now."

Within a few minutes, he was starting up his truck, still surprised Quinn had managed to talk her way into the passenger seat. She wouldn't take no for an answer. He didn't know if having her up at Hidden Rock was a good idea or a terrible one, but a small part of him was relieved he wouldn't be in the old house alone with Grandma.

He turned onto Main Street and fire trucks were lined up in front of Haute Coffee, lights flashing and hoses spread along the sidewalk. Sawyer's sheriff's SUV was there too. From the front it didn't look like the damage was extensive, but time would tell. He hoped for Edie's sake they'd gotten there in time.

Quinn pressed a hand to her mouth. "That's so sad. Edie has clearly thrown her heart and soul into that shop. The building is old though. Must have been some sort of faulty wiring problem."

Unease prickled along the base of his spine. He had a feeling, and even though he wasn't a firefighter anymore, it was hard to ignore the instinct that something was wrong, especially when that instinct had saved his life not a few times.

"You don't think it was an accident, do you?" Quinn swiveled in her seat, turning to regard the scene with a furrowed brow.

"I didn't say anything."

"There's an awful lot that you communicate with that face of yours." She reached back and stroked his cheek. "And I can't believe you were the boy from the fair. I've thought of you, you know. How old were you?"

"Sixteen."

"Yeah, that makes sense. It was right around when I turned ten. You were really going to run away from home?"

He bit down on the inside of his lower lip, hard enough to taste a coppery tang. "Yeah."

"Why?"

He turned and their gazes locked. Time hadn't dulled the memory of those soft, observant brown eyes. He was surprised he didn't recognize her the moment they met.

He'd done it this time.

Blood bloomed down the front of his shirt and the thick, metallic taste in the back of his throat made him gag. He spat in the hay and knocked his head against the stall. Yeah. He'd really gone and fucking done it this time. Grandma had made it crystal clear that if he got into another fight he'd be packed off to military school. His cousin, Kit, never shut up about enlisting, but that wasn't Wilder's path.

The problem was he didn't know anything about his path.

"Stupid." He punched the stall. It hurt but not bad enough. He punched again and again until his knuckles split, bleeding just like his nose.

"Stop that!"

He froze at the high-pitched voice. A kid stood watching him. A girl clutching a stick of cotton candy and wearing round glasses that magnified her eyes and made her look like a baby owl. Her hair was braided into two long pigtails.

"Get out of here," he snapped. Last thing he wanted was to have some kid playing twenty questions.

"What happened?" Her nose crinkled as she took in all the blood. "You need a Band-Aid or something?"

Yeah, I need something all right. "Don't think they make Band-Aids big enough to suit me, kid."

"What hurts the most?" She sat on a hay bale and crossed her legs.

"Everything is pretty damn equal."

"Were you kicked by one of the horses? Daddy always said that if I'm around horses to never stand behind their—"

"I wasn't kicked by a horse. Got into a fight."

Her eyebrows shot up. "People beat you up?"

He glared through a puffy eye. "Bet they look worse. I think I broke Garret King's arm. Why are you bothering me anyway?"

"Daddy is working." She shrugged. "He's an electrician and they needed his help over at the bandstand so he gave me five bucks and said not to get into trouble."

"Then best clear out of here because that's all I am."

"Why were you fighting?"

"Garret and his friends were picking on someone who couldn't defend herself. Doris Higsby's daughter."

"Lola? She's my cousin, has Down syndrome."

"Yeah. Well. She can't help it and those guys were being assholes."

"So you punched them." She crammed a big bite of cotton candy into her mouth.

"I might look shitty but I promise they look worse. But now I'm fucked. Sorry, kid."

"You can say fuck, I don't mind."

"Your daddy lets you swear."

"No way. But I'm not the one saying bad words. You are."

"Look, I'm not in the mood to play Mary Poppins. Take what's left of that cotton candy and run along. Go barf on the Tilt-a-Whirl or something."

She giggled. "You're gross."

"I'm a lot of things."

"And you've been crying."

"Have not."

She glanced at the ceiling. "Doesn't look like it's been raining in here."

He gouged at his eyes with two fists. "Jesus. Don't tell anyone."

"I won't. You might knock my teeth out."

"I'd never hit a girl."

"Why not tell your grandma what happened? She'll understand. People can't be mean to Lola. It's against the rules."

"You are acting like my grandma is a reasonable person. And hell, maybe she is, but not where I'm concerned. Fuck it, I'm not going to sit around and wait for her to ship me off. I've got fifty bucks in my wallet. I'll get out of here tonight. Hitchhike."

"And go where?"

"Who cares? Any place is better than here. I could wash dishes under the table in San Francisco. Or pick fruit at a farm near the coast. Or maybe go to the Rockies. Idaho. Montana. Be a lumberjack."

"Or say sorry."

"It ain't that simple."

"Ain't isn't a word, and yeah it is."

"I mess up. It's what I do." He clenched his jaw. "What I've always done."

She swallowed her next bite of cotton candy. "My dad says it's no use crying over baked beans."

"That doesn't even make any sense."

"Does too. Why cry over baked beans? It's silly. There's no point. And there's no point sitting in here talking about running away. You did nothing wrong."

"That's not how my grandma will see it. She hates me."

"Here." She stuck out the cotton candy cone. "Take some."

"I don't want your candy. Don't even know where your grubby fingers have been."

She thrust her shoulders back. "I wash my hands and they haven't been anywhere bad. Go on. You'll feel better."

He didn't feel like arguing with the little brat so he grabbed some fluffy spun sugar. "Happy?"

"Yeah."

"You're a bossy little thing."

"I'm the tallest girl in my class. And the number one reader," she said proudly.

Wilder stuffed the candy into his mouth. The sweetness masked the bitter copper flavor of blood.

"See. Look. You feel better already."

"Bizzy? Bizzy Bee, you in here?" a man called out.

The girl's eyes widened. "That's my daddy. I have to go."

She jumped up and turned to go. Before she left the stall, she paused. "Whatever your grandma says, I'm glad you hit those bad boys."

Then she was gone.

CREAK. CREAK. CREAK. Grandma Kane rocked next to the fire. Quinn turned the page of the *Ranching Life* magazine she was skimming. "Hey, listen to this," she said to the quiet room. "Did you know cows produce more milk if they listen to soothing music? Scientists did a study and apparently R.E.M.'s 'Everybody Hurts' caused the most lactation."

"Sounds like a bunch of cockamamie, if you ask me," Grandma muttered.

Wilder didn't say a word.

Tough crowd.

Time for plan B.

"Who'd like a cup of tea?" Quinn asked, rising to her feet. "Mrs. Kane?" Calling her Grandma felt way too familiar. "Want some Egyptian licorice?"

The older woman peered over the top of her turquoise bifocals. "Egyptian licor-what?"

"Or plain black? Simple? Classic?"

That received a brief, pursed-mouth nod. Quinn gave Wilder the "help me out a little" eye. He knew she was doing it, so he looked everywhere but in her direction. Darn him.

"Boy," Grandma snapped. "Will you kindly acknowledge your girlfriend before she gives me a turn with all that nervous twitching?"

Her throwaway use of the word *girlfriend* did a better job of snagging Wilder's attention. He jerked out of whatever gloomy stupor he'd been trapped in.

"We're just friends," Quinn said quickly. Yeah, he was a real good friend to her girl parts.

"Just friends?" Grandma snorted, catching her blush. "Hah. I might be over eighty with a busted hip and be able to remember when Roosevelt was president, but that doesn't mean I lost my marbles. I have friends, missy, but none that know what I look like out of my drawers."

Quinn had a sudden terrible image of Grandma Kane in a pair of drawers, white ones with pink flouncy ruffles on the butt. The idea made a titter well up in her throat, no, worse, a giggle, wait, crap, a guffaw. Yeah, a full-scale guffaw was imminent and there was nothing she could do to stop it.

She tried to turn it into a sneeze and that just made everything ten times worse. The escaping noise was a mash-up between a wheeze, snort, hiccup, and chortle. The entire thesaurus could have a field day trying to describe the sound that stress, uncertainty, sex, and the glare of a dowager rancher could pull from her body.

"Is this one all right in the head?" Grandma Kane asked Wilder, speaking out of the side of her mouth.

"The same as anyone," Wilder responded, adding, "And for the record, when you talk like that, everyone can still hear you."

Grandma's gaze was frostier than the White Witch of Narnia's.

"Wasn't sure if you were aware." Wilder shrugged. "When I was a kid you used to do it to cashiers in the checkout aisle, talk about their moles or the fact that you were going to be covered in moss if they moved any slower."

That sent Quinn off on a fresh round. She grabbed her water glass off the coffee table and took a swig. Maybe that would help.

"I'm sorry," she gasped, bending over and bracing her knees.

"Here I thought Annie Carson was the kooky one but you might take the cake," Grandma said, shaking her head.

"Guess we all have our moments." Quinn wiped her eyes.

"I'll make the tea." Wilder rose and went straight to the kitchen without waiting for anyone to tell him no. He was using his cane less and less.

The fire crackled in the hearth, otherwise silence reigned supreme. Strange, seeing as this was an old house. No creaks.

"You have a lovely home," Quinn said at last.

"Don't get any big ideas," Grandma barked. "It's going to Archer and Edie."

"Excuse me?" Quinn bristled.

"You're a Higsby, aren't you?"

"Yes, but I don't see what that has to do with—"

"Everyone knows a Higsby is the worst kind of fool. You're the one who works in the bookstore, aren't you?"

"Yes. You come in every Wednesday with the other Chicklits, but I don't see what that has to do with—"

"Go to the mantel." Grandma pointed to a thick leather-bound book on the end.

Quinn rose and trudged over. What a shrew. No wonder Wilder didn't like spending time with his family. She glanced at the title. "*Brightwater: Small Town, Big Dreams*?"

"That right there is the town history," Grandma Kane said. "You like to read? You should give it a try. The pages are riddled with the exploits of Higsbys, half-baked ideas, inventions. Did you know your great-aunt Helen tried to sell a baby mop?"

Quinn wasn't sure if she should be amused or horrified, so she settled somewhere in between. "Excuse me?"

"A baby mop. It was a mop head but instead of a stick, a crawling baby was attached to it. She thought she'd put her children to good use. Considering she had enough of them, you could almost not blame her. Higsbys are a fertile lot, after all." Grandma gave her an appraising stare. "And you have the family's birthing hips."

"I'm not sure if I ever want to have kids." Quinn willed her voice to stay steady. It wasn't that she didn't love kids. She did, at least most kids, unless they ate their boogers or threw fits on an airplane. Still, if she carried the early-onset gene, she couldn't reproduce. No way would she saddle another person with a fifty-fifty future like the one she faced.

"No children?" Grandma's frown deepened, her eyes narrowing into suspicious slits. "But what about keeping the family alive, growing the herd?"

"Leave her alone," Wilder said, carrying two mugs of tea. He set one next to Grandma and carried the other over to Quinn.

Grandma made a tsk sound. "Use a—"

"Coaster. I know. You only told me that for as long as I lived here," Wilder muttered as he set the cup down.

Grandma Kane crossed her arms and stared at her grandson. "I told you a lot of things but never saw it do much good."

Wilder walked over, grabbed a log, and threw it onto the fire with more force than the situation called for.

Quinn watched both their faces. Wilder was hurt, masking it with anger, whereas Grandma Kane was like a junkyard dog who'd caught a pant leg and was physically incapable of letting go.

"You want to pick on somebody, pick on me," Wilder said. "How about a game of chess?"

"It's getting close to my bedtime. Aren't you supposed to make sure I'm tucked in at a sensible time?"

Wilder dug out the chessboard from under the coffee table. "Save your smarts for the game—you're going to need them."

The two of them engaged in serious trash talking. The dynamic was impossible to figure out. A tug of war was going on, a power play. One Quinn didn't understand and was glad she didn't have to get involved in.

Instead, she cozied onto the couch with Brightwater's history. She'd never really devoted much brain space to wondering about the town's past or the fact that her family really did tend to have a lot of kids. More than the Kanes if that was possible.

She flipped around, pausing at a strangely titled chapter. "The Curious Case of the Castle Falls Phantom."

She read through the short entry, her stomach in knots. Déjà vu wasn't a feeling that she had much experience with, but there'd been a Castle Falls hermit before Wilder?

Why? And what happened to him? Quinn tried to lose herself in the story, but her thoughts kept drifting to Wilder.

He was stuck in the past while she fixated on the future. Was there a way they could both figure out how to live in the present?

Chapter Fourteen

GRANDMA BEAT WILDER, best two out of three games. He played hard but she was wily, didn't miss a trick. Never had. She always was one step ahead of him. It used to scare him how she seemed to understand what he'd do before he did.

She'd gone to bed smug in her victory before Archer and Edie returned, tired and a little rattled.

"The fire started inside the kitchen," Edie said, taking a spot next to Quinn. "Luckily the damage was minimal. I'll have to replace some appliances but it could have been worse. A lot worse."

"Was it set on purpose?"

Edie bowed her head, a troubled look crossing her refined features. "The only person with a real axe to grind against me is my ex and he's in jail now. Unless he somehow got out and . . ."

"He didn't get out, Freckles." Archer had walked

behind the couch and began kneading her shoulders.

"My guess is that this wasn't about you at all," Wilder said.

"I'm exhausted on a cellular level." Edie stretched. "So tired even getting a back rub feels like work. Thanks for helping out at the last minute. Did Grandma keep you on your toes?"

"She's a tough old bird," Archer said. "I'm glad you spent some time together, although I wish it were under better circumstances."

When Wilder got Quinn out to the car, he paused. "Grandma *is* a tough old bird. Sorry about what she said, about you having kids."

"It's fine."

"Not really. She hurt you."

"People accidentally hurt each other all the time."

"Still doesn't make it right. You can bear more than most people. But that doesn't mean it's okay or that you should have to. When is the last time anyone took care of you?"

"I . . ."

"Do you trust me?"

"I—yeah I do, so help me."

"I want to take you someplace special. It's near my house."

"Now you've gone and gotten me all intrigued."

He turned on the radio and "Little Drummer Boy" was playing.

"This is my favorite Christmas song," they both said at the same time.

"For real?" Quinn said, surprised. "Why do you love it?"

Wilder was quiet for so long she wondered if maybe he'd never answer. "Guess I like how the little boy played his best, and everyone stood there, watching, waiting. He stepped up to the challenge."

Quinn tried and failed to swallow the lump in her throat. "You know you're the same way, right?"

"Trouble, I've pretended that for a long time, but now I know better. I've been running scared for years."

"Your accident changed so much about your life. But look how well you are doing. Honestly, you should be proud."

"There is so much I'm not proud of."

"Everyone makes mistakes sometimes. Did you know part of the reason why I moved here is because I got fired. I thought my boss was being friendly, inviting me inside his house in Laurel Canyon after his big premiere. He was in his late fifties—it never even occurred to me that he might think of me in *that* way." She took off her glasses and polished the lenses. "He said that I'd been doing a great job, that he wanted to thank me. I was picturing a glass of wine before driving back to my apartment. I mean, he had daughters my age. Instead, he wanted to show his appreciation in a different way."

"He fucking touched you?" Wilder gripped the wheel so hard she was afraid it would rip off.

"He wanted to, tried even. But instead, I touched him. In the nose. With my fist."

He rumbled his approval. "Good girl."

"His cries woke his wife up. I'm so stupidly naïve. I

thought that she would jump to my defense. It wasn't her fault she married a creep. Instead, she called me a . . . how did she put it again?" Quinn tapped the side of her chin. "Ah, yes, 'a home-wrecking whore,' I believe was the phrase. She was more worried that he'd have facial bruising for his big advertising shoot the next day than the fact that he tried to tune in Tokyo with my boobs. This was right after my dad started going downhill fast, and it seemed like the universe was telling me in a very nonsubtle way that I needed to get to Brightwater."

"I'm sorry that happened to you. But I'm not sorry you're here." He cracked his neck, the pop audible over the music. "Which is a shitty and selfish thing to say."

"No. No, it's not. I'm glad I'm here too. Don't get me wrong, there are a lot of fun aspects to working in Hollywood, but the thing is, eventually everything feels superficial, plastic. I would have had to get away eventually. The only reason I moved there was because my mom's sixth husband got me a job right out of college. I figured my public relations résumé would look better if I had A-list cred. But the thing I learned was that I didn't even really like PR. I don't enjoy spin."

"You wouldn't. You are one of the least bullshit people I know."

"I'm working at A Novel Experience and trying to figure out what I want to do with my life. I'll know more in two weeks. After the test results come in."

"Will the results change your plans?"

"They must. I'm living with an axe over my head." She mimed a chopping action.

"What if . . . what if . . ." He sounded like he was choking on the words.

"The test is positive?" She let out a long, slow breath. "I still want to be there for Dad, but I'll need to make a bucket list. Except I guess it should be called the Loose Marbles List."

"Don't joke," he snapped. "Not about this."

"It's like whistling in the dark." Her smile held no humor. "If I can't laugh while facing terrible things then I don't have any weapons at all. If I can look at the worst and still find a way to smile, maybe I'm keeping some of the power for myself. Maybe the bad guys don't get a chance to win everything. Except the bad guy in this scenario is still me." She gave her forehead a rueful tap. "Or at least my asshole brain."

He balled his hand into a fist and knocked the side of his leg. "Don't talk like that."

"Fine, but it's still true."

He turned down Castle Lane and then, just before his driveway, made a quick right onto an unmarked road that Quinn hadn't noticed. "My mom used to take me here. I was the oldest so I used to get picked by her when she went collecting."

"Collecting?"

"She was into dried flowers as a hobby, would make botanical plates, or put them in homemade soap or do bookmarks for Christmas and birthdays. I was her assistant. Sawyer and Archer would stay home. Dad would take them on a horse or throw the ball around with them. She said she liked us having special time. It wasn't like I was her favorite or anything. She had a thing she liked to do with each of us."

"She sounds really wonderful."

"She was." He turned off the engine. "I've come back here since but never gone in. Never felt right, until now."

"Gone in?"

"You'll see." He got out, walked around, and opened her door, taking her hand. "The snow looks like it's a little deep in places but we should see fine with the moon this full."

"What about you and walking?"

He arched a thick brow. "I'll lean on you if I have to."

She smiled. "That's good, I'd like that."

Their boots crunched the snow. Up ahead a cluster of dark shapes appeared in a circle. Deer.

"What are they doing?" she asked, watching as they stood in a circle, heads down, pawing at the snow.

"I leave them cracked corn," Wilder said. "Helps them during the winter. I've never told anyone about this place. I guess people know, but I like to think it's mine." He helped her over a fallen log and the river became louder. "Here we are, Obsidian Hot Springs."

"Hot springs?" The clearing was small, canopied by wide branches, heavily laden with a thick dusting of snow. In the river's eddy was a small pool ringed by large stones stacked into a curving wall. By rights the water temperature should be freezing, but visible steam wafted up into the dark. "You want to skinny dip?" She glanced around nervously.

"No one else is going to come here tonight."

"I've never done this before."

"It's simple." He stepped forward, grinding down her jacket's zipper. "You. Me. Nothing else."

"I'm nervous."

"I've seen you naked before."

"I know it's stupid."

"No, I get it. It's different to get naked in front of someone not in the heat of the moment. I'm nervous too. Nervous you'll look at my body and laugh."

"Just as an FYI, laughing isn't the first thing that comes to my mind when I see you naked."

He kissed her then, soft, slow, nothing urgent. He kissed her like they had time, as if they were two lovers who had a future in front of them.

"This isn't just sex between us," she breathed into his mouth.

"Not on your life." He peeled back her jacket and hung it off a nearby branch. "I've done the no-strings sex thing. That's all I've ever done."

"You've never had a girlfriend?"

"I've hidden myself, my heart." He kept undressing her. "Hidden from anyone who might expose me for what I am. Not a badass but just another guy who doesn't have all the answers. It's easier to be feared."

She was in her bra and panties when he helped her to the edge, hooked his thumb in her silk and lace, and eased it down. "But that's all I feel like we do to each other, expose everything."

"Yeah. Crazy as it sounds there's something inside of me that didn't exist before I met you." He offered her a hand, eased her into the water until it pooled around her thighs in a sultry caress. "Or if it did, I ignored it."

"Which is?"

"Now is the time to do what we want. Now is the time to live. Now is our time."

His next kiss wasn't gentle. With every plunge and stroke of his hot tongue he showed her what he meant by being in the present.

"Come here," she said.

"Why do you want me?"

"Maybe because you're broken on the outside and it matches my insides? Or maybe because I've discovered that I like my men dark and broody with a little bit of scowl that hides how inside they are nothing but a marshmallow."

"Marshmallow? The hell you say."

She sank into the water, wanting to applaud when his shirt came off. She could stare at him all night. His beautiful build. That mouth, the full lower lip in particular. She wanted to bite it, suck it into her mouth while digging her fingers into his skin. Pull him close until he pushed his way in, greedy and relentless, taking from her but also taking her to a place where she didn't feel alone. That's what he did. Stomped in and all that niggling fear and uncertainty and regret flew away, burned off by his passion, his consuming self.

He bent to deal with his leg and the moon's glow shined over his strong shoulders, the narrow taper of his waist, the hard bulge of his biceps.

He squatted, balancing on his hands, easing himself into the water. "You were staring."

"Yes, sir, I certainly was."

"You say the leg doesn't bother you but . . ."

She slid toward him. "Because it's hard to notice when everything else about you is so overwhelming. The crazy part is that you aren't even my type."

"Really."

"Big, tough with a touch of mean. Yeah, no. I should stay away."

"But you keep coming closer." He made a deep, rumbling sound in the back of his throat when she took him in hand, tugged his length from root to tip, the mineral content of the water working to ease the friction.

"You're a mistake." Her other hand skimmed his thigh to cup his balls, thick and heavy in her hand. "The worst kind or the best, I can't make up my mind."

He lifted her up, set her on his right thigh, pushing her a little to indicate that she needed to start moving.

She ground against him, increasing her strokes, her clit rubbed in tight strokes, drawing back her hood, reaching the bud of hot nerves.

He settled his lips against her forehead. "You like it hard."

It wasn't a question.

"Yes. So much." Her body grew increasingly feral, as if outside here beneath the late-autumn moon she finally felt *in* her body. Not gangly. Not the girl next door. But someone who was going crazy, hot and stripped bare of everything but need.

"Can that sweet mouth play dirty?" He lightly bit her shoulder, his teeth softly scraping her sensitive skin, mouth hot in contrast to the cold night air. He braced himself, shifting her weight to get more comfortable. "Come on, Trouble, let's see what you've got."

"Okay. Okay. You asked for it." She braced his face between her hands, tangling her fingers in his hair, loving the rough graze of his stubble over her palms. "I want to suck you down to the back of my throat, until you're giving me everything and I take it. I take it all."

He moaned. "Jesus."

Her hair fell in her face and she realized dimly it was starting to snow. Little flakes were hitting the hot water and melting. She was the snow. He was the heat. She wanted to melt all over him. But she wouldn't take him in her mouth—not yet—she had other plans for him tonight. She shifted and he was there. Right there.

"What are you doing?"

"What I need. What you need."

"But we're in the water, we don't have . . ."

"Wilder." God, even saying his name did things to her. Some men had a name that was meant to be screamed. He wasn't a Philip. Or a Reggie. Or a Jimmy. No, you moan *Wilder*. You groan it with every last bit of sanity left to you.

"Wilder. I want to do this. I want you inside me. Do I have permission to come aboard, sir?"

"Aye, aye," he ground out, tugging her down. She slid until there was no more room. Until she was full and he was deep.

"You feel that?"

"So much that I almost can't stand it."

"Why is it so good, so hard to bear?"

"Don't know, Trouble." He stroked the side of her neck, tracing her clavicle, his voice gruffly tender. "But let's see how much we can take."

She braced her knees on either side of his hips, his ass firmly set against the hot spring's sand. Wind trembled the trees' overhanging branches while just beyond the pool, the water raced, not paying them any attention, and they stayed in their own little eddy, lost and churning against each other.

"You're so fucking sexy," he ground out.

She rode him harder, the water splashing against him. He stared and she was glad. Her heart seemed like it was expanding, filling her chest, rattling her rib cage. His gaze couldn't tear away from her, and she wasn't sure if he'd blinked. Good, let him see what he did. Let him never think he wasn't man enough.

Once she'd ridden on the swings at an amusement park and after the ride was over didn't want to get off. The ride operator was too busy texting to notice so she stayed on for another go and then another. Until the world got a little lopsided, surreal as if somehow everything kept spinning in a mad orbit and she stood apart from that, observed, watched.

That's how she was now, dizzy, seeing herself from a slight distance, watching her body filled with Wilder. Never had it been this way, these constant contractions.

"Be here." He slammed into her. "Be here now, with me." The ragged rhythm of his breath was punctuated by a rough huff. His hold on her tightened and he threw his back into it, pumping harder.

Every thrust broke against her barriers, the ones that said, "Don't let him in. Don't let him in." Too late. Maybe it was a mistake but he was here. A cry of pleasure burst from her throat as his hold increased. A hot jolt shot through her body. God, she was close, right there and yet as much as she loved the anticipation, she wanted more, longer.

"Don't let me come yet."

"Why not?"

"Don't want this to stop."

His teeth grazed her earlobe. "Doesn't have to."

"What do you—oh. Oh God."

He gripped her ass, keeping her grinding pressure right there, right at the edge.

"Trouble, you come for me now like a good girl and I'll let you come again."

"Again?"

"Fuck, honey. You know you can do this all night, right? You aren't a guy."

"I've heard that, but my body doesn't work that way."

"Wanna bet?" Two more thrusts and he had her right where he wanted, plunged into the fire, every nerve tingling. He fanned the flames of her desire, burning off her need to reveal the core, the looming power that rose up. Her thighs trembled as she clamped down, milking his shaft in powerful currents.

"That's it. That's it exactly."

She shut her eyes and fell forward, wanting to rub her cheeks on his pectorals' hard swell of muscle.

"Oh, we're just getting started." He shed all vestiges

of gentleness, set a rhythm that was fast, almost brutal, but exactly what she wanted. "You like that, don't you?" He smirked at her whimper because she did, she loved it.

"You don't come once with me," he said. "It's too good watching you lose that pretty head."

"I've never—"

"No past. No future, remember?" He pumped his hips harder. "Just you, feeling what I give you until I say you come again."

"So bossy." Her head lolled and it started to happen, impossibly, her body so spent with pleasure began to fill again, like a bucket in the well. The friction and his filthy words bringing her back as if she hadn't just come her brains out.

"But this—if I—it might kill me."

"Nah, I'm going to take you to heaven." He grabbed her ass, bracing her in place as he rolled against her.

She studied the place where they were joined, the slick glide of their flesh, then turned toward his face where he stared back with an elusive smile and a heavily lidded gaze. Amazed that this brutal man possessed her and yet she didn't feel threatened or frightened; if anything she was free.

He let out a grunt as she inwardly gasped. If she did this again, she might implode or explode, hard to know if coming with Wilder was a burst out, or an inward push.

"Quinn." He was strong, big, and suddenly vulnerable here at the end, ragged in his need. "Are you with me? Are you with me, Quinn?"

And she was. Her body was responding, except this

time, it was more—more intense, more powerful, more consuming, more everything.

"This still a mistake?" he gasped.

"The best."

"Am I the best you've ever had?"

Had there been others? Of course there had, but they seemed like nothing now, far away and out of focus, a memory that she never lived but was only told about.

"Best ever."

"Goddamn right." His mouth slanted over hers, sucking in her gasp. There was a last flurry of thrusts and the world shrank away until all that was left was her blood pulsing in her ears and his hard body.

"Now, now, baby, please."

It was the *please* that put her over, that pulled from her what she didn't know she could offer. If the last orgasm cracked her in two, this one shattered her into pieces that would never fit back together. Everything she had thought and planned for these last few months was gone and there was only Wilder, holding her close as he pulsed against her, teeth set as if he were in pain, contrasting with the fierce triumph in his gaze.

The world began to return but she was anchored here, to his shaft still half thick and buried within her.

He rested his cheek against hers with a heavy sigh. "So this is what it feels like." His tone was soft, reverent even.

"What it feels like?"

"Living."

And as their hearts pounded against each other she grinned. "Yeah. I think so."

"It's good."

"Perfect." She glanced up and there beside the moon was a small star. At least she thought it was. *Please don't be a satellite.* She wanted to make a wish. A simple wish really. All she wanted was for everything to work out. For her brain not to fall apart, for Dad not to run away again, and for Wilder to choose peace.

Let us have a shot, she wished. *Please give us the chance.*

Maybe it was a mistake to have hopes and dreams given everything she was up against, but this guy in her arms was worth the risk.

Chapter Fifteen

FOR THE NEXT week and a half, it seemed like Quinn had gotten her wish. Dad stayed calm and even smiled a few times while watching *Ghostbusters*. Wilder accompanied her on visits to Mountain View Village, sitting beside her in Dad's room, holding her hand, barely watching the movie because all he did was stare at her.

It was good. Perfect really.

And if sometimes she woke in the night, fear squeezing her heart and uncertainty sucking away the room's oxygen until she could barely breathe, with Wilder's arm heavy over her waist and the pesky old idea "this is a mistake" ringing through her skull, it was gone by morning light.

Mostly.

So far her phone didn't ring, at least not with a call from the doctor. Each day without news was another to kick the can of worms further down the road.

It turned out that Edie's bakery sustained minimal damage, to the relief of the townsfolk who had come to depend on her baked goods as a normal part of their daily routine. The shop had been closed for a few days while a thorough check was done to determine everything was safe.

As it was Wednesday again, the Chicklits were meeting at the big table in the back of A Novel Experience arguing over next month's selection. They'd decided it was time for a romance and there was a strenuous debate over whether a billionaire BDSM should trump a sweet friends-to-lovers contemporary romance. Quinn took a sip of water from her bottle and accidentally splashed some down her "Reading Is Sexy" t-shirt. Wiping at it, she called out, "Maybe you guys can just split the difference? The half of you rooting for whips and canes can choose that book and the other half that wants movie dates and walks in the rain can go that route."

"That's not how this works," a woman in a pair of faded overalls piped up. "This is about consensus."

"We're the thirteen musketeers," interjected another woman with painted eyebrows. "We're all in. One for all. However it goes."

"By all means, carry on—only making a suggestion," Quinn said in a fake hoity tone.

"Is that the pretty one who's dating your grandson?" Painted Eyebrows' stage whisper was impossible to ignore. "That still working out? If not, mind if I try to set her up with my Roger?"

Grandma Kane held court at the end of the table like

a dowager countess. Annie had dropped her off for book club before ducking in the *Brightwater Bugle* offices to finish an article.

"I don't pretend to know what, or whom, my grandson is doing." Grandma's frosty tone didn't inspire much in the way of confidence.

"I've heard his truck has been parked in front of her house most every night."

"I heard that they were spotted in the grocery store together buying hot fudge."

"I heard that they were seen kissing in the town square and that tongue was most definitely involved."

Quinn's cheeks flamed. She knew small towns had a reputation for busybody behavior, but had someone followed her around the last two weeks with a handheld camera?

Finally she glanced up from her stack of inventory. "Um, ladies. I can hear you."

They all burst out laughing.

"Course you can," Grandma Kane said. "They're trying to get a rise."

"Just trying to have some sorely needed fun, Dorothy. This weather has been giving me a bad case of the grumps," the woman in overalls said.

"Have your fun with someone else's family, Beryl. Not mine. Meeting is adjourned." Grandma rapped her knuckles on the table.

"But we haven't decided on a title," Painted Eyebrows protested.

Grandma furrowed her brow. "We're doing the contemporary. The hero on the cover reminds me of Chris Pratt."

"Chris Brat?" Another piped up. "Who's that?"

"Pratt," Grandma snapped. "P like *phenomenal*."

"But that sounds like an F."

"Sounds like but isn't."

"What's a Pratt?" another member asked, turning up her hearing aid, the high-pitched squeak making everyone jump.

"He's an actor. *Guardians of the Galaxy*?" Quinn interjected. "*Jurassic World*?"

Twenty-four eyes stared blankly at her.

"Good taste, Mrs. Kane." Quinn gave a thumbs-up.

Grandma ignored her.

P also stands for poleaxe. Grandma Kane had quite the hatchet face. Imagine having been raised by her—no wonder Wilder ran out of town. But then, Sawyer and Archer seemed to regard her with real affection, and she returned it.

What had happened between her and her oldest grandson?

The contemporary romance winners moved on from bickering over phonetic pronunciations and began high-fiving each other over their victory while the BDSM fans marched out grumbling under their breath. It looked like Grandma had the final say even outside of Hidden Rock Ranch.

And as the shop emptied, it also looked like the two of them were going to be alone for a bit. Quinn gave the wall clock a covert glance.

"Still fifteen minutes until Annie is due to fetch me."

"I wasn't—"

Grandma smiled tightly. "Don't feed me a line, dearie. I can smell your fear a mile away."

"Fear?" Quinn lifted her chin. "You think I'm scared of you?"

"Everyone is."

Quinn laughed despite herself. "Now I know where Wilder gets it from."

"Gets what?"

Quinn arched a brow. "That tough-as-nails routine."

"Hrumph." Grandma opened up her purse and made a careful study of its contents.

"Wilder wants to make you proud, you know."

"Know? Know?" Grandma's voice rose an octave. "What would I know about Wilder Kane? There's a boy that doesn't want to be known, pushes everyone away. Always has."

"He does." Quinn came out from around the counter. "He does that so much."

"You think you can roll around in the hay or whatever it is you do for a couple of weeks and presume to tell me how it is with a boy I've known since he was whizzing in diapers?"

Quinn paused, before nodding slowly. "Yeah, I think I can. Sometimes a situation can be better assessed with a fresh pair of eyes."

"Doesn't look like your eyes see all that great." Grandma sniffed, waving her hands in the direction of Quinn's glasses.

"Wow." Quinn took a seat. "You really bring out the heavy artillery to keep people at bay, don't you?"

"I don't know what you are yammering about." Grandma returned to her handbag rummage. "I'm just going to sit here and wait for my harebrained daughter-in-law to fetch me. No, wait, not daughter-in-law because right now she's living in sin with my Sawyer."

Quinn propped her hand on her chin. "They seem serious."

Grandma wrinkled her nose in response. "Serious is when he sticks a ring on her finger and gives me some legitimate grandbabies."

"Legitimate?" Quinn smothered a smile. "We aren't in the middle ages anymore."

"This is Brightwater, not Hollywood. Traditional family values still matter here. At least to the old-time families."

"Hey now, I'm a Higsby, remember?"

"To a degree." Grandma pulled out an *Us Weekly* from her purse. No wonder she was current on all the hot young actors.

"Hey!" An idea occurred to her. Good or bad was impossible to say, but worth a shot. She didn't need this woman to bless her relationship, but sensed it would mean the world to Wilder. "Would you be willing to come to my house?"

Grandma glanced over the top of the magazine with a startled expression. "Now why would I want to do that?"

"I'd like to make you and Wilder dinner. The three of

us. You and I can get acquainted and you and he . . . well, you can get reacquainted?"

"Does that boy know about your cockamamie idea?"

"Of course." It was a little startling how smoothly the lie rolled off her tongue. "In fact, it was his suggestion."

Grandma shook her head. "Now I know you're telling tales out of school."

"I'm serious. How does tomorrow night sound?"

The bells to the front door tinkled.

"Evening, ladies. Brrrrrrr, it's freezing outside." Annie came in pink cheeked and bright eyed, her small frame buried under a bright yellow jacket, red wool scarf, and ladybug winter boots. Somehow the whole eclectic combo looked perfect on her.

"I was just telling Grandma here how Wilder and I wanted to have her over to my place for dinner tomorrow night."

"Oh." Annie blinked as if to say "Are you sure about that?" Instead, she managed to say, "What a wonderful idea. She'd love that."

"My hip might be bum but I have a pair of perfectly functioning vocal cords," Grandma snapped. "And *wonderful* and *love* aren't the words I'm searching for."

"I know you aren't driving much these days on account of your fall last summer but how about Wilder comes and picks you up at six?" Quinn crossed her fingers under the table. *Please don't let him kill me.*

"Six? Won't work. I eat at five," Grandma said grimly.

Annie clucked her tongue. "Isn't it fun to try new things, step out of the ho-hum routine?"

Grandma slammed her hat on her head, a purple felt one with a plastic bird stapled to the side. "Change gives me indigestion."

"Five is perfect." Quinn smiled. "So Wilder will pick you up at four-thirty and we'll eat then. I don't work tomorrow. I'm going to spend the afternoon with Dad."

"Fine." Grandma heaved a hefty sigh. "As long as you don't serve none of that kombooty."

"Excuse me?"

She pointed an accusing finger at Annie. "Kombooty. This one tried to poison me with it last week."

"Kombucha," Annie replied patiently. "It's full of probiotics."

"Smelled like infected cat pee."

"No kombucha, promise. How about pan-fried pork chop and baked potatoes?" Quinn could manage that, just. "I'll pick up a yummy dessert from Edie's shop."

"She's another one." Grandma shook her head. "Can't that girl bake a chocolate cake, plain and sensible? No, she has to go adding a ganache. What is a ganache anyway?"

"It's a French glaze," Annie answered promptly.

"Foreign food." Grandma huffed. "Why not good old American buttercream?"

"Grandma, are you having a low-blood-sugar moment because I have some snacks in my car." Annie's tone seemed sweet but Quinn could tell she enjoyed baiting the older woman.

"You're trying to kill me off with those snacks. Dried coconut chips, blue corn chips, and homemade granola? No thank you." What's more, Grandma enjoyed being baited.

Annie grinned. "All the more kale for me then."

Grandma shook her head but couldn't restrain her own smile. Needling Annie seemed to be how she showed affection. Interesting.

"I look forward to seeing you tomorrow night," Quinn said in her most chipper tone.

"Just once, just once I'd like one of my grandsons to settle down with a sensible girl. Do you have sense, missy? And how is your father?" Grandma continued, not waiting for a reply to her first question. She shoved her magazine back in the bag and rose. "Damn shame what happened to him. He was a fine man, a good man. They don't make them like that in this day and age."

"Thank you," Quinn said. "I miss him, which is strange to say because he's right there in front of me."

Grandma reached across the table, grabbing her wrist with a surprisingly strong hand. "There's a part of him that knows. You have to trust that. He might not act like he gets that love, but somewhere deep inside he does."

Quinn glanced up and Grandma's eyes misted. Maybe it was a trick of the light because then she was standing up, thrusting her handbag at Annie, imperious as a queen.

"Tell that boy I'll see him at four-thirty sharp."

"Will do," Quinn said as Annie mouthed "good luck" behind Grandma's back.

After they left the shop, Quinn stayed seated at the table, staring thoughtfully at the wall. In theory, Grandma was talking to her, but she couldn't shake the feeling that the older woman was also talking to herself.

As she locked up, she glanced at the sky. The clouds were covering the moon and stars, but just in case anyone was listening, she offered up a small prayer. "Please."

That was all. Please let everything work out for the best. As she walked to her truck, a little warmth blazed in her chest and she hugged herself. Maybe everything would work out okay. Maybe Brightwater would end up being a surprise happy ending after all.

Just as she got her key in her car door, a feeling prickled over her, one she'd had the last few days in the store, as if someone watched her. Every time she scanned Main Street, no one was there. But this time, a flash of high beams swept over her. She shielded her eyes as a small nondescript car flew past her, missing her by less than five feet. The driver was hunched low, face obscured by the steering wheel.

"Hey," she yelled at the disappearing taillights, "watch where you are going."

She shivered, the warm feeling replaced by an ominous prickle. All of a sudden it felt like danger could exist around every corner, and you never knew when it would slam into you without warning.

Chapter Sixteen

WILDER SAT AT Quinn's little kitchen table, conscious of the scrape and clink of his silverware. Today her shirt said, "I Read the Book before It Was a Movie." Cute and funny, but falling flat with this crowd. The conversation was nonexistent despite Quinn's valiant attempts at small talk. When she told him what she was planning, a bonding dinner between him and Grandma, he almost said not to bother. But she looked so hopeful that the idea of disappointing her about killed him.

She wanted so much to believe that everything would work out, have a happy ending like one of those old books she favored. What could he do, tell her how the world really worked and rain on her parade? Not happening. She'd been kicked in the teeth enough, by her old job, by her dad being sick. He didn't want to show her what it was really like to be kicked in the ass, how those scars never heal. How eventually the wounds fill with poison until nothing looks good and you're angry every day, from the first breath when you wake up until you fall into another uneasy sleep.

Grandma, on the other hand, knew . . . all too well. From time to time during the dinner, she caught his gaze, her eyes still sharp behind those turquoise bifocals. She never missed a trick. That night of the house fire, after she got Sawyer and Archer tucked into beds at Hidden Ranch, she came to him, sat on the edge of his bed.

"You going to tell me what really happened?" she had asked.

She always knew the worst about him.

"So." Quinn wiped her mouth with her napkin and set it on the table. "Everyone's plates are empty so looks like my questionable cooking skills turned out okay this one time. Pork chops were my dad's favorite meal—he taught me how to make them when I was thirteen years old. It's either this, canned soup, or macaroni and cheese so don't expect any more from me in the way of culinary greatness."

"Meat was a little overcooked," Grandma muttered.

Wilder tossed his fork on his plate. "Jesus, Grandma."

"Hey, I don't mind," Quinn soothed. "Well, maybe a *leetle* more sugar-coating would be nice, but hey, at least we're all talking now, right? Better than just staring at our plates and listening to the light bulb hum." She glanced up. "Those fluorescent bulbs in there are noisy when there's no sound, huh? Anyway, I have an idea."

Wilder had to give her points for sheer tenacity. This dinner was a bust but she wouldn't admit defeat, was going down punching, and that deserved respect.

"What are you thinking, Trouble?" he asked, gentling his tone.

"A game."

"Do I look like a game player to you?" Grandma said skeptically.

Quinn looked between them. "Everyone likes board games."

"Looks like you found the two exceptions to the rule," Wilder muttered.

"Good lord, you really are both cut from the same cloth," Quinn said, standing to grab the plates and waving Wilder back into his seat. "No. Butt in chair, mister. There's a dishwasher in this kitchen and I intend to put it to good use. We are going to eat cake and play a game and there will be no ifs, ands, or buts about it. Understood?"

The two faces stared back at her with identical expressions of shock and awe. She felt like she was a lion tamer in the ring. Exhibit a trace of fear and they'll eat you alive. Better to show them who is boss.

She stalked to the kitchen, loaded the dishwasher, and cut heaping slices of the cake Edie insisted on giving her for free. "A donation of goodwill," she had said. "Listen, I've lived with the woman since summer time, and all I can say is don't be fooled into thinking she can be tamed. She's like a barn cat. If she likes you, she likes you, but her mood is unpredictable and you can't take it personally."

But of course this was personal. Grandma Kane didn't have to like her, but she had to respect her.

She set the cake slices before them and scanned the games on the bookshelf. *Risk? Too long. Scrabble? No, not quite right. Hungry Hippos? Ah, thumbs-up for child-hood nostalgia, but again, no. Monopoly? Maybe. Wait a second. What's this? Yes. Yes, perfect.*

"The Game of Life," she announced, grabbing the box off the bookshelf and walking back to the table.

Grandma glared at the brightly colored lid before forking the last bite of cake into her mouth. Ganache or not, she hoovered the slice like it was going to sprout legs and scurry away. "When you get to my age you learn life's not a game. It's a joke."

"Now, now." Quinn clucked. "Nothing ages a person faster than being set in their ways."

Grandma snorted. "You're saying that if I play this here board game, I'll push back my date with Saint Peter?"

"Who's to say?" Quinn spread out the board as Wilder picked up a tiny car, frowning.

"What's this thing do?"

"Jesus, take the wheel," Grandma muttered.

Quinn refused to lose her grin. These party poopers would have fun tonight or she'd die trying. "You mean to tell me that you've never played Life either?"

"I'm with Grandma on this one. Not big into games."

"That is all about to change." She gave Grandma a red car. "Now find a little plastic person, either blue or pink. Sorry, this game doesn't really take gender ambiguity into consideration."

They both stared as if her neck had sprouted a new head. These two might have different features, but something about the way they held their heads and set their mouths marked them unmistakably as kin.

Quinn pointed to the dial. "Then we spin the wheel and start."

"And what's the point?" Wilder asked, sticking a blue man into the driver's seat.

"To win at life." She left off the duh part of her statement but it managed to hang there regardless.

"Hah," Grandma muttered. "There is only one winner in life and that's the Grim Reaper."

"Enough." Quinn slammed her own car down so hard that her little pink stick figure flew across the table in a perfect arc, landing in Grandma's lap. "I'm adding extra rules. No cynical comments and that includes under-the-breath grumbles. No snorting. No checking your watch. We are going to have fun even if it hurts because today, right now, we are all alive, we are all more or less in good health, and we are all together, so we might as well make the best of it."

Grandma Kane stared at her with an unfathomable expression. Quinn restrained the urge to gulp and rubbed an invisible speck off the table. She'd gone and done it now, gone too far, the lion was opening its mouth, coming in for the bite . . .

"You have gumption." Grandma thought for another moment. "Yes, I'm giving you that, missy. More grit than any other Higsby I've ever met."

"Thank you." Quinn wiggled her feet in a secret under-the-table happy dance. She had conquered the lion. It was giving her a begrudging lick and purr. "Now spin the wheel and let's see who goes first."

Chapter Seventeen

IT WAS ALMOST midnight when Wilder drove Grandma back to Hidden Rock Ranch and for once they had actually spoken. Not about anything deep and meaningful—he asked about her hip rehab after it was broken in July and she checked in on the status of his leg.

But it was a start.

"We're a pair, aren't we, boy?" she'd said as he pulled up in front of the old homestead she now shared with Archer and Edie. The house she'd taken him and his brothers into after his parents died, the house that never quite felt like a home, at least for him. "Survivors."

Quinn had made rum-spice apple cider halfway through the board game. He'd declined because he was driving but Grandma had sipped a mug. Maybe she'd snuck another and the tipple was making her emotional?

"Let's get you inside before you catch a chill." He got out and limped to her side of the truck. He'd abandoned his stick for the last week and it felt damn good. His gait wasn't as surefooted as it used to be yet, but it was as if he'd turned a corner, and in the distance was a light, one Quinn had lit. It was like she was his own spitfire guardian angel. She wasn't the type to hold your hand and tell you everything would be okay. No, she'd kick your ass until sense was knocked into your skull.

He offered Grandma his arm and got her up the front steps, the same ones she had tumbled down. Archer stepped up after the accident, took on the running of the ranch, Grandma, and a serious relationship with his typical easy stride. It wasn't hard to see why people loved Archer. He knew how to make you feel good, just by being close to him.

Wilder had always been more of a porcupine.

He had the door half open when realization hit him with a jolt.

Quinn was right. He and Grandma were cut from the same cloth.

"Hey. Can I say something?" he said.

Grandma set down her handbag and sniffed. "You smell that?"

Wilder inhaled deeply, catching faint traces of cinnamon, brown sugar, and apples. "Yeah and it's making me hungry all over again."

Edie ducked out of the kitchen door, Archer hot on her heels. Her red hair was a mess and she looked suspiciously flushed while his little brother had a telltale smirk.

Jesus Christ.

Wilder didn't feel any jealousy, just a vague sense

of amusement. Plus, Edie's shirt was on backward and Grandma was going to notice in another few seconds.

"I'm gonna tell you two lovebirds the same thing I told Sawyer." Grandma shrugged off her coat and hung it on the brass peg. "At my age, my wants are straight-forward. Grandbabies, grandbabies, and more grand-babies. But I want it done proper. Children who carry the Kane name."

"Hold up now." Archer's cheeks were a near match to Edie's. "Grandma, I—"

"And please, for the love of all that's holy, tell me you didn't get up to anything on the kitchen table. That's where I eat my Cream of Wheat."

"Grandma," Edie yelped, clapping her hands to her chest. "It's not what you think."

Wilder tugged at his shirt, waggling his eyebrows and Edie glanced down, her silvery eyes bugging out of her head as she realized the seams were on the outside.

The front door burst open. "You're here. Thank God," Sawyer said, taking a deep gulping breath.

"Course I'm here. This is still my home," Grandma snapped.

"Not you, him." Sawyer thumbed at Wilder. "Saw your truck parked out front while I was driving by. You got to come with me, pronto."

Wilder frowned, the old adrenaline rush setting in, putting his senses on high alert. "Another fire?"

"Oh no," Edie gasped, grappling for Archer's arm. "Please not at the bakery again."

"No. You were right." Sawyer clenched his jaw. "The

fire was in an occupied home this time. Quinn's home. The call just came in."

Wilder took a step backward. The room disappeared. The roof caving in. The scream. The damn scream frozen in his head for twenty-five years filled his senses. Smoke choked his lungs. A chill shot down his spine.

"Is she . . . is she . . ."

"All I know is that she was taken to the hospital. One of the firefighters rescued her."

A hand brushed his arm. "I'm so sorry," Edie said.

"I'm coming with you." Grandma marched back to her jacket, slinging it on.

"Grandma, no." Sawyer held up a hand. "Stay here."

"Let her come," Wilder choked out. It had come at last. Payback. He'd taken so much from her.

But when she looked at him, there wasn't a glimmer of justice or malicious glee. Only concern. "Come," she said, holding out a hand. "You don't need to face this alone."

Archer stepped forward and clasped his shoulder. "We're coming too. Family sticks together." He turned to Sawyer. "Edie and I are following behind, man."

Wilder moved in a daze. His limbs propelled him out into the wintry night but he wasn't in control, autopilot had taken over. He paused on the front porch, turning to face his family. "The fire spared me this summer, but I'd rather burn a hundred times over than have a single hair on that woman's head be scorched."

"True words, brother," Archer said with a nod. "I feel the same way."

"Me too," Sawyer said.

"One question." Wilder gave voice to a niggling idea. "Any chance the fireman who pulled Quinn from the house was Garret King?"

Sawyer blinked. "Yeah. Why?"

Wilder ground his teeth. He'd been thinking about who the arsonist could be for weeks and only one name kept repeating itself. "Because I'm going to kill that son of a bitch."

"King? He's an asshole, but that hasn't changed since we were in elementary school, man. Remember when he ate the fish out of the fish tank in the school lobby?"

Wilder didn't crack a smile. "Has the ATF given you an arson profile yet?"

Sawyer knit his brows. "Report should be coming in any day."

"King's a volunteer firefighter," Grandma Kane butted in, joining the conversation.

"You think he is responsible?" Archer asked, puzzled. "But why?"

"Hero complex," Wilder said tightly. "He gets to be a big shot. People buy him drinks at The Dirty Shame. Slap his back when he walks down the street. He likes to impress, always has."

"There's a hell of a big difference between being a show-off and putting lives in danger." Sawyer crossed his arms, staring off in the distance, thinking. "I'm not saying you're wrong but why target Quinn?"

"He's pursued her, and he sniffed around her place not long ago, unable to get the memo that she wasn't into him."

Sawyer shook his head. "That means he's a fucking creep, not a potential murderer. Arson is a serious accusation, man."

"I've been at this a long time, brother." Wilder clenched his jaw. "Where there is smoke, there is always fire. Something with Garret is off. There's a connection."

He and Grandma got into Sawyer's truck while Archer and Edie followed behind. For once, Wilder was glad to have them close. The woman he cared about was in danger.

It didn't make sense that this would happen. Why would she be targeted? Sawyer was right—arson wasn't an allegation to be thrown around lightly. But he had a gut-deep certainty King was connected to these fires.

The drive was tense, quiet, and when they got to the Brightwater Hospital, Grandma's huffy breath puffed out in the cold air as she threw open the door. "Not looking forward to seeing the inside of this place again."

"That was a long two months," Edie said, nodding sympathetically. Grandma had been hospitalized from July to September with a broken hip and complications from pneumonia. Since then, she'd scaled back her duties on the ranch but didn't show any signs of slowing down in the busybody department.

They walked into the emergency room and Wilder pulled up short. There was Trixie Higsby, one of Quinn's cousins, sitting next to none other than Garret King.

The room vanished in a red haze. Wilder's hand flexed, clenching into a tight fist.

"Easy, brother," Sawyer said, resting a hand on Wilder's

elbow. "Even if what you say is true, and I'm not saying it's not, starting a fight here isn't going to help Quinn. It's only going to land your ass in hot water."

"I'll handle this," Grandma snapped, storming over.

"Shit," Sawyer said. The three brothers stood shoulder to shoulder, powerless in the wake of a crotchety old woman.

"Mrs. Kane," King said, looking solemn. "News travels fast."

"I want to see that girl."

"Family only." Trixie glanced at Garret under downcast lids, her lower lip giving an attractive tremble. "With her daddy in his bad way, Garret called our house as next-of-kin and I volunteered to come right down."

"How is she?" Wilder ground out.

"Oh, I haven't been able to bear going in yet." Trixie gripped Garret's bicep as if to absorb his strength. "I get white-coat anxiety. Hospitals make me all kinds of scared."

"You mean to tell us that you haven't been back to check on Quinn?" Wilder stormed forward. "Is she . . ." He couldn't bring himself to say the words flashing red in his brain. *Hurt. Scared. Or worse.*

She shot Wilder a suspicious look and scooted closer to Garret, practically crawling onto his lap. "The doctor came out about a half hour ago and said she'd be perfectly all right. They were just going to run a bunch of tests."

Grandma Kane lowered her chin and steam was almost visible from her flaring nostrils. "Trixie Higsby, you get your milksop, pansy butt back there and tell us how our girl is doing."

Trixie's mouth opened and closed as if she was in cha-
rades and had been assigned the role of "goldfish."

"I don't give a fig about your white-coat whatchama-
callit. There is a weakness in the Higsby line. Your people
might be long-lived, fertile, and loyal, but Quinn is the
first one of you that's shown any real spine or gumption."

"Now see here, Mrs. Kane." Trixie pulled a tissue from
her sleeve and dabbed her nose. "People who live in glass
houses shouldn't throw stones."

"Excuse me?"

"Oh? Oh!" The young woman looked triumphant.
"You don't know, do you?"

"Know what?"

"She doesn't know," she repeated to Garret. "It's hard
to see what's right in front of you sometimes, isn't it?"

"You fool of a Higsby, spit it out."

"*He's* got some nerve showing up here."

Wilder glanced around before realizing Trixie's finger
was pointed directly at him.

"Me?"

"Lucky the sheriff is here because this freak should be
arrested."

"On what charges?" Sawyer approached, a muscle
twitching in his temple.

"Arson." Garret stood up, his hands balled into two
big fists. "You almost killed an innocent woman tonight,
you fucking animal."

Chapter Eighteen

"CAN I PLEASE go home now? It's almost three a.m.," Quinn said to the nurse. "My biggest problem is that I'm exhausted and you've sucked me dry with all those needles."

"Do you have a place to go?"

"Yes. My friend's house. Boyfriend actually." When she got to the hospital, she asked Garret to notify Wilder of her whereabouts. He hadn't been back to see her yet but the nurse had said visitations were restricted to family only.

"Boyfriend?" The nurse looked troubled.

"Wilder Kane." Saying the words out loud felt a little strange, but it's what he was for better or worse. In fact, he was a whole heck of a lot more. She wasn't going steady. He wasn't a crush. In his grumpy, quiet way he'd stolen her heart and she didn't ever want it back.

The nurse's eyes widened. "So you don't know."

The warmth ebbed from her chest. "Know what?"

"He was taken to the sheriff's office. Didn't anyone call you?"

"My phone was burned in the fire, no one can call me. What happened?"

"Oh my, there was almost a big fight in the emergency waiting room. Sheriff Kane took two men into custody. One was his own brother and the other was the guy who saved you, Garret King." The nurse paused. "I thought he was your boyfriend, seeing as how you're so pretty and he's so handsome. The other one. He's, well, he's sort of scary with all those scars and that attitude. Wait, what are you doing? You can't leave—"

"Says who?" Quinn yanked out her IV and slid from the bed, beelining to her clothes folded on a plastic chair in the corner.

"The doctor hasn't discharged you."

"I didn't suffer a single burn. I might be deaf from the smoke alarm, but it saved my life. The house is the one in trouble." And all her belongings. She pushed the thought from her mind. Who cared about stuff? Comic book collections and board games meant nothing when Wilder was at the sheriff's office. What was Sawyer thinking? Obviously Wilder didn't set the fire. He'd left her house to take his Grandma home after helping her clean up the dinner dishes. She'd taken a mug of rum cider to bed and was playing around on her phone waiting for him to return. Instead, she dozed off and woke to the high-pitched whine of the smoke alarm. When she got to the bedroom door, the knob was hot to the touch.

Rather than opening it and risking flames, she'd climbed out the window. It was one-story so while the snow was cold underfoot it wasn't tricky. By the time she'd run to the front of the house, the first fire truck was pulling up. Garret King had leapt out, scooping her in his arms as if she were a ragdoll, ignoring her orders to be set down that instant.

While other volunteer firefighters fought the blaze he insisted on staying by her side, riding in the ambulance with her.

While she was grateful for the fire department's fast response and the fact they did their best to salvage the house, Garret had continued to be too overbearing. As she was taken in to the ER, she'd asked him to get in touch with Wilder as soon as possible, and if he didn't have his number to contact the sheriff.

She was whisked off before he could answer but she hadn't expected him to ignore her wishes entirely.

"Miss Quinn." The nurse sharpened her tone as Quinn yanked off her hospital gown. "I must insist you stay here."

"There's been a terrible mistake and I have to help put it right." Quinn changed into her clothes at the speed of light.

"This isn't how things are done," the nurse continued. "If you won't cooperate I'll have to fetch the doctor."

"Do whatever you need to do because I'll be doing the same." Quinn tore through the open door and jogged down the hall. What had Wilder and Garret done to get themselves in trouble? And how was she going to help?

The hospital was a mile out of town, a long lonely stretch of highway at this time of night. How would she get all the way back to Main Street?

She burst through the emergency room double doors as cries of "Wait! Come back!" rang out behind her.

Edie and Grandma glanced, startled, from two plastic chairs in the corner.

"Told you she'd come," Grandma said triumphantly, rising to her feet. "That girl has gumption."

"You can't leave," the nurse repeated, coming into the waiting room.

"Do you have keys?" Quinn asked Edie.

"Yes to Archer's truck. He left with the guys," Edie replied.

The nurse cleared her throat. "I said—"

"You said your piece and last time I checked it was a free country," Grandma snapped. "And I know you. You're Dinah Kane's little girl, aren't you?"

"Yes, Mrs. Kane." The women shrunk back. "Bonnie."

"Well, Bonnie, I suspect you know that Dinah is in the Chicklits and the Lady's Guild. It would be such a shame for her to be dishonorably discharged."

Bonnie gasped. "Are you blackmailing me with my mama?"

"Blackmail? Oh. No. That's got a harsh ring to it, don't you think?" Grandma affected a sugary sweet tone. "I prefer to call it negotiating. We go now without a fuss and you don't ruin your dear mama's fun. She's a nice lady, if a bit of an airhead."

Bonnie gasped. "You're straight from the mafia."

"There are two things I care about in life." Grandma held up her forefinger and middle finger. "My tomato patch and my grandsons."

Quinn gave Bonnie a tight smile. "I'll come back in tomorrow if I'm feeling out of sorts. Promise."

Bonnie's mouth gaped.

"Don't let the flies in, dearie," Grandma snapped, leading the charge to the front doors.

Edie grabbed Grandma's handbag and flashed Quinn a look of quiet concern. "Are you really okay?"

"Course she's not," Grandma called over her shoulder. "Her house burned down and Wilder is in the slammer."

"What happened?" Quinn trotted behind. For her bad hip, Grandma certainly moved fast tonight.

"What happened is that Trixie Higsby is a damn fool, and I'd like to put that Garret King over my knee and give him a proper hiding."

Edie unlocked the truck door, helping Grandma inside before turning. "In translation, your cousin was notified as next of kin after the fire. She and Garret King accused Wilder of arson, claimed he's been responsible for the other two house fires and what happened at Haute Coffee. Claimed he had a history of bad behavior and that none of the fires had started before he returned to Brightwater."

Quinn stiffened. "And do you believe them?"

"Of course not." Edie smiled gently. "But then Wilder blamed Garret in return and the two of them almost got into a fight. Sawyer and Archer grabbed both of them and left for the sheriff's office so they can cool down and get to the bottom of everything."

"That's exactly where we are going," Grandma said stiffly, pushing her glasses up her nose.

Quinn climbed into the truck and looked over at the older woman beside her on the bench. "Are you okay? You look like you've seen a ghost."

Grandma's smile was troubled. "Tonight is a night for ghosts, I'm afraid. Someone better call Annie and tell her to wake up and come down too."

"Annie?" Edie asked, starting the truck. "What's she got to do with anything?"

"Nothing," Grandma replied. "But Sawyer will need her. I hate to admit being wrong, but those boys all chose the right women. Tonight they are all going to need you like they've never needed you before."

SAWYER SET HIS elbows on his plain wood desk and leaned in. "I'll ask again and somebody better start talking. What the hell happened back at the hospital, fellows?"

The Brightwater sheriff's office wasn't big, a single room, but tonight if someone dropped a pin in one of the two empty holding cells in the back, the clatter would be deafening.

"I have alibis for tonight." Garret broke the silence at last, folding his arms and glaring at his boots.

Wilder shrugged, keeping his body tilted left, away from the asshole seated on his right like they were two bad kids in the principal's office. He didn't have much to contribute. Garret had always been a bully. A big kid

BEST WORST MISTAKE 217

who pushed others around. Wilder was a fighter too, but never had Garret's charm. Or talent for picking on defenseless people. Instead, Wilder would pick on Garret and his crowd, and that dynamic is what almost got him thrown out of high school half a dozen times, not to mention that it had caused the fight that first introduced him to Quinn all those years ago.

Quinn.

Wilder closed his eyes. They'd gotten enough out of Garret to understand that she hadn't suffered any great injury, but she'd come close, too close, to danger. And this asshole beside him was somehow involved.

A hand clasped his shoulder. "Easy, tiger," Archer said, pausing from his round-the-room pacing. "I see you tensing up. Sawyer's a patient man and he'll wait this out until someone starts talking."

"I got nothing to say," Wilder said.

"Maybe not but I do." Grandma Kane burst through the sheriff's office door. Wilder turned to see Edie and Quinn hurrying in her wake. His chest relaxed and he could finally take a full breath again. Quinn looked tired, out of sorts, her hair in a messy ponytail and glasses a little cockeyed, but there was no denying she was the most beautiful woman he'd ever seen.

Wilder started to stand when Sawyer shook his head. "Sit."

"Want to try and make me, little brother?" Wilder flew around, all his pent-up frustration directed at his brother who remained calm as usual. Always so goddamn collected and in control.

"Hey, calm down. No need to start anything," Archer said.

"He can't help it." Garret sneered, slamming his feet to the ground. "He's unhinged."

"That's it," Wilder ground out. Someone was going to feel some pain, and he didn't care who it was, even if that person was him. Better to bleed than suffer the numb hollow fear gnawing at his gut.

"Boy." Grandma stepped in, her hand raised in warning. "Don't let your fist write a check your butt can't cash."

Everyone fell silent.

"What does that even mean?" Garret grumbled.

"Means keep your trap shut unless you want me fixing you a knuckle sandwich," Grandma shot back. "Now I have a few things that need saying."

The door opened again. "This is a three-ring circus," Sawyer muttered, scrubbing his jaw.

"Circus?" Atticus stumbled in, his white-blond hair poking out in irregular tufts.

"What are you doing here?" Sawyer asked, straightening.

"Grandma Kane called." Annie covered her mouth with her hand to stifle a yawn. "She said there was a family emergency and you'd need me."

Grandma silenced Sawyer's protestation with a clap of her hands. "Everyone take a seat and shut your pie holes. I have the floor."

Wilder met her gaze and realized in an awful flash of certainty what she was about to do. "No, don't, please. You don't have to . . ."

"For twenty-five years I've kept silent," Grandma said, looking him in the eye, as if willing him to understand. "For a long time, so help me, I believed it was the right thing to do, that forgetting would heal us, but instead, forgive me, I caused hurt, bad hurt, the kind that I'm not sure can ever be undone."

Wilder didn't know what to say. Where to look. Her words pounded him, although they didn't pierce, like he was wearing a bulletproof vest. He was left breathless, aching as if he'd been punched.

"Forgive me." Grandma's voice quavered. "Please, forgive me, child."

Wilder's gaze blurred as he slammed back in his seat. Grandma was asking for *his* forgiveness? But that didn't make sense.

"Can someone please tell me what's going on here?" Sawyer said.

"It wasn't your fault," Grandma said. "You were nothing but a little boy acting like a little boy. Bridger should have known better than to drink too much, fall asleep like that."

Archer rubbed his temples. "It's been a hell of a long night. Is it just me or is anyone else confused?"

Annie and Edie both raised their hands. Atticus sat in the corner with his feet hitting the edge of his chair. Boom. Boom. Boom. Wilder focused on that noise, it anchored him, as did the warm brown glow in Quinn's gaze. She looked at him as if he was a good man. As if she believed in him.

He closed his eyes wanting to commit that expression

to memory. No matter how much it hurt in the empty years ahead, he wanted to keep it treasured.

Because he was going to lose her now. Lose her for good.

"It was me who started the fire," he mumbled.

"I knew it." Garret punched his fist into his opposite hand. "I told you all."

Quinn's mouth opened and shut. "I don't believe you. It's impossible."

"Not the fire tonight," Grandma snapped.

"The one at Edie's store?" Archer asked quietly, all trace of his characteristic good humor gone.

"No. None of those," Grandma continued.

"Then what?" Sawyer tilted back his chair, folding his arms behind his head.

Wilder cleared his throat. "The fire that killed our parents."

The room fell into utter silence. Atticus stopped tapping his feet.

"Dad had a poker game that night and it kept me awake. After his buddies left, I went downstairs to check on him. He'd drunk too much. He liked to have a good time, he was always the life of a party." Wilder couldn't look up. He couldn't face them while he did what he had to do, tell the story.

Instead, he fixated his gaze on a small hole in the plaster, just above the baseboards. Might be a mouse hole. Too bad he couldn't shrink down and run away. Instead, he was living out his worst nightmare, but somewhere deep down he understood that this would eventually

happen. Someday they'd all know and their fear of him
would turn to something far worse.

Hate.

"Dad was asleep in his chair, snoring a little. I thought
about waking him up, didn't want to leave him there because then he'd get in the doghouse with Mom. But the
table was covered with cards and beer bottles. I drank
out of one but didn't like the taste. Someone had left out
a pack of cigarettes.

"I opened up the pack and inside were two . . . and a
book of matches. I'd seen Dad strike a match before but
never tried for myself. The first one didn't light, but the
second did. I watched the flame until it burned my fingers and then shook it out. The next one I dropped and
it sparked a fire. They'd been keeping score on the table
and there were crumpled sheets of paper everywhere. I
tried to wake up Dad but he didn't budge. The flames
covered the table, bigger and bigger, and I didn't know
what to do. I ran to the kitchen and got a cup of water,
but the splash didn't do a thing.

"That's when I went upstairs and got Mom. She was
fast asleep and didn't wake easily. Said I was having
a nightmare and to go back to bed. I kept shaking her
and finally she got angry and yelled at me. But by then
the smoke was already coming up the stairs. She got to
your room," he told his brothers. "Pulled Archer out of
bed and told Sawyer he'd have to walk. Both of you were
sleepwalking and started throwing temper tantrums.
When we got to the stairs, there were flames closing in
but still room to get out the front door. Mom shepherded

us outside a safe distance from the house. Asked me to hold both your hands, then she went back for Dad.

"I begged her not to go. Not to leave us. But she said Dad was in there. She said everything would be okay. She promised. And I believed her. She always kept her word.

"It was an old house. The fire must have gotten inside the walls. Everything destabilized fast. I didn't know it then. I was just a kid. You two were crying and I was just staring at that door, willing them to come back. To be safe.

"Finally the door swung open and I knew everything would be okay. I might be in trouble forever but everything would be fine.

"That's when the roof collapsed. Through the open door came Mom's scream. It . . . it didn't last long, only a few seconds, but I've never been able to get the sound out of my head."

And then he could say no more. Only bury his head in his hands.

"Oh, Wilder," Quinn said.

"Why didn't you ever say anything?" Sawyer asked after a moment.

"No one knew the cause of the blaze," Grandma said. "The official ruling was that my son must have fallen asleep smoking. Wilder confessed everything to me that night but I told him never to speak of it. I hoped he'd forget in time."

"I never could." Wilder choked. "I can still see it like I was there."

"It was wrong of me not to let you talk it out," Grandma said. "But that's not the way I was raised. It's not what I know. Feelings weren't things you shared; they are things you keep out of sight. A private matter."

"I killed our parents," Wilder said. "I killed our parents and hated myself. Eventually I had to leave Brightwater. The guilt got too much to bear. I figured, out of sight, out of mind. You'd all forget about me in time. What good could I bring you? I'd torn from your life the two people you loved the best in the world."

"Stop talking like that. Stop it right now." Grandma crossed the room and grabbed his chin, forcing him to look at her. "You were six years old and had an accident. I didn't know what to do and made the wrong choice. Once you got bigger, I realized that you wanted to fight the world to get people to react and punish you. And what did I do? I came down harder. Threatened you. Told you I'd ship you off to military school. And then you did leave and I realized what a damn fool I'd been. I've lived with that regret for a long time, Wilder, and I will live with it for as many years are left to me.

"What your father did was stupid, leaving cigarettes and matches out. Drinking too much when he had three little boys. He loved you all but he had a reckless streak a mile wide."

"I'm sorry." Wilder looked around the room. "I'm sorry I never manned up and told you. I could barely speak the words to myself."

There was the sound of a chair sliding back. Sawyer walked toward him, his boots loud against the floor. His brother pulled off his hat and threw it down on his desk.

"I don't know what to do," he said.

"Throw a punch, I can take it," Wilder said. "Do what you need to do. I owe you a lot more than that."

Annie rushed forward and Sawyer held up a hand. "I don't want to hit you." He rubbed his stomach for a moment. "Shit. I feel like I'm going to be sick."

"There's nothing I can do to make it up to you."

"No. That's not it. Wilder, I don't blame you. You were just a kid, the same age as Atticus."

All eyes turned to the little boy who had taken out a Matchbox car and was pushing it along the bench lost in his imaginary Formula 1 race.

"It hurts to know that's what's been eating at your insides for so long."

"You don't . . . hate me?" Wilder couldn't believe that he didn't see anger in Sawyer's face, only sadness.

"Hell no," Archer said. "And you either, Grandma. What happened to our family was a tragedy, but Wilder was too young to understand what he was doing and, Grandma, you handled the situation how you thought best. In hindsight it was a mistake, but you acted out of love for Wilder. You hoped he'd forget and move on."

Grandma nodded, stiffly. "My heart wasn't as tender as it should have been. But know this, I loved you boys with every ounce of strength in this skinny body."

"And we love you, Grandma." Archer slung his arm around her narrow shoulders and pecked her cheek. Sawyer did the same. Then they both looked at Wilder.

"I heard you and your grandma fighting," Garret said. All heads swiveled to him; Wilder had forgotten he was even there.

"After our fight at the fair, my mom sent me to apologize to you. I heard you and your grandma arguing in the barn. You said, 'You know I burned the house down and killed my parents. I did that. Me.' "

Grandma shook her head. "It was the only time we ever spoke of it."

"I thought you were a killer, man," Garret said. "When you came back into town covered in burns, I was suspicious. Then the fires started."

"Sawyer said you were almost always first on the scene," Wilder said.

"That's true, but there aren't many of us on the Brightwater force. It's not hard to be the first responder."

Wilder raked a hand through his hair. "If it wasn't you setting the fires, and it wasn't me, then who the fuck was it?"

Sawyer shook his head. "I'll call ATF tomorrow morning and light one hell of a fire under their ass, pardon the pun. We can't have some sort of nut job running around town setting fires."

"Guys, PG language, please," Annie said, reaching out to take Sawyer's hand and nodding at Atticus.

Wilder rubbed his chin. "I still think it's someone associated with the fire department."

Garret shook his head. "Besides me, every other guy is a family man. What would be the motive?"

"To be a hero." Wilder leaned back with a frown. "Or make one of you the hero."

Quinn stepped forward. "What about Lenny?"

"What about Lenny?" Garret scoffed, wrinkling his

brow. "He might be a joker, but he's also a friend. Plus no way does he have it in him."

"I'm not so sure about that." Wilder glanced over at Quinn with dawning awareness. "You're a genius."

She winked. "Tell me something I don't already know."

"You're modest."

"Are you serious? Lenny?" Garret glanced between them as if they'd each sprouted an extra head and announced an intention to take up tap-dancing. "That doesn't make sense."

"Think about it. He was your lap dog all through high school," Wilder said. "Always idolized you. What better way to set up a hero than to make him someone the whole town can get behind?"

"You might be on to something," Annie replied slowly, turning to Sawyer. "He was the one who contacted the paper and suggested that I do that story on Garret."

"Does he happen to drive a Honda Civic by any chance?" Quinn asked, remembering the car that scared her recently in the A Novel Experience parking lot.

"That's his mom's car," Garret replied. "He still lives at home. But I'm telling you, he's harmless, not our guy."

Wilder folded his arms. "Go to his house and I'll bet you'll find everything you need. I might have been wrong thinking Garret was the culprit, but Lenny fits the bill. He wanted to make his buddy a hero so he could bask in the limelight."

"A hypothesis does not a search warrant make," Sawyer said. "I say we all get on home and in the morning I'll look into everything."

"Remember the milk jugs?" Wilder pushed.

Garret jerked. "What about milk jugs?"

Wilder studied him. "That's what started the fires. Gasoline was poured into milk jugs as an accelerant and a cotton sock was used as a wick each time to light it."

"We never found a milk jug," Garret said.

"You didn't look, or rather, didn't know what to look out for. We had a few arsonist situations on and off in Montana over the years and one's method of choice was the milk jug."

"Lenny is allergic to dairy," Garret muttered, "but I saw him buying two gallons last week. Didn't think much of it at the time."

"Think you can keep your trap shut, not alert him that he's a suspect?" Sawyer said with a layer of menace.

"Sure thing, Sheriff. But are you sure about Lenny?" Garret shook his head. "This guy makes more sense." He jutted a thumb at Wilder.

"*This guy* isn't sitting in the hot seat for one second longer," Quinn said, reaching out a hand. "He's coming home with me."

Wilder blinked at her hand. She still wanted him? "Home?"

Shit. That was a hell of a thing to say.

"Your home," she clarified.

Grandma nodded. "I knew I liked this one."

Wilder glanced down at Quinn's beautiful, trusting gaze and knew what he felt was a good deal more than like.

Chapter Nineteen

QUINN STARED AT Wilder's back as he bent, big hands braced on his kitchen counter. He was a powerfully built man, no doubt about it, with shoulders that could carry more than his fair share of the load. Morning was still a ways off. "The darkest hour is just before dawn," she whispered.

"What's that?" he asked, his voice distant.

"Sharing your story with your brothers tonight was brave. I am proud of you."

"Feels like a dream." He shook his head. "I always thought that if they knew, they'd hate me as much as I hated myself."

Quinn walked to him, rested her hand on the small of his back, and felt the big muscles tense and bunch at her touch.

"Your mother sounded like she loved you very much. She was a brave woman."

"I wonder if she can see me ever." Wilder shook his head. "If she looks down and sees the man I've become. Whether I've disappointed her."

"I don't know where she is, or what she sees, but I do know one thing. You are the kind of man any mother would be proud to claim. You're a hero—"

"No."

"Yes," Quinn retorted firmly. "You protected vulnerable people when you were younger, even if the fight wasn't your own. You had a job where you jumped out of freaking airplanes to battle wildfires. You leave out cracked corn for deer in winter and worry if they are getting enough to eat. You were kind to a strange man who needed a helping hand, and as much as you might say you're a fighter, you're also a lover." She gave a naughty smile. "And a darn good one at that."

He turned around and faced her full-on. "Can I ask you for one thing, Quinn?"

"Of course." Her stomach rolled at his use of her name. This sounded serious.

"Hold me?" he asked gruffly.

God, this man knew how to melt her. "Come." She took him by the hand, led him into his room. There in the quiet dark, they removed their clothes. Not fast or urgent, but as if they'd done this a hundred times before. Wilder set his leg against the dresser. "Same as leaving out a glass of water," he said ruefully.

She leaned out and stroked his injured leg as he sat, his thigh muscle still rock hard and solid. "When I look at this injury, I do feel sadness. Sadness that you suffered and even illogical fear because while you are safe beside me, warm and alive, I can't believe you lived after a freaking parachute malfunction dropped you into a fire. The idea has given me a couple of nightmares."

"Me too." He buried his face in her hair and inhaled deeply. "But when I sleep beside you, hold you close, and smell the wildflower scent in your hair, I'm taken to a world where there is no smoke, no fire. I'm safe."

"You'll always be safe here, in my arms, next to me." She tried to ignore the shiver shooting down her spine. The one that worried he was attached. That she was too attached. Wilder was beginning to dismantle his walls, open up, and believe the world might hold something good for him after all. What if she was the one to snatch that newfound hope away?

Her test results still hadn't come in.

She wanted him to keep walking toward the light, not be pulled back into the darkness of a bad diagnosis. He was a good man. If the worst was true, he'd want to stick by her, he'd try and do the right thing even if it came at the cost of his own future.

She couldn't ask him to give up his life for sacrifice or suffering. Determination bloomed through her. No, she would never ask for that, but she could hold him until the sun rose and the earth spun to a new day.

He pressed his length against her and they adjusted their bodies until they found the perfect fit, their ribs rising and falling in synchronicity, fingers laced, foreheads touching. He wasn't physically inside her and yet he was still imbedded deeply.

She knew that the fact she was willing to let him go was proof that this feeling filling up her insides, however illogical, was real.

"I'm falling in love with you," she murmured.

He squeezed her hand. "Good, because I've been on my ass about you since the night you walked into my house during the worst storm in half a decade and started arguing."

"That's all it took?"

"That and this pretty backside." He slid one of his hands down to squeeze the top of her rump.

"Stop, I'm serious," she said with a giggle.

"I can't say it was love at first sight, Trouble. More like love at first challenge."

She leaned down, pressed her lips to his neck, sucked softly as he let out a soundless moan—his ribs swelled, but no sound escaped.

I love you. I love you. I love you. She branded the words into every nip and suck of his skin. This wasn't a love that had been battle tested, polished by years and shared experience. It was new, jagged on the edges, and had the potential to slice through her like a ninja throwing star.

But this wasn't affection or mere attraction. It was a recognition of his intense fragility beneath the intimidating attitude. It was the fact that his innate cockiness also carried a recognition of his own fallibility. He was a mess of contradictions, but stripped to his core, he was the kind of guy who could have gone bad, made rotten choices, and in some ways she wouldn't have blamed him. No kid should be expected to suffer what he did.

Instead, he dug in, through sheer stubbornness, and if all of his choices weren't perfect, that only rendered him more human.

He pulled her head back, bracing her face between his hands.

"What is it?" she asked. "What's wrong?"

"Nothin'. Need to taste you." He tugged her close, his lips parting hers, his tongue pressing inside with hard, thick thrusts, rough and needy, holding just enough recklessness to make her respond to the challenge.

The moment she whispered her assent, he released a soft grunt as if in relief, as if she really meant it, as if he was finally home and that's what she wanted to be for him. But not yet.

God.

Why couldn't anything be simple for five seconds?

"Quinn?" He said her name as a question, sensing the change in her.

She ignored him and went in for another kiss. Soon it would be day. Who knew what news the sun might bring? Best savor the connection here in the darkness.

"No." He held her back even as his cock pressed into her thigh, long, hard, and insistent.

"It's nothing. I'm being stupid."

"You're a lot of things, Trouble, but stupid isn't one. What's going on?"

She took a deep breath. "I'm scared."

"Of me?" He pulled back an inch. "Because I'd never hurt you—"

"Not you." She wiggled closer, closing the gap. "Never you. I'm scared of being the one to hurt you."

"How?"

"I am going to find out my test results soon," she said softly. "Maybe even today. And what if it turns out I carry the gene and that sometime in the distant, but not-too-far-off future, I'm going to get sick? I can't ask you to sign on for that. We only just met and as much as this here—me and you—is amazing, important, life changing even, I want you to start living. Have the best chance at happiness, every good thing."

He passed his fingers over her lips, in a smooth, strong, and unmistakably stop-talking gesture. "You're tired so I'm going to chalk it up to that."

"Chalk what up?"

"Acting crazy."

She yanked away his hand. "Crazy? I'm being practical. I'm trying to help you—"

"Do you trust me?" he asked evenly.

"What?"

"Do. You. Trust. Me?"

"Of course."

"Then trust me to decide what I can handle." He stroked her hair back from her forehead. "Trust me to know what I can or can't bear." He shoved his arms under her arms, grabbing her back and rolling her on top of him, grazing his fingers across the dimples bracketing the base of her spine. This time his kiss held a savoring quality, breathing her in. His scruff rasped her cheek as he slid inside her, gently, carefully, inch by inch.

"You like me here?"

"Yes," she whimpered helplessly. "Yes, so much. But—"

"Anything could happen, Trouble. Any second of any day. You could get that test result tomorrow and find out everything is fine, then be struck by a bolt of lightning or trampled by a moose in Montana."

She took him deeper, faster. "A moose in Montana?"

"I'm taking you to Montana someday, Trouble. Need you naked, wet, and wanting under all the Big Sky."

Her hips rose and rolled. "God, this feels good."

"And it feels good to feel good, doesn't it? All I care about right now is me and you. How you're moving on me, how I'm moving in you. The rest is details."

"Details?"

He reached back, grabbing the headboard, driving his hips up. "Look what we do together." A pale light began to seep in. The first hint of morning after a long sleepless night. "Eyes down. I want you watching me, seeing what we're doing to each other."

She looked, and couldn't stop staring. She'd never watched anything more fascinating than their bodies joining. She wanted to laugh and cry and didn't know why.

"I don't know what's going to happen to us. I don't know what waits ahead. But I want to find out the next chapter while standing beside you."

Everything dissolved into slow, drawn-out friction. They took their time as if the day couldn't scare them, as if the past and future didn't matter, drawing out their pleasure until they trembled, quaking as if they were joining on a fault line. Pressure rose within her and she knew that once it gave way, she would never be who she'd been. Nothing made sense and why did it have to?

What if there were no mistakes, only events that serve as stepping-stones to a never-imagined place?

What if there were no mistakes and her entire life had been leading to this moment?

Every mistake had brought her here, to Wilder, to this dawn in his bed, two hearts beating to the same strong rhythm.

THEY WERE HAVING breakfast, looking over the "1001 Books to Read before You Die" list. "You're going to have to let me make some additions to this," Quinn said, sighing as Wilder worked his hand over her sole. He insisted on giving her a foot rub while she drank her coffee and far be it from her to tell him no. It was eleven and she wasn't sure when she'd ever slept in so late. Soon there would be calls to insurance companies, her property management company, and her mother. A visit to Dad. A call from the hospital. But not now. Not yet.

Soon she'd need to handle so much that in this quiet late-morning moment, when Wilder asked to handle her, it was enough. It was as close to perfect as life could get.

Outside the world was white, pure, like the most perfect Christmas card with snowcapped peaks, and pines heavily laden.

"Look, there." She pointed. Three deer moved noiselessly past the window.

"Move in with me," he said, watching her instead.

"What?" she squeaked, and the deer jumped, reacting to her yelp, even from within the cottage.

"You don't have a place to live and I like you in my bed."

"Um, that's great and all, but what about me burning dinner? I'm serious; my failed superhero alter ego is Kitchen Disaster Girl. You will lose weight and I'll miss all those big strong muscles."

"I'll still want to kiss the cook and sneak a dirty peek under her cape."

"Or what about the fact that I leave wet towels on the bathroom floor? Or the fact I'll totally nag when you leave the toilet seat up?"

"Towels can be picked up and I never leave the toilet seat up."

"Even as a bachelor?"

"Grandma Kane drilled that rule into us boys from the get-go. I couldn't leave a seat up if I tried."

"You're serious?"

"There's nothing to joke about here. I want you, want this." He tickled her foot. "My alter ego is Ornery Bastard, but he's met his match."

"So no more hermit?"

"When I turned my back on the world, I missed some pretty damn fine sights."

"Okay, Wilder Kane, then I need to ask you a question and I want the answer to be yes."

He pulled her little toe. "Sure, as long as it's not a proposal."

She jerked. "That's not what I was going to ask, but hang on. Are you saying you don't want to make an honest woman out of me? Grandma Kane might have words to say on that subject."

"It means that I'm going to be asking you, but I want to do the asking. I'm old-fashioned like that."

Uncontrollable heat coursed through her abdomen. He was seriously considering spending his life with her? "Are you going to expect me barefoot in the kitchen?"

"No, unless you're frying us up some pork chops and the rest of you is bare too."

She giggled. "We'll see if that can be arranged."

"Because I'd have to hit it before we got to the meal."

She pointed at her frames. "Can't hit a girl with glasses."

"Really? What if she looks really fucking sexy in glasses?"

"I guess there's an exception to every rule." She cleared her throat. "Now let's be serious."

"Okay." His face lost its teasing humor.

She nibbled the corner of her lower lip.

"You look serious."

"I am. Wilder Kane, do you solemnly swear that you'll read with me in bed, every night, through sickness and in health?"

He gave a solemn nod. "I do."

They grinned at each other as her phone rang. She glanced down and the screen read, "Brightwater Hospital."

Chapter Twenty

WILDER KEPT HIS hands shoved in his pockets in the recreation room in the Mountain View Village's Alzheimer's Unit. This wing could only be entered with a code. Quinn was informed that her test results were in and she was set to meet with a doctor in an hour. She'd asked to come here first to see her dad.

Quinn hadn't said much after the call, tried to put on a happy brave face, asking what he'd like for Christmas as they drove through the downtown. Every streetlight was adorned with a wreath, and in the square was a giant Christmas tree. The official lighting was set for tonight with the mayor doing the honors of hanging the traditional mistletoe. For the next few weeks, Brightwater couples would sneak under the bough and make out through the New Year.

Tonight he could be there kissing her, or they might be back huddled in his cabin, facing an uncertain future.

Quinn gripped her dad's hand, staring blankly while he watched the DVD she'd brought over, Bill Murray's *Scrooged*.

"I'm going to grab you a cup of tea," Wilder said. Each second on the clock was torture for her.

Why hadn't they just given her the results over the phone?

Better to deliver bad news in person?

He shook the fear away.

"That would be great, thanks." She gave him a quick glance that twisted his gut. He hated that she looked worried for him, as if measuring how much he could withstand.

He limped down the hall, wishing for once he had his stick back. He could bear anything happening to himself, but for someone he loved to suffer? Who had that kind of strength?

"Dig deep, man," he answered, bracing a hand on the wall, wiping his brow.

All the resident rooms had framed glass cases next to their doors. Inside were black and white photographs, war medals, figurines, and other family knickknacks. He paused and stared into one. The sepia-toned picture was of an attractive blonde and a smiling man cutting a cake. They stared at the camera with beaming faces, as if their future had nothing but happiness waiting for them. The next photo was a posed family photograph in front of the Hoover Dam; three little girls in smock dresses who all looked exactly like the woman. The next picture was more recent, at the Brightwater football field, a young blonde woman standing between her mother and grand-mother, clearly the woman from the other two images, Mount Oh-Be-Joyful rising behind them.

A card said "Happy Birthday, #1 Grandma."

Whoever this woman was, she'd had a good life, family who loved her. As he stepped forward to keep walking, he glanced into the room. An older woman, clearly the woman from the pictures, sat in a recliner, staring out the window.

He didn't know why he did it, but his hand found its way to the door frame and he knocked.

She glanced over. "Hello," she said with a gentle smile. "I'd wondered if you'd come in."

Shit, she must have seen him lurking outside her room. He hoped he hadn't scared her.

"Sorry to intrude, ma'am, I just wanted to say . . ." What? He was sorry? He hoped she knew how much she was loved. That who she used to be must live on in many people's memories. "I wanted to say you have a fine-looking family."

She laughed then, an infectious sound that made her sound like a mischievous young girl. "Of course we do, silly. But that's because their daddy is a looker." She winked before tipping back in her chair, rocking in a slow rhyth-mic pace. "Oh, Bill, we did have a good time, didn't we?"

His throat grew tight. She thought he was someone else. Bill. Her husband probably. Damn it, coming in here was a mistake. He didn't know if this Bill was even still alive. Probably not.

He glanced to the hallway. He could leave now and

she wouldn't know, would forget they ever spoke. Instead, he stepped closer and settled a hand on her thin, fragile shoulder. "We did indeed."

She nodded with satisfaction, gazing up at him, her eyes a mist of tears. "Life's a beautiful thing." She gave a little yawn before turning to look out the window again. "You always loved the snow, dear."

He stood silently as her rocking grew slower and her eyes fluttered closed, her chest rising and falling in the natural rhythm of sleep.

For the next few minutes, even when it was clear she had dozed off, Wilder didn't move, only continued to watch the snow falling outside, dusting the parking lot. He wasn't able to form anything close to an articulate thought, only that if Quinn was to get the news she dreaded, he would do everything in his power to make sure that she always felt safe, cherished, and protected. The heat between them burned but he'd never let it go out. He didn't care about anything else—having kids, protecting his heart—if it meant he couldn't be with her.

For once, he was proud of the man he was. "I mean to love her no matter what," he murmured to himself, to his mother and father if they were listening. "In good times and bad." Then he went to get the tea with the decision sinking into his heart.

He knew what he had to do.

WHAT WAS TAKING Wilder so long? He'd left to get tea fifteen minutes ago and hadn't come back. They'd need to leave soon. She glanced over at Dad and he was staring at the screen. Was there a part of him, however locked away, that remembered watching this movie with her every year? This was Christmas to her. The smell of Dad's bay rum soap, watching old movies. What she really loved best was hearing him laugh. He was normally reserved, but had the sort of laugh that vibrated through you until everything felt good, safe, protected.

She hadn't heard that laugh in a long time. She'd never hear that laugh again except in her memories. Reaching out, she took his hand and held it. "I miss you," she whispered. "I miss you so much."

He glanced over and stared. Nothing registered on his features but his fingers gave a small reassuring squeeze.

Take it as a good sign.

Wilder came into the rec room and Quinn turned, the only person in the room who seemed to register that a new person was here.

"Your tea," he said, handing her a paper cup with the lid on.

She took it between her hands, holding it up to take a sip. "Peppermint? Yum. Thank you. I'd wondered what happened to you."

He gave her a strange look. "I had to hunt down someone in the kitchen."

"To make the tea?" She frowned. "But didn't you remember that there is a coffee and hot water station near the nurse's desk?"

"I know," he said simply. "But that's not what I needed to see the dietary department for."

"So what's up?" she pushed. "You got hungry for a snack?" How could he think of eating? The very idea of putting food in a ten-foot radius of her mouth right now made her insides churn.

"I needed aluminum foil," he answered.

"I'm so lost right now—Oh. My. God." She covered her mouth as he dropped to the couch beside her and held up an aluminum ring, twisted to make a circle.

"Quinn Alexis Higsby, I want you to know that, though I might not be able to go down on one knee just yet, I do know this. People use the phrase 'other half' and I've never known what that means, never understood it until you came into my life. When you are around, you complete me. You make me want to be my best self, the man I never thought I could be. Even as you cause a fire in me, you cool me down. No matter what happens today, I want you to know that you can count on me, all the way, to support you and walk alongside you no matter how hard the path or how uncertain the destination. Mr. Higsby, sir, you raised a heck of a woman, and I promise you here and now that I will treat your princess like a queen."

"Wilder." Her throat swelled. "I don't know what to say. This is all happening so fast. We talked about the future a little but in such abstract terms."

"For so long I've been putting what I want out of the equation. I want you for as long as our forever will be. One day. One year. One long and healthy lifetime. Whatever news you are about to get won't change that. Surely there could be complications, but me loving you feels like the simplest answer of all."

"Yes," she said. "Yes a million times over."

The words came out before she could overthink or analyze. It felt perfect and even though the little aluminum ring wasn't what she had imagined during the occasional daydream when she'd pictured a handsome suitor sweeping her off her feet, the reality was that while Wilder was no Prince Charming, he was the prince of her heart and if she wanted a happy ever after, it would be with him.

He slipped the foil ring on, pressing it against her skin. "I'll buy you a ring soon," he said. "I promise to do this right."

"You already have," she murmured, leaning in to brush her lips against his. "You've done better than right. You've done amazing."

"I needed you to know that I'm in this no matter what, because I want to be," he said before she could say another word. "Because I don't want to be a hermit anymore."

Quinn turned to her dad and touched his arm. "Thank you for being such a good man, for teaching me to believe more good men were out there. I doubted I'd ever find a real-life hero, but because of you, I never settled. I love you."

Wilder glanced to the wall clock. "It's time."

The hospital was close. Her heart sped up but when Wilder slid his hand into hers, the strength of his grasp pressed that thin sliver of aluminum foil against her skin and it made her feel less alone.

"I'll see you soon, Daddy." She leaned forward and kissed his forehead. She hadn't called him Daddy in years but right now she felt reduced to a scared little kid, the one who used to cower when thunderstorms roared over the mountains. He'd always tell her the angels were bowling and even though she knew it was silly, the image made her giggle and pushed the scary feelings away.

After they got to the hospital, she took a seat in the waiting room, and passed Wilder a magazine.

"I'm okay," he said.

"Sorry, I meant please read to me." She was desperate for distraction.

He glanced down. "*Country Homemaker*. Okay, let's see what we can do."

For five minutes his low voice rumbled about how to make the perfect fruit cake. She clung to every detail from soaking the dried fruit in rum to when to add the molasses.

"Quinn? Quinn Higsby?" a woman called from the doorway.

Quinn stood and Wilder's hand settled on her waist. He didn't have to say a word. His touch told her everything that she needed. He was here.

The fact let her keep walking even though it felt like she was on a pirate ship in the Caribbean, tiptoeing along a plank and not looking down. No point making eye contact with the hungry sharks. They'd have their turn soon enough.

The nurse smiled and Quinn tried to evaluate it. Was this a happy smile? Or sympathetic? Stop. She probably didn't even know.

By the time they were shown into a small waiting room, her heart was beating so loud that she couldn't hear what Wilder said. His lips moved. His brow furrowed in concern.

"What?"

"Are you all right?"

"I . . ." She had this handled, right? No. Maybe? God, how does anyone handle these last few moments of waiting without coming out of their skin? "I'm going to throw up."

He dragged over a garbage can and went to the sink, taking a paper towel and running it under the tap. He gave it a quick, efficient squeeze before handing it over. "Wipe your face, it will help make you feel better."

She wanted to argue but didn't have the strength. Instead, she did what he said and found that it did feel better. A little cool water on her flushed cheeks. Who knew?

"When I was in the fire," Wilder said, "I thought the worst would happen. Dying in a fire was my biggest fear and there I was, looking at it happening. And it seemed like my entire life had boiled down to that moment. The thing that scared me, the burning shadow that haunted all my nightmares was going to come true."

"What did you do?"

"For a moment I gave up," he admitted. "I decided this was it. I rolled on my back and all I wanted to see was the sky. I figured if I could go out seeing blue then at least that was something. But instead all there was was smoke, thick and heavy, and while it sucked it was good because it cleared my head."

"What did you do?"

"I said I wasn't going to be beaten. If it was my day to go, that was fate's business, but I'd fight until the end."

"What if I'm afraid?" Quinn's voice broke.

His features were gentle. How had she ever thought them mean? "Being afraid and fighting back is the true meaning of courage."

There was a knock on the door and Quinn squared her shoulders. "Okay then. I'll fight, no matter what."

"Of course you will," Wilder murmured as the door opened. "It's who you are."

The doctor entered, looking over her chart. "Looks like you had quite the night."

"Excuse me?" It took Quinn a minute to realize she was talking about the fire. Good lord, how crazy was her mental space if the fact her house burned down was something she'd already forgotten about?

"There's a note in the system that you left before finishing your complete physical."

"I felt fine," she said. "I had to go last night, for personal reasons."

"Yes. Mmm. Now for the test results. Well, I might have a few surprises."

Seriously? This is how they were going to tell her that she was going to have Alzheimer's, with a surprise! This wasn't like a five-year-old's birthday party.

"The Alzheimer's test came back negative."

It took a second for the words to sink in. "Negative?"

The doctor smile gently. "You aren't a carrier."

"Oh. Oh my God. My God." She started crying and reached for Wilder. He pulled her close in a bear hug, and even though his grip was strong, she felt the tremble course through his body.

"But I haven't gotten to the surprise yet. But perhaps it is not a surprise?"

"Wait, okay." Quinn scrubbed her eyes. She wasn't out of the woods yet. "Is this a nice surprise?"

"You're pregnant."

"Pregnant?" She reeled back, unable to keep her voice even semi-steady. "But how? I'm not even late and am taking birth control."

"It's very early." The doctor's mouth tilted at the right in a small half-smile. "The blood work was done as part of your physical last night. It can detect pregnancy six to eight days after ovulation."

The examination table felt suddenly wobbly. "Are you sure?"

"Why don't I leave you two alone?" the doctor said. "We're not busy today so take as much time as you need."

The door opened and closed, and Quinn slowly lifted her gaze, unsure what to expect in Wilder's eyes.

Chapter Twenty-One

THERE WAS A LONG, awkward silence.

"Say something," Quinn begged, taking his hand. "Please. A single word so I know you're still alive."

"Baby." It didn't seem real. Quinn pregnant?

"I really am on birth control," she said quickly. "I wasn't trying to trap you or anything. I guess there isn't a perfect statistical track record with taking the pills and—"

"Stop." It was as if the smoke cleared and he finally saw his life's purpose in crystal clarity. "Stop trying to explain."

"I'm sorry."

Shit. He hadn't meant to raise his voice. "Wait, I—"

"I can handle this on my own." Her voice was flat.

"Handle this?" He took by both her shoulders. "In five minutes we've learned you won't get sick and we are going to have a child."

She nodded tearfully. "It's a lot to take in."

He pressed a hand against her cheek, running his thumb over her bottom lip. "The best damn day of my life."

Her brows flew upward. "Are you sure? I mean, it's one thing to call me Trouble as a joke but this will change everything for you."

"I never thought this would happen. I'm scared shitless, but a family is what I've wanted more than anything." He pressed his other hand over her flat stomach. "After the fire I thought my purpose was gone. I didn't realize that the past had to burn for a new future to grow. You. Us. This baby. This is my real life."

"You're really happy?" A small sob broke her lips as she rested a hand over his, cradling the small life within.

"Happy doesn't cut it." His voice was clear, confident. "We'll have to stop at your bookstore and pick up a thesaurus so I can find a whole new vocabulary."

She pulled his collar. "Kiss me."

And he didn't stop until the nurse knocked at the door.

THEY LEFT THE hospital in a daze. The sun still shined overhead, the snowdrifts sparkled so brilliantly that it was hard to see. He tightened his grasp on her hand. "We should go check in with Sawyer."

As surreal as the last few hours had been, the real world was still out there, and it would only be pushed away for so long.

"Yes," Quinn said. "And as for our news . . . do we tell everyone now? Or keep it a secret for a little while?"

"I'm tempted to say nothing, but this is Brightwater. I feel like people will somehow figure it out no matter what. There's some collective town mind-reading power."

"Okay, it's better we get out in front of this. My dad would have loved to be a grandfather. Mom? She's going to shit a brick when I call. I'm pretty sure she told her latest husband that she's fifteen years younger than she actually is. She'd rather have me be her sister, take bikini selfies by the pool, than be a doting diaper-changing grandma."

"Let's give her a chance. What if she does the right thing?"

Quinn stared. "Who are you and what have you done with my grumpy fiancé?"

The word made him grin ear to ear. "I've expected the worst for so long and it never got me anything good. Why not expect the best for once?"

When they got to the sheriff's office, Sawyer's desk was empty. Kit turned down the radio. "Well, well, well. Look who the cat dragged in."

"Cousin," Wilder said with a curt nod.

"Your ears must be burning. Nobody has stopped talking about the pair of you all day."

"What's the current situation?" Wilder asked.

"Sawyer went looking for you. Your phones have both been turned off. Garret King has been officially cleared as a suspect; he had a watertight alibi last night. A lady friend. Or rather two. Guess somebody had to pick up

Archer's mantle now that he's settled down." Kit whistled low. "The Kane boys are dropping like flies, but not yours truly. I'll be buzzing free for a long time yet."

"Are you comparing me to a fly swatter?" Quinn asked with mock annoyance.

Kit chuckled. "Hey, don't take anything I say personal. I talk straight out my ass."

"Good to know some things never change," Wilder said.

"I'll call the boss, let him know you are around. He'll want a chat. Warning, he's not all that happy about your disappearing act."

"We've had a heck of a day," Wilder said. "He can deal."

Kit made a quick call and gestured to a few chairs. "Can I offer you folks some refreshments?"

"I'm a little hungry actually," Quinn said as Wilder eyed the window, waiting for Sawyer's patrol car to pull up. If Garret had an alibi that checked out, then whoever set those fires was still out there. And that meant Quinn and the baby were at risk.

The baby.

It was more like a floating sea monkey at this stage but he didn't care. What if it was a boy? Wilder'd take him fishing, camping. Teach him chess. If it was a girl he could do the same, but if she looked like her mother, she'd wrap him around her pudgy little finger in no time.

"I keep Girl Scout cookies stashed in my desk," Kit said with a conspiratorial wink. "You want to come see my selection?"

"Do you have Thin Mints by any chance?"

"Hell yeah."

"Then you're my favorite of Wilder's relatives." He handed her a cookie sleeve and she took a few. "Want one?" She waved one at Wilder.

"I'm good." He couldn't eat. He couldn't do anything except focus.

If not Garret, who?

Fucking who?

Could it really be Lenny?

Quinn traded good-natured banter with Kit until she asked if anyone had gotten in touch with Marigold Flint and let her know that the cottage had burned.

Wilder noticed the change in the room. Tension grew and Kit's face lost his easy smile.

"Yeah, yeah. We got in touch with her around lunchtime."

"I hear she can have quite the temper." Quinn's brow crinkled. "I hope she doesn't blame me."

"You? Course not. She was horrified on your behalf. But I almost feel sorry for whoever is responsible. Goldie is cutting her trip short to fly home. If they find the guy, he'll be begging to be put behind bars rather than deal with that she-lion."

Quinn smiled. "I'm sure she's not that scary."

Kit shoved another cookie in his month in response.

To say his cousin and Goldie Flint had a tempestuous history was an understatement. When they had it out at town football games, the fans in the bleachers stopped watching the field and munched popcorn while watching them invent curses that made the crowd gasp in awe or cheer whenever they struck a particularly good low blow.

They were aware of the attention, played to the crowd sympathies like they were starring in a Shakespearean play. But then Kit enlisted and was gone, and Goldie went quiet. A scary quiet because every once in a while it erupted into a tongue-lashing.

Those two had history, but Wilder always guessed it was their business.

The patrol car pulled up and Sawyer climbed out. His gaze went right to the window. Wilder knew from the way the sun hit the glass that his brother couldn't see him, but he still knew he was there.

And what if he had a change of heart after last night's conversation?

The door swung open and Sawyer stomped the snow off his boots. "Glad to see you out in the world," he said. "Was beginning to think you both went underground."

"How are you, brother?" Wilder put a hell of a lot of meaning into the question.

Sawyer nodded thoughtfully. "Good, man. Worried about your dumb ass, mostly. And you," he said to Quinn. "Apparently the fire investigator for our region quit recently. Had a heart attack and decided to retire early. Got a guy coming over from Sacramento but that might not be for another day or so."

"Quit," Wilder said. "So there's a vacancy?"

"Posted this morning," Sawyer said, frowning slightly. "Too late to be of much use here I'm afraid. But ATF did send a profile over."

"Can I take a look?" Wilder said.

Sawyer handed over the two-sheet form and Wilder read through it quickly.

"Anything spring to mind?" Sawyer said. "You got a look on your face."

"Maybe. Yeah," Wilder said as his heart sank to his gut. "Tonight's the Christmas tree lighting, isn't it?"

"Yeah, why?" Realization dawned on Sawyer's face. "Aw, hell, you don't think there'll be trouble?"

"I got a feeling."

Sawyer gave a grim smile. "You sound like Grandma."

"About time I realize we're a lot alike," Wilder said with a curt nod. "I have a plan. It's a long shot, but here's what we can do."

Chapter Twenty-Two

QUINN HELD HER hands over the truck's heater.

"You sure you won't go wait in the bookstore?" Wilder asked for the third time in as many minutes. "I promise to come back and get you before the lighting."

"Positive. I've never been on a stakeout before." She scanned the Save-U-More parking lot. "You've got Kit watching the Kum & Go gas station and we're here. Care to let me in on the secret?"

Wilder gave her a side eye. "Thought you liked fishing."

"I do." She bristled. "But I like to know what I'm setting the line for."

"Like I said last night, it looks like all the fires have been started using a milk jug. It's a long shot but I'm watching to see if the suspect is going to stop by. Then we'll follow him."

Quinn stared around the half-full parking lot. One of her cousins walked past but didn't look over. "Lenny?"

"Shit." Wilder ducked, drumming his fingers on the steering wheel. "He's right there."

"You really think he's capable?"

Wilder scratched his scruffy jaw. "He hero worships King. If King wasn't setting the fires, he was responding to them and getting lots of praise in the process. Praise that eventually could trickle down to the best buddy."

"That's sort of crazy."

"I said it was a long shot."

"No, I mean it in a good way. That's his car, huh?" She pointed at the nondescript grey Civic.

"Guess so, why?"

"I saw that car. It was acting weird, sort of casing me out one night, but I chalked it up to my imagination. Lenny was always with Garret when he was trying to hit on me and, for the record, probably the worst wingman ever."

"So he set a fire in your house, hoping King would rescue you, and—"

"That I'd fall for him."

Lenny emerged carrying a single gallon of milk.

"Whoa." Quinn gasped. It was as if the oxygen had just been sucked out of the car.

"He needs to be caught in the act," Wilder said, waiting for Lenny to drive off before beginning the tail. "Otherwise he's going to be able to claim that he wanted to make a banana fucking milkshake or eat a bowl of cereal. Buying a gallon of two percent isn't a crime."

Wilder made a quick call to Sawyer. "He's going down Main and taking a left on Laurel Street. Shit, he's turning into an alley. I can't follow without alerting him but that's right near the town square. Where there's smoke there's fire, man. I think we've got our boy." Wilder nodded a few times. "Got it. Yep. Agreed."

He did a U-turn and headed back toward Main Street.

"What's the plan?"

"I'm not law enforcement so can't go all vigilante on that asshole. We're going to the square. Have to leave this to Sawyer and Kit."

She rubbed his stiff shoulder. "This is killing you a little, isn't it? Not being involved?"

Wilder's muscles loosened. "Yes and no. You and Sea Monkey are my priority."

"Sea Monkey?" She wrinkled her nose. "That's what you are calling the baby?"

"I have in my head, but can stop if you don't like it."

Quinn giggled. "Actually it's perfect. Our darling little Sea Monkey."

"I'm thinking about something. I won't do it if you say no."

"Lay it on me."

"What Sawyer said about the fire investigator position opening up . . . How would you feel if I went for the job? I have good savings, but I can't live on them forever. Now I've got you and Sea Monkey to take care of and—"

Quinn cupped the side of his cheek. "You'd be brilliant at it."

He grimaced. "I'm no genius. Remember, I suspected King first."

"You saw a link with Garret that no one else did.

That's a start. You said yourself that catching an arsonist is like finding a needle in a haystack."

"You won't mind if I get back into fire?"

She gave him a sympathetic smile. "That is always going to be a part of you, Wilder. But this is a way to move forward. This way you'll be helping protect people."

"I don't have the job yet."

"Maybe not officially, but you do in my mind. They'd be crazy not to want you."

"Speaking of crazy . . ." Wilder yanked the wheel toward the curb and hit the brakes. Lenny burst between Higsby Hardware and Bab's Boutique, running full speed. Kit and Sawyer gave chase but he was headed straight in their direction.

Before Quinn could say a word, Wilder jumped from the car. "Hey, Lenny," he barked. "Going somewhere?"

The smaller man pulled up short, chest rising and falling from exertion. "Get the hell out of my way, freak," he snapped, glancing over his shoulder at the approaching law enforcement.

"No. I don't think I will." There was a crunch as Wilder's fist made contact with Lenny's snub nose and the man went down faster than a domino. "That's for putting my woman at risk," Wilder growled.

Sawyer approached, shaking his head. "I'd lecture you on slugging a suspect but if I gave Archer a pass last summer, guess you get one too."

"He's out cold," Kit said, nudging the unconscious man with his boot. "You pack one hell of a punch, dude."

"What happened?" Wilder asked.

"He had emptied the milk and filled it with gasoline, stuffed a sock in just like you said. We surprised him when he was sneaking over to the generator box."

"Son of a bitch," Wilder spat.

"An S.O.B. that's going to wake up to a world of hurt and a shitload of trouble," Sawyer said, hauling Lenny to his feet.

"Thank you," Quinn said, rubbing Wilder's arm. "Didn't I once tell you that every blue moon someone deserves a hard knock in the nose?"

"Yeah, you did, Trouble." Wilder planted a kiss square on her forehead. "You're safe now, and I'll keep you safe forever."

"You two get a room," Kit said as Sawyer began hauling Lenny away. The shorter man moaned insensibly.

"Nah, I'm taking her to watch the Christmas tree lighting," Wilder shot back. "That is, if you're in the holiday spirit."

"You know what?" Quinn gave him a long look. "We have a lot to celebrate. Why not?"

It took another hour for the square to fill and the sun to drop behind Mount Oh-Be-Joyful. The sky turned as red as a poinsettia while the Brightwater Children's Choir sang "Little Drummer Boy."

Quinn glanced at Wilder to share the moment but he was staring over her shoulder. "Come on," he said, taking her hand. "Let's go this way."

It was crowded with residents bursting with festive holiday cheer. Red Rudolph noses, antlers, and Santa hats abounded. Quinn gave a soft inward sigh. Maybe

Wilder wasn't quite ready to say a complete goodbye to the hermit life he'd inhabited for so long.

Disappointment tugged at her while they walked but at the same time, she couldn't expect him to change who he was. She had to love him with eyes wide-open.

He pulled up short. "Close your eyes."

She cocked her head. "What is going on?"

"Please?" He fidgeted. "It's a surprise."

"I never thought I'd say it but I might be a little surprised out."

"You'll like this one," he murmured.

"Okay." She closed her eyes and waited.

The mayor finished giving his speech and the crowd began to count down, "Nine . . . eight . . . seven . . . six . . ."

Wilder kissed her, soft, gentle, and with a sweetness that made her rise up on her tiptoes as he slowly withdrew.

The people around them began to clap as the holiday lights turned on, illuminating the big tree. A woman shouted, "Atta girl." Quinn grinned at Natalie's voice.

"What was that for?" she asked dreamily as the choir broke into "Have Yourself a Merry Little Christmas."

"Thought it was obvious. For having the most kissable lips in the town." He gave her chin a playful chuck. "And look up."

Overhead was a sprig of mistletoe dangling from a red velvet ribbon.

She grinned. "Something tells me this holiday is going to be extra holly jolly."

It HAD BEEN a long, hard winter but Wilder barely noticed. Quinn had moved in and over the months his heart swelled alongside her growing belly. June arrived in all its sunny glory and he'd taken the day off work as the fire investigator for the Eastern Sierras to attend something that a year ago would have sent him running in the opposite direction.

A baby shower.

What a difference three hundred and sixty-five measly days made. Quinn sat in a lawn chair behind the cottage holding a green hand-knit baby blanket.

"This is absolutely adorable," she said.

"I had to pick green since you won't find out if it's a boy or a girl." Grandma tried to grumble but it was hard to do when a huge smile tugged the corners of her mouth. He and Quinn married on Valentine's Day, a simple wedding at city hall. Her dad, had given a soft, wistful smile

BEST WORST MISTAKE 263

at the sight of her white dress, as if grasping the magnitude of the day. Mom had sent a dozen pink roses and a tersely worded card chastising her for not having a blowout celebration, but with Sawyer and Annie, Archer and Edie, Kit, Margot, Grandma, and Atticus in attendance, everything felt complete. It felt like a family and they wouldn't have had it any other way.

Archer and Edie were getting married in a few weeks and everyone was buzzing because Archer had picked Kit to be his best man and Edie had asked Goldie Flint, who was back from her travels, to be her maid of honor. Her cousin, Quincy Bankcroft, was allowing his home, The Dales, a historic mansion and the biggest home in the county, to be the reception site.

Bets were being exchanged at Haute Coffee and The Dirty Shame Saloon as to how long into the ceremony it would take before Kit and Goldie were dueling with pistols. The current average estimate was eight minutes and twenty-six seconds.

"Everyone! Everyone! Guys! Come quick, you have to see this." Atticus tore from the forest edge, Sawyer and Archer tagging after him. Wilder had foregone their trip down to the falls in favor of games like "How Fast Can the Plastic Baby in the Ice Cube Melt?" "Guess the Baby Food," and the homemade "Pin the Sperm on the Egg" that Grandma brought.

That was the only one that sent Wilder into the house for a beer.

"Are you okay, sweetheart?" Annie asked, jumping to her feet. She was going to be Edie's matron of honor, and

Quinn had been leaning on her as a big sister, gleaning everything from labor tips to must-have baby gear.

"It's so cool." Atticus took a puff from his inhaler. "The mystery is back."

"Mystery?" Annie glanced to Sawyer with a quizzical expression.

"Sorry to break in on all your fun, ladies, oh, and gent." Archer tipped his hat at Wilder. "But this is well worth a gander."

"Gander?" Edie said, lacing her fingers with his. "Have you turned old-timer on us?"

"Nothing wrong with that," Grandma said, hobbling forward.

"Right this way." Wilder offered Quinn his arm.

The baby shower party walked through the forest. The sound of the falls grew louder and louder. Upstream, not far from Wilder's hot spring, were three perfect circles of wildflowers.

"Well, I'll be damned," Grandma said.

"Fairy rings!" Annie clapped her hands. "Just like in the old tale. I'll have to do a story on it for the *Bugle*."

Wilder frowned, puzzling over the sight. This is where he'd left the cracked corn out. Perhaps the very same night that Sea Monkey started growing inside her.

The supplemental food attracted the deer and their trampling had created circles in the snow. Now that the late-spring wildflowers were coming into bloom, they were growing thicker in the places that had been so friendly to them all winter.

He glanced at Quinn. "The deer?" she murmured, putting two and two together.

Everyone wandered, exclaiming, trying to guess how it happened.

"Looks like whoever the hermit of Castle Falls was, he also had a good heart," Quinn said, bending down and picking a pale purple blossom. "And your mom was right all those years ago."

"How's that?" he asked.

"No act of kindness, however small, is ever wasted," she said, tucking the flower into his buttonhole.

He put his arm around her shoulders and rested his head against her. The flowers waved in the light breeze and all around them good things were taking root.

Can't wait for more of Lia Riley's
Brightwater series?
Keep reading for an excerpt from the
hilarious second book in the series,

RIGHT WRONG GUY

Sometimes two wrongs can make a right. . .

BAD BOY WRANGLER, Archer Kane, lives fast and loose.
Words like responsibility and commitment send him
running in the opposite direction. Until a wild Vegas
weekend puts him on a collision course with Eden
Bankcroft-Kew, a New York heiress running away from
her blackmailing fiancé . . . the morning of her wedding.

Eden has never understood the big attraction to cowboys.
Give her a guy in a tailored suit any day of the week. But
now all she can think about is Mr. Rugged Handsome,
six-feet of sinfully sexy country charm with a pair of
green eyes that keep her tossing and turning.

Archer might be the wrong guy for a woman like her, but
she's not right in thinking he'll walk away without fighting for her heart. And maybe, just maybe, two wrongs
can make a right.

Available Now from Avon Impulse!

An Excerpt from
RIGHT WRONG GUY

ARCHER KANE PLUCKED a dangly gold nipple tassel off his cheek and sat up in the king-sized bed, scrubbing his face. Overturned furniture, empty shot glasses, and champagne flutes littered the hotel room while a red thong dangled from the flat screen. He inched his fingers to grab the Stetson resting atop the tangled comforter. The trick lay in not disturbing the two women snoring on either side of him. Vegas trips were about fillies and fun—mission accomplished.

Right?

"What the?" A dove dive-bombed him, swooped to his left, and perched on the room-service cart to peck at a peanut from what appeared to be the remnants of a large hot fudge sundae. Who knew how a bird got in here, but at least the ice cream explained why his chest hair was sticky and, farther below, chocolate-covered fingerprints framed his six-pack. Looked like he had one helluva night. Too bad he couldn't remember a damn thing. He should be high-fiving himself, but instead, he just felt dog-tired.

He emerged from beneath the covers and crawled to the bottom of the bed, head pounding like a bass drum. As he stood, the prior evening returned in splintered fragments. Blondie, on the right cuddling his empty pillow, was Crystal Balls aka the Stripping Magician. The marquee from her show advertised, "She has nothing up her sleeve." Dark-hair on the left had been the assistant . . . *Destiny? Dallas? Daisy?*

Something with a D.

How in Houdini they all ended up in bed together is where the facts got fuzzy.

A feather-trimmed sequined gown was crumpled by the mini bar and an old-man ventriloquist's dummy appeared to track his furtive movements from the corner. Archer stepped over a Jim Beam bottle and crept toward the bathroom. Next mission? A thorough shower followed by the strongest coffee on the strip.

Coffee. Yes. Soon. Plus a short stack of buttermilk pancakes, a Denver omelet, and enough bacon to require the sacrifice of a dozen hogs. Starving didn't come close to describing the hollow feeling in his gut, like he'd run a sub-four-hour marathon, scaled Everest, and then wrestled a two-ton longhorn. His reflection stared back from the bathroom mirror, circles under his green eyes and thick morning scruff. For the last year a discontented funk had risen within him. How many times had he insisted he was too young to be tied down to a serious committed relationship, job . . . or anything? Well, at twenty-seven he might not be geriatric, but he was getting too old for this bed-hopping shit.

"What the hell are you doing?" he muttered to himself.

The facts were Mr. Brightwater wasn't looking his best. His second cousin, Kit, gave him that nickname after he graced the cover of a "Boys of Brightwater" town calendar last year to support the local Lions Club. He'd been February and posed holding a red cardboard heart over his johnson to avoid an X rating, although as his big brother Sawyer dryly noted, "Not like most women around here haven't already seen it."

In fairness, Brightwater, California, didn't host a large population. For a healthy man who liked the ladies, it didn't take long to make the rounds at The Dirty Shame, the local watering hole. Vegas getaways meant variety, a chance to spice things up, although a threesome with Crystal and Donna—*Deborah? Deena? Dazzle?*—was akin to swallowing a whole habanero.

He reached into the shower and flicked on the tap as a warm furry body hopped across his foot. "Shit!" He vaulted back, nearly going ass over teakettle, before bracing himself on the counter. A bewildered white rabbit peered up, nose twitching.

"You've got to be kidding me." He squinted into the steam with increased suspicion. Hopefully, Crystal's act didn't also involve a baby crocodile or, worse, a boa constrictor. He hated snakes.

The coast was clear so he stepped inside, the hot water sending him halfway to human. There was a tiny bottle of hotel shampoo perched in the soap dish and he gave it a dubious sniff. It smelled like flowers but would do the job of rinsing away stale perfume and sex. He worked a dollop through his thick hair, shoulder muscles relaxing.

He'd always prided himself on being the kind of good-time guy who held no regrets, but lately it seemed like there was a difference between dwelling on past mistakes and reflecting in order to avoid future ones. Did he really want to live out these shallow morning-after scenarios forever like some warped version of *Groundhog Day*?

The hair on the back of his neck tingled with the unmistakable sensation of being watched. He swiped suds from his eyes and turned, nearly nose-to-nose with the blank stare of the old-man ventriloquist's dummy.

"Fuck," he barked, any better word lost in shock.

"Great Uncle Sam don't like it when menfolk cuss," the dummy responded in a deep, Southern drawl. Other than the puppet on her hand, Dixie-Dorothy-Darby wore nothing but a suggestive smile.

"Uh . . . morning, beautiful." Thank God for matching dimples, they'd charmed him out of enough bad situations.

"No one's ever made me come so hard." The puppet's mustache bobbed as he spoke and more of last night's drunken jigsaw puzzle snapped into place. Desdemona-Diana-Doris had gone on (and on) about her dream of becoming a professional ventriloquist. She'd brought out the puppet and made Great Uncle Sam talk dirty, which had been hilarious after Tequila Slammers, Snake Bites, Buttery Nipples, and 5 Deadly Venoms, plus a few bottles of champagne.

It was a whole lot less funny now.

"Hey, D, would you mind giving me a sec here? I'm going to finish rinsing off." When in doubt, he always referred to a woman by her first initial, it made him sound affectionate instead of like an asshole.

"D?" rumbled Great Uncle Sam.

Damn. Apparently an initial wasn't going to cut it.

Okay think . . . Dinah? No. Two rocks glinted from her lobes—a possible namesake. "Diamond?"

Great Uncle Sam slowly shook his head. Maybe it was Archer's imagination, but the painted eyes narrowed fractionally. "Stormy."

And so was her expression.

Not even close.

"Stormy?" he repeated blankly. "Yeah, Stormy, of course. Gorgeous name. Makes me think of rain and . . . and . . . rainbows . . . and . . ."

"You called it out enough last night, the least you could do is be a gentleman and remember it the next morning!" Great Uncle Sam head-butted him.

Add splitting headache to his current list of troubles.

Archer scrambled from the shower before he got his bare ass taken down by a puppet. You don't fight back against a woman, even if she is trying to bash your brain in with Pinocchio's demented elderly uncle.

"Get the hell out." Stormy's real voice sounded a lot more Jersey Shore than genteel Georgian peach farmer. She wasn't half bad at the whole ventriloquist gig, but now wasn't the time to offer compliments.

He threw on his Levi's commando-style while Stormy eyed his package as if prepping to go Category

Five hurricane on his junk. Scooping his red Western shirt off the floor, he made a break for the bedroom. His boots were by the door but his hat was still on the bed, specifically on Crystal's head. Her sleepy expression gave way to confusion as Stormy sprang from the bathroom, Great Uncle Sam leading the charge.

"What's going on?" Crystal asked as Stormy bellowed, "Prepare to have your manwhore ass kicked back into whatever cowpoke hole you crawled from."

Hat? Boots? Hat? Boots? Archer only had time to grab one. He slung his arms through the shirt, not bothering to snap the pearl clasps, and grabbed the hand-tooled boots while hurtling into the hall. Yeah, definitely getting too old for this shit.

"Pleasure to make your acquaintance," he called over one shoulder as the dove swooped.

He bypassed the elevator bay in favor of the stairwell. Once he'd descended three floors, he paused to tug on his boots and his phone rang. Pulling it out from his back pocket, he groaned at the screen. Grandma Kane.

He could let it go to voice mail. In fact, he was tempted to do just that, but the thing about Grandma was she called back until you picked up.

With a heavy sigh, and a prayer for two Tylenol, he hit "answer." "How's the best grandma in the world?" he boomed, propping the phone between his ear and shoulder and snapping together his shirt.

"Quit with your smooth talk, boy," Grandma barked. "Where are you?"

"Leaving church," he fibbed quickly.

"Better not be the Little Chapel of Love."

"What do you—"

"Don't feed me bullhickey. You're in Vegas again."

Sawyer must have squeaked. As Brightwater sheriff, he was into upright citizenship and moral standing, nobler than George Washington and his fucking cherry tree.

"Did you forget about our plans for this weekend?"

"Plans?" He wracked his brain but thinking hurt. So did walking down these stairs. Come to think of it, so did breathing. He needed that upcoming coffee and bacon like a nose needed picking.

Grandma made a rude noise. "To go over the accounts for Hidden Rock. You promised to set up the new purchase-order software on the computer."

Shit. His shoulders slumped. He had offered to help. Grandma ran a large, profitable cattle ranch, but the Hidden Rock's inventory management was archaic, and the accounting practically done by abacus. In his hurry to see if an impromptu Vegas road trip could overcome his funk, the meeting had slipped his mind. "Let me make it up to you—"

"Your charm has no currency here, boy." Grandpa Kane died before Archer was born and Grandma never remarried. Perhaps he should introduce her to Stormy's Great Uncle Sam. Those two were a match made in heaven, could spend their spare time busting his balls.

He closed his eyes and massaged his forehead. "I'm sorry, I completely forgot, okay?" Not okay. Grandma counted on him and he let her down.

"Funny, guess you're probably too busy using women like disposable silverware." Her tone sounded anything but amused. "Even funnier will be when I forget to put you in my will."

Grandma's favorite threat was disinheriting him. Who cared? The guy voted Biggest Partier and Class Flirt his senior year at Brightwater High was also the least likely to run Hidden Rock Ranch.

The line went dead. At least she didn't ask why he couldn't be more like Sawyer anymore.

Whatever. Archer had it good, made great tips as a wrangler at a dude ranch. His middle brother took life seriously enough and he hadn't seen his oldest one in years. Wilder worked as a smoke jumper in Montana. Sometimes Archer wondered what would happen if he cruised to Big Sky Country and paid him a surprise visit—maybe he had multiple sister wives or was a secret war lord.

Growing up after their parents died in a freak house fire, they all slipped into roles. Wilder withdrew, brooding and angry, Sawyer became Mr. Nice Guy, always the teacher's pet or offering to do chores. Archer rounded things out by going for laughs and practical jokes and causing trouble because someone had to remind everyone else not to take life so seriously. None of them were getting out alive.

He kept marching down the flights of stairs, tucking in his shirt. Grandma's words played on a loop in his mind. "Using women like disposable silverware."

Lord knew—those women used him right back. It was fun, didn't mean anything.

Meaningless.

He ground his jaw so tight his teeth hurt. Casual sex on pool tables, washing machines, countertops, and lawn chairs filled his physical needs, but these random hook-ups were starting to make him feel more and more alone.

On the ground floor, he slammed open the stairwell door. There were two corridors ahead. He turned left for no reason other than that's the hand he favored. Seemed like he chose wisely because a side entrance gave him a quick exit. He walked out, wincing at the morning sun even as he gulped fresh air, fresh for the Vegas Strip, but a far cry from the Eastern Sierras's clean mountain breeze. His heart stirred. He'd have some breakfast and hit the road. As much as he liked leaving Brightwater, he always missed home.

Archer reached to adjust his hat and grabbed a hand-ful of wet hair instead. Twelve stories above, a stripping magician had found herself a mighty fine Stetson.

He stepped onto the street, jumping back on the curb when a city bus turned, the side plastered with a shoe ad sporting the slogan, "Can You Run Forever?"

Hell, he'd been running from accountability, stability, and boring routines his whole life.

Another thought crept in and sank its roots deep. Was he really running from those things, or was he letting his fears of commitment and responsibility run him instead?

**See where it all started in the first wonderful
installment in the Brightwater series,**

LAST FIRST KISS

A kiss is just the beginning. . .

PINTEREST PERFECT. OR so Annie Carson's life appears
on her popular blog. Reality is . . . messier. Especially
when it lands her back in one-cow town, Brightwater,
California, and back in the path of the gorgeous six-
foot-four reason she left. Sawyer Kane may fill out those
Wranglers, but she won't be distracted from her task.
Annie just needs the summer to spruce up and sell her
family's farm so she and her young son can start a new
life in the big city. Simple, easy, perfect.

Sawyer has always regretted letting the first girl he loved
slip away. He won't make the same mistake twice, but
can he convince beautiful, wary Annie to trust her heart
again when she's been given every reason not to? And as a
single kiss turns to so much more, can Annie give up her
idea of perfect for a forever that's blissfully real?

Available Now from Avon Impulse

About the Author

After studying at the University of Montana-Missoula, LIA RILEY scoured the world armed with only a backpack, overconfidence, and a terrible sense of direction. She counts shooting vodka with a Ukrainian mechanic in Antarctica, sipping yerba mate with gauchos in Chile, and swilling fourex with station hands in Outback Australia among her accomplishments.

A British literature fanatic at heart, Lia considers Mr. Darcy and Edward Rochester as her fictional boyfriends. Her very patient husband doesn't mind. Much. When not torturing heroes (because c'mon, who doesn't love a good tortured hero?), Lia herds unruly chickens, camps, beach combs, daydreams about as-of-yet unwritten books, wades through a mile-high TBR pile, and schemes yet another trip. Right now, Icelandic hot springs and Scottish castles sound mighty fine.

She and her family live mostly in Northern California.

Discover great authors, exclusive offers, and more at hc.com.

Give in to your Impulses . . .
Continue reading for excerpts from
our newest Avon Impulse books.
Available now wherever e-books are sold.

THE BRIDE WORE RED BOOTS
A SEVEN BRIDES FOR SEVEN COWBOYS NOVEL
By Lizbeth Selvig

RESCUED BY THE RANGER
By Dixie Lee Brown

ONE SCANDALOUS KISS
AN ACCIDENTAL HEIRS NOVEL
By Christy Carlyle

DIRTY TALK
A MECHANICS OF LOVE NOVEL
By Megan Erickson

An Excerpt from

THE BRIDE WORE RED BOOTS
A Seven Brides for Seven Cowboys Novel
by Lizbeth Selvig

Amelia Crockett's life was going exactly the way she had always planned—until one day, it wasn't.

When Mia's career plans are shattered, the always-in-control surgeon has no choice but to head home to Paradise Ranch and her five younger sisters, cowboy boots in tow, to figure out how to get her life back on track. The appearance of a frustrating, but oh-so-sexy, former soldier, however, turns into exactly the kind of distraction she can't afford.

He studied her as if assessing how blunt he could be. With a wry little lift of his lip, he closed his eyes and lay all the way back onto the blanket, hands behind his head. "Honestly? You were just so much fun to get a rise out of. You'd turn all hot under the collar, like you couldn't figure out how anyone could dare counter you—the big-city doc coming to Hicksville with the answers."

The teasing tone of his voice was clear, but the words stung nonetheless. Funny. They wouldn't have bothered her at all a week ago, she thought. Now it hurt that he would ever think of her that way. She hadn't been that awful—she'd only wanted to put order to the chaos and bring a little rationality to the haywire emotions after her mother and sister's awful accident.

"Hey." She turned at the sound of his voice to find him sitting upright beside her again. "Amelia, I know better now. I know you. I'm not judging you—then or now."

Pricks of miniscule teardrops stung her eyes, the result of extreme embarrassment—and profound relief. She had no idea what to make of the reaction. It was neither logical nor something she ever remembered experiencing.

"I know."

To her horror, the roughness of her emotions shone through her voice, and Gabriel peered at her, his face a study in surprise. "Are you crying? Amelia, I'm sorry—I was just giving you grief, I wasn't—"

"I'm not crying." Her insistence held no power even though it wasn't a lie. No water fell from her eyes; it just welled behind the lids. "I'm not upset. I'm . . . relieved. I . . . it was nice, what you . . . said." She clamped her mouth closed before something truly stupid emerged and looked down at the blanket, picking at a pill in the wool's plaid pile.

A touch beneath her chin drew her gaze back up. Gabriel's eyes were mere inches from hers, shining with that beautiful caramel brown that suddenly looked like it could liquefy into pure sweetness and sex. Every masculine pore of his skin caught her attention and made her fingers itch to stroke the texture of his cheek. The scent of wind-blown skin and chocolate tantalized her.

"Don't be anything but what and who you are, Amelia Crockett."

His kiss brushed her mouth with the weightlessness of a Monarch on a flower petal. Soft, ethereal, tender, it promised nothing but a taste of pleasure and asked for nothing in return. Yet, as subtle as it was, it drove a punch of desire deep into Mia's core and then set her stomach fluttering with anticipation.

He pulled back but his fingers remained on her chin. "I'm sorry. That was probably uncalled for."

When his fingers, too, began to slide from her skin, she reacted without thinking and grabbed his hand. "No. It's . . .

It was . . . Gah—" Frustrated by her constant, unfamiliar loss for words, she leaned forward rather than let mortification set in and pressed a kiss against his lips this time, foregoing light and airy for the chance to taste him fully. Beneath the pressure, his lips curved into a smile. She couldn't help it then, her mouth mimicked his and they clashed in a gentle tangle of lips, teeth, and soft, surprised chuckles.

"Crazy," he said in a whisper, as he encircled her shoulders and pulled her closer.

"Yeah," she agreed and opened her mouth to invite his tongue to meet hers.

First kisses in Mia's experience were usually fraught with uncertainty and awkwardness about what should come next, but not this one. Kissing Gabriel seemed as natural and pleasurable as walking along a stunning stream full of rapids and eddies and satisfying things to explore. She explored them all and let him taste and enjoy right back. When at last they let each other go, her head continued to spin with surprise, and every nerve ending sparkled with desire.

An Excerpt from

RESCUED BY THE RANGER

by Dixie Lee Brown

Army Ranger Garrett Harding is new in town—but not necessarily welcome. The only thing Rachel Maguire wants is to send this muscled military man packing. But when the stalker who destroyed her life ten years ago reappears, Rachel hits the road hoping to lure danger away from those she loves. Garrett won't let this sexy spitfire face trouble alone. He'll do anything to protect her. Even if it means risking his life—and his heart.

Pressed tight to the wall, Garrett waited. As she burst from cover, looking over her right shoulder and away from him, he stepped toward her. Catching her around the middle, he swung her off her feet and up against his body, holding her tightly with both arms. "It's me, Rach. Take it easy. I just want to talk."

She stopped struggling, so he loosened his hold as he set her back on her feet. Mistake number one. She dug her fingernails into his forearm, scratching until she drew blood. As soon as he leaned over her shoulder to grab her hand, she whacked his jaw with the back of her head, hard enough to send him stumbling back a step. He shook his head to clear the stars in time to see her swing that black bag.

"Wait a minute, Rachel!" Garrett tried to duck, but her shorter height gave her the advantage. She caught him across the side of the head, and there was apparently something heavy and damn hard in her bag. He staggered, lost his balance, and went down.

She looked surprised for a second before determination steeled her expression. "I told you not to look for me. What didn't you understand about that?" Shifting her bag onto her shoulder, she turned, and started running down the alley.

"Well, shit." Garrett glanced at Cowboy and damned if it didn't look like he was laughing. "Okay, already. You were right. Saddle up, Cowboy."

The dog took off, his long strides closing the distance to Rachel's retreating back easily. Garrett stood, brushing the dirt off and taking a moment to stretch the ache from the wound in his back. Then he jogged after the girl and the dog. He'd seriously underestimated Rachel today. Cowboy had his instructions to stop her, but keeping her there would require a whole different set of commands—ones that Garrett would never utter where Rachel was concerned.

Ahead of him, the dog ran circles around her, making the circle smaller each time. When she finally stopped, keeping a wary eye on the animal, Cowboy dropped to a walk, his tail wagging as he angled toward her. Though she didn't move, her body, tense and ready, said she was on high alert. Garrett picked up his pace to reach them.

Rachel looked over her shoulder, obviously noted the diminishing distance between them, and grabbed for her satchel. The next thing he knew, the damn hard object she'd hit him with—a small revolver—was in her hand and she was pointing it at Cowboy.

"You need to stay where you are, Garrett, and call your dog or . . . I'll shoot him."

"Cowboy, chill." The dog dropped to the ground, watching Garrett carefully. "This is what it's come to then? You want to get away from me so bad you're willing to shoot my dog?"

She shook her head dejectedly. "That's not what I want, but I will if I have to."

"I don't believe you, Rach. That dog's just following orders. My orders. Shoot me if you want to hurt somebody." Garrett moved a few steps closer.

Rachel laughed scornfully. "Did you miss the part where I tried to leave without anybody getting hurt?"

"No. I get that you're worried about Peg, Jonathan, and the rest of the people at the lodge, but damn it, Rachel, they love you. They want to understand. They want to help if they can, because that's what people do when they love someone. They don't sneak off in the night, leaving their *family* to wonder what happened."

"I can't—" She lowered the weapon until her hand hung at her side. Her eyes closed for a second, then she sat abruptly amidst the grass that bordered the alley.

Garrett walked up to her and knelt down. Prying the gun from her fingers, he placed it back in her bag and zipped it up. "Yes, you can. I'll help you." He tilted her chin up so he could see the sheen of her expressive green eyes. "Give me a chance, Rachel. What have you got to lose?"

An Excerpt from

ONE SCANDALOUS KISS
An Accidental Heirs Novel
by Christy Carlyle

When a desperate Jessamin Wright bursts
into an aristocratic party and shocks the
entire ton, she believes it's the only way to
save her failing bookstore. The challenge
sounded easy when issued, but the one thing
she never expected was to enjoy the outrageous
embrace she shares with a serious viscount.

For the hundredth time, Jess called herself a fool for agreeing to Kitty Adderly's ridiculous plan for revenge against Viscount Grimsby. Kissing a viscount for one hundred pounds sounded questionable at the time Kitty had suggested it. Now Jess thought perhaps the jilted heiress had put something in her tea.

Initially she made her way into the crowded art gallery unnoticed, but then a woman dripping in diamonds and green silk had questioned her. When the lady's round husband stepped in, it all turned to chaos before she'd even done what she'd come to do. The deed itself shouldn't take long. A quick peck on the mouth—Kitty had insisted that she kiss the man on the lips—and it would all be over. She'd already handed the money over to Mr. Briggs at the bank. Turning back now simply wasn't an option.

She recognized Lord Grimsby from the gossip rag Kitty had shown her. The newspaper etching hadn't done him justice. In it, he'd been portrayed as dark and forbidding, his mouth a sharp slash, his black brows so large they overtook his eyes, and his long Roman nose dominating an altogether unappealing face. But in the flesh every part of his appearance harmonized into a striking whole. He was the sort of man she would have noticed in a crowd, even if she hadn't been seeking him, intent on causing him scandal and taking unimaginable liberties with his person.

He was there at the end of the gallery, as far from the entrance as he could possibly be. Jess continued through the gamut and a man snatched at her arm. Unthinking, she stepped on his foot, and he spluttered and cursed but released her.

Lord Grimsby saw her now. She noticed his dark head—and far too many others—turned her way. He was tall and broad shouldered, towering over the man and woman beside him. And he did look grim, as cold and disagreeable as Kitty had described.

Jessamin turned her eyes down, avoiding his gaze. Helpfully, the crowd parted before her, as if the respectable ladies and gentlemen were unwilling to remain near a woman behaving so unpredictably. Every time she raised her eyes, she glimpsed eyes gone wide, mouths agape, and women furiously fanning themselves.

Just a few more steps and Jess stood before him, only inches between them. She met his gaze and found him glaring down at her with shockingly clear blue eyes. Furrowed lines formed a vee between his brows as he frowned at her like a troublesome insect had just spoiled his meal.

She opened her mouth to speak, but what explanation could she offer?

Every thought scattered as she studied her objective—or more accurately, his lips. They were wide and well-shaped but firmly set. Not as firm as stone, as Kitty claimed, but unyielding. Unwelcoming. Not at all the sort of lips one dreamed of kissing. But Jess had given up on dreams. Her choices now were about money, the funds she needed to keep the book-shop afloat for as long as she could.

Taking a breath and praying for courage, Jess reached up and removed her spectacles, folded them carefully, and hooked them inside the high neckline of her gown.

His eyes followed the movement of her hands, and the lines between his brows deepened.

Behind her, a woman shouted, "How dare you!" A hand grasped her from behind, the force of the tug pulling Jessamin backward, nearly off her feet. Then a deep, angry male voice rang out and stopped all movement.

"Unhand the woman. Now, if you please." He'd spoken. The stone giant. Lord Grim. He glared past her, over her head. Whoever gripped her arm released their hold. Then Lord Grim's gaze drilled into hers, his eyes discerning, not cold and lifeless as she'd expected.

For several heartbeats he simply watched her, pinning her with his gaze, studying her. Jess reminded herself to breathe.

"Are we acquainted, madam?"

The rumble of his voice, even amid the din of chatter around them, echoed through her.

She moved closer, and his eyebrows shot up. Oh, she'd crossed the line now. Bursting uninvited into a room filled with the wealthy and titled was one thing. Ignoring a viscount's question could be forgiven. Pressing one's bosom into a strange man's chest was something else entirely.

A surge of surprise and gratitude gripped her when he didn't move away.

Assessing his height, Jess realized she'd have to lift onto her toes if the kiss was to be accomplished. She took a step toward him, stretched up tall, and swayed unsteadily. He reached an arm out, and she feared he'd push her away. Instead he gripped her arm just above her elbow and held her steady.

A woman said his name, a tone of chastisement lacing the word. "Lucius."

Then she did it. Placing one hand on his hard chest to balance herself, Jess eased up on the tips of her boots and touched her lips to his.

An Excerpt from

DIRTY TALK
A Mechanics of Love Novel
by *Megan Erickson*

Brent Payton has a reputation for wanting to have fun, all the time. It's well-earned after years of ribbing his brothers and flirting with every girl he meets, but he's more than just a good time, even though nobody takes the time to see it. When a new girl walks into his family's garage with big thoughtful eyes and legs for days, this mechanic wants something serious for the first time.

Ivy Dawn is done with men, all of them. She and her sister uprooted their lives for them too many times and she's not willing to do it again. Avoiding the opposite sex at all costs seems easy enough, until the sexy mechanic with the dirty mouth bursts into her life.

Brent was the middle brother, the joker, the comic relief. The irresponsible one.

Never mind that he'd been working at this shop since he was sixteen. Never mind that he could do every job, inside and out, and fast as fuck.

Never mind that he could be counted on, even though no one treated him like that.

A pain registered in his wrist and he glanced down at the veins and tendons straining against the skin in his arm where he had a death grip on a wrench.

He loosened his fist and dropped the tool on the bench.

This wallowing shit had to stop.

This was his life. He was happy (mostly) and free (no ball and chain, no way) and so what if everyone thought he was a joke? He was good at that role, so the type-casting fit.

"Why so glum, sugar plum?" Alex said from beside him as she peered up into his face.

He twisted his lips into a smirk and propped a hip on the counter, crossing his arms over his chest. "I knew you had a crush on me, sweet cheeks."

She narrowed her eyes, lips pursed to hide a smile. "Not even in your dreams."

He sighed dramatically. "You're just like all the ladies. Wanna piece of Brent. There's enough to go around, Alex, no need to butter me up with sweet nicknames—"

A throat cleared. And Brent looked over to see a woman standing beside them, one hand on her hip, the other dangling at her side holding a paper bag. Her dark eyebrows were raised, full red lips pursed.

And Brent blinked, hoping this wasn't a mirage.

Tory, Maryland, wasn't big, and he'd made it his mission to know every available female in the town limits, and about a ten mile radius outside of that.

This woman? He'd never seen her. He'd surely remembered if he had.

Gorgeous. Long hair so dark brown, it was almost black. Perfect face. It was September, and still warm, so she wore a tight striped sundress that ended mid-thigh. She was tiny, probably over a foot smaller than him. Fuck, the things that little body made him dream about. He wondered if she did yoga. Tiny and limber was his kryptonite.

Narrow waist, round hips, big tits.

No ring.

Bingo.

He smiled. Sure, she was probably a customer, but this wouldn't be the first time he'd managed to use the garage to his advantage. Usually he just had to toss around a tire or two, rev an engine, whatever, and they were more than eager to hand over a phone number and address. No one thought he was a consummate professional anyway, so why bother trying to be one?

He leaned his ass against the counter, crossing his arms over his chest. "Can I help you?"

She blinked, long lashes fluttering over her big blue eyes. "Can you help me?"

"Yeah, we're full service here." He resisted winking. That was kinda sleazy.

Her eyes widened for a fraction before they shifted to Alex at his side, then back to him. Her eyes darkened for a minute, her tongue peeked out between those red lips, then she straightened. "No, you can't help me."

He leaned forward. "Really? You sure?"

"Positive."

"Like, how positive?"

"I'm one hundred percent positive that I do not need help from you, Brent Payton."

That made him pause. She knew his name. He knew he'd never met her so that could only mean that she heard about him somehow and by the look on her face, it was nothing good.

Well shit.

He opened his mouth, not sure what to say, but hoping it came to him when Alex began cracking up next to him, slapping her thighs and snorting.

Brent glared at her. "And what's your problem?"

Alex stepped forward, threw her arm around the shoulder of the woman in front of them and smiled ear to ear. "Brent, meet my sister, Ivy. Ivy, thanks for making me proud."

They were both smiling now, that same full-lipped, white-teethed smile. He surveyed Alex's face, then Ivy's, and holy fuck, how did he not notice this right away? They almost looked like twins.

And the sisters were looking at him now, wearing matching smug grins and wasn't that a total cock-block. He pointed at Alex. "What did you tell her about me?"

"That the day I interviewed, you asked me to recreate a Whitesnake music video on the hood of a car."

He threw up his hands. "Can you let that go? You weren't even my first choice. I wanted Cal's girlfriend to do it."

"Because that's more appropriate," Alex said drily.

"Excuse me for trying to liven it up around here."

Ivy turned to her sister, so he got a better glimpse of those thighs he might sell his soul to touch. She held up the paper bag. "I brought lunch, hope that's okay."

"Of course it is," Alex said. "Thanks a lot, since someone stole my breakfast." She narrowed her eyes at Brent. Ivy turned to him slowly in disbelief, like she couldn't believe he was that evil.

Brent had made a lot of bad first impressions in his life. A dad of one of his high school girlfriends had seen Brent's bare ass while Brent was laying on top of his daughter before the dad ever saw Brent's face. That had not gone over well. And yet this one might be even worse.

Because he didn't care about what that girl's dad thought of him. Not really.

And he didn't want to care about what Ivy thought of him, but dammit, he did. It bothered the hell out of him that she'd written him off before even meeting him. Did Alex tell her any of his good qualities? Like . . . Brent wracked his brain for good qualities.

By the time he thought of one, the girls had already disappeared to the back room for lunch.

FOREVER

Fall in love with more great reads from
Lia Riley

FALL 2015

*The only way to move forward is
to let yourself fall...*

THE OFF THE MAP SERIES

Upside Down   Sideswiped   Inside out
Carry Me Home   Into My Arms

Love is an uncharted territory...